D0720419

LOVE MATCH

"I'm in need of a wife, and you're in need of a respectable burial for your father. If you'll marry me, I'll see to his burial and give you a comfortable home."

This was the last thing Lacey had expected to hear. She stared openmouthed at the stranger's lean, bronzed face. Had he recently fallen off his horse and addled his brains? Or was he just plain loco?

"Look," she pointed out, "we don't know each other. What if we don't match?"

Trey ran a fast glance over Lacey's body. Her hips were gently curved and he thought that her breasts were just big enough to fill a man's hands.

There was not a hot glint in his eyes when he looked back at Lacey and said, "We'll match."

NORAH HESS

Lacey

LEISURE BOOKS   NEW YORK CITY

A LEISURE BOOK®

April 1996

Published by

Dorchester Publishing Co., Inc.
276 Fifth Avenue
New York, NY 10001

To all my wonderful readers who continue to buy and enjoy my books. Your faith in my writing is greatly appreciated.

Lacey

Chapter One

1865-Julesburg, Nebraska

Her face strained with exhaustion and anxiety, eighteen-year-old Lacey Stewart guided the old mule up the rutted street of Julesburg, Nebraska. The last warm sunshine of October shone on her tawny hair and formed a film of perspiration on her sun-browned brow above the dark leaf-green of her eyes.

Lacey pulled the weary mule to a halt just short of a livery stable at the end of town. There was no need to tie him up, she thought as she left the hard seat she had bounced on all day and climbed into the back of the wagon. The old fellow was too tired to move.

Lacey knelt beside a pallet of striped ticking

filled with straw, and picked up the thin, frail hands of the gravely ill man lying there. She gently rubbed the long hands, willing the warmth of her palms to warm her father's cold hands.

For the past ten years, Lacey and her father had traveled throughout the Western frontier in their once gaudy, but now faded painted wagon. The last five years of that time, Miles Stewart had fought off the tuberculosis that was slowly draining the life from him. Now, at age fifty-four, Miles Stewart was dying.

As Lacey gazed down at the face of her beloved parent, her thoughts went back ten years to when she was eight years old. Her mother had caught pneumonia that winter and passed away within the week.

Her father had been like a crazy man during the first months after his wife was laid to rest. Theirs had been such a close relationship, there were times when Lacey felt she was intruding in their lives. Nevertheless, she had always known that she was loved dearly by both of them.

As her father continued to mourn his loss, young Lacey decided that they must leave St. Louis and its bittersweet memories. It took her a while to convince him, and when he finally agreed that they should move, his plan was not at all what Lacey had envisioned.

Miles had decided that they would go on the road, making their living by peddling his herbal medicines as they traveled along. He had out-fitted a box-like wagon that was to be their home.

His friends thought that he had lost his mind in his grief, but eight-year-old Lacey had thought it a grand idea after she was allowed to see the inside of the wagon.

In the back of the vehicle were two narrow mattresses of straw. At the foot of each pallet was a small trunk to hold their clothing. Fastened to one wall of the wagon was a wide shelf with a small mirror hung over it. Beneath the shelf, on the floor, was a wash basin and a box that held soap, comb, brush, and shaving material. Stacked next to those items were towels and flannel washcloths.

On the opposite wall hung pots and skillets, and beneath them were Miles's carefully packed bottles of herbal medicine. Wedged in beside them were stacks of books. Tin plates and cups and eating utensils were stored in a box affixed to the back of the seat.

Miles had painted the wagon a bright red, embellishing it with white and blue flowers around the edges. When the paint had dried, he printed on both sides, in big bold letters: "Dr. Miles Stewart—Herbalist. Pure Vitamins. Will Enrich the Blood & Help Fight off Colds and Pneumonia & Other Ailments."

The morning they left St. Louis, friends and neighbors had gathered in the yard of the small house Miles had sold. They were there to wish

---

father and daughter well on their adventure, though many expressed their doubts about Miles's undertaking.

Especially the women. "What about Lacey's schooling?" one asked. "Are you going to let her grow up ignorant?"

Another had asked, "How is she ever to meet a nice young man and get married, traveling all the time?"

Yet another wanted to know, "What if you're set upon by Indians?"

Miles had answered that he was quite capable of teaching his daughter and that by the time she was of marriageable age they would most likely be settled down someplace. As for Indians, he had read in the newspaper that they were no longer a danger in the west.

Papa had cracked his whip over the back of the mule, which was young and strong then, and they rolled down the street, good-byes and good wishes following them.

Lacey sighed. Bucko, the mule, was old now; his face was beginning to turn gray. The brightly painted wagon of ten years ago was now faded, the paint peeling. As for the excitement that had gripped that young girl on that early June morning, it no longer existed. After a year of traveling through blistering heat, lightning storms, and blizzards, all the excitement had shriveled up inside her.

She didn't, however, tell her father that her dearest wish was to live in a house again.

Poor Papa, Lacey thought sadly as she smoothed the hair off his feverish forehead. His medicine hadn't sold as well as he had thought it would. They barely scratched out a living. He was too honorable a man to make false claims, as some other medicine men did, swearing that their potions would cure anything from baldness to rheumatism.

Business had picked up some when she was fifteen years old. She had noticed in their traveling that the other medicine wagons they competed with always had a woman or two standing beside the man who barked his wares. They were scantily dressed, their hair frizzed and their faces heavily painted. Men always lined up to buy the bottles, which were filled with raw whiskey and sulfur molasses.

She had wondered why a good many of those men followed the women into the back of the wagons for a short while. They never seemed to be carrying any extra bottles with them when they left.

After several days of mulling over an idea that had come to her, she had gotten up the nerve to approach her father about it. What did he think about her dressing a little fancier and using some paint on her face? Before Miles could respond, she pointed out that it might induce the men to buy their vitamins.

Miles's answer was vehement. "No! Those women have low morals. Do you know why they take the men into their wagon?"

Lacey shook her head. "No, I don't. I've wondered about it, though. Why do the women take their customers into the wagons?"

"Well," Miles snorted, "they don't take them in there for tea and conversation."

When she looked questioningly at her father, waiting for him to continue, he stamped away, muttering to himself.

Lacey didn't bring up the subject of the women again, but she did continue to urge her father to let her buy a new dress and some paint for her face.

Finally, worn down from her pleas, Miles had reluctantly given in. He was worried that they were selling less and less of his herb mixture. Most of the towns they traveled through these days had a doctor to prescribe remedies. There was also the fact that his health was slipping.

Nevertheless, it was with much misgiving that Miles watched his daughter take the small box from the trunk in which they kept their carefully hoarded money.

"It will be all right, Papa," Lacey assured him, a small portion of the money in her wrist bag as she climbed out of the wagon.

Lacey couldn't remember now the name of the town where she had bought the dress. There had been so many towns and villages. But she had found a dressmaker's shop and had entered it, her palms wet with nervous sweat.

A pleasant-faced woman in her mid-fifties, dressed in a stylish blue challis dress with a white cloth rose at the high-necked collar, smiled at her from a highly polished counter.

"What can I do for you, miss?" she asked, taking in Lacey's drab, worn dress and her scuffed shoes. "I have some bright calicos that would go beautifully with your auburn hair."

When Lacey left the shop a short time later, she carried a package containing a pair of cheap but shiny black slippers and the red dress she had chosen.

The dress was cut wide across the shoulders, exposing her creamy flesh, and it barely hung below her knees. Papa would be scandalized when he saw it, she thought, hurrying along, but they had to try something. If sales continued to be so poor, they would starve to death come winter.

Lacey continued down the street, walking toward the end of town. She was looking for what she knew every town, large or small, had. A brothel.

She had almost come to the conclusion that this town didn't have a house of prostitution when she spotted a two-story house off by itself in a stand of cottonwoods. The red-painted door told her she had found what she had been seeking.

There was no movement around the place, no sound coming from inside. Lacey began to wonder if she had been mistaken about who lived there. Shouldn't she be hearing the loud voices of men?

She continued to stand in front of the building, clutching the package to her breast. An inward voice pointed out, "You'll never find out who lives here by standing outside like a frightened prairie dog."

Firming her lips, Lacey stepped up onto the narrow porch and knocked on the red door.

She rapped twice before a woman's rough, querulous voice called from inside, "Whoever you are, you ought to know that my girls don't work in the daytime. They have to rest sometime."

When Lacey answered that she wasn't looking for a girl, her voice came out in a squeak and she had to repeat herself.

The door opened then, and she looked into the coarse features of a large woman. Hard blue eyes ran over Lacey's slender figure, which was just beginning to show soft curves.

A quickening interest lightened the madam's features. She could make a lot of money from this fresh, beautiful young girl. She smiled and opened the door wider.

"Come in, dearie. If you're lookin' for work, I always have room for one more girl. Let's have a cup of coffee, and I'll explain my rules to you."

Lacey didn't know whether to be amused or angry that this woman thought she was a whore looking for employment.

She stepped inside a room that still bore a resemblance to the parlor it had once been. But the bright plush covering of the sofas and chairs was now stained and rubbed bare in spots where many men had sat while waiting their turn to escort one of the madam's girls upstairs.

When the door closed behind her, Lacey lost no time in disabusing the hard-looking woman. "I'm sorry if I led you to believe I was seeking employment," she said politely. "I only want to ask if you'd sell me some face paint and teach me how to use it."

The hard blue eyes stared at Lacey. "Why should I show you how to pretty up yourself so that you can go out on your own and steal my customers away from me?"

"I have no intention of doing that," Lacey answered quickly. "I'll be leaving town in a couple of days. My father and I have a medicine wagon, and sales of our wares haven't been too good. I thought if I fancied myself up a bit, we would attract more men to buy our herbal vitamins."

The madam studied Lacey's face closely, especially her eyes. She was looking for deceit or trickery. She had dealt with all kinds of people in her business and could spot a liar in a minute.

She decided the girl hadn't lied, and she was a greenhorn if ever she had seen one. She would attract the men all right, but she had no idea that it wouldn't be her father's medicine they'd be interested in. And this innocent would sell nothing else.

The madam gave Lacey a sincere smile. She'd had her own hard times. "Sit down, honey," she invited, "and Madam Rose will show you how to improve on the beauty you already have."

Lacey was taught how to use rice powder, kohl and a rouge pot. Half an hour later, after having refused the money offered her, the big woman watched Lacey walk down the street, wishing her well.

Lacey remembered now how very upset Papa had been the first time he saw her in the red dress with her face painted.

"Take that Jezebel dress off and scrub your face," he had thundered at her.

She had finally mollified him by explaining that she would only wear the skimpy dress and face paint when they were trying to lure customers to their wagon.

Lacey's idea had not worked quite the way she had hoped. For though her new appearance had attracted the men to their wagon, it wasn't her father's vitamins they were interested in purchasing.

They wanted to buy an hour of her time and were willing to pay handsomely for it. She could have made enough money to keep her and Miles through two winters. She now knew why those other women took customers into their wagons. As for herself, she would starve before she sold her body.

Lacey always kept the men's lewd offers from her father. She continued to put on the red dress, because some of the younger men bought bottles of her father's remedy while they were getting up the nerve to proposition her.

Over the years, the red dress had been re-placed several times, first because she had grown taller and filled out until the dress had crept up to her knees and her breasts threat-ened to spill out of the neckline. The other red dresses had simply worn out. As for face paint, she had always found some madam willing to sell it to her.

After Papa was gone, would she still be wear-ing a red dress and paint her face? Lacey won-dered bleakly, looking down at the gaudy attire she'd put on just before they entered Julesburg. Should she try to go on alone? How long would the rickety old wagon hold out? And how many more miles did the poor old mule have in him? And how safe would it be for her to travel alone?

But if she looked for work, what kind of em-ployment could she seek? Papa had seen to it that she had a good education, but the things he had taught her from the stack of books in the wagon hadn't prepared her to earn a living. She only knew how to cook simple meals over a campfire, and she had no idea how to run a house or take care of children. Her only hope was that somewhere, in some town, she could find a teaching position. She would be very good at that.

The sudden slight pressure of her father's hand in hers brought Lacey swiftly back to the present. His pale lips moved, and she leaned closer to hear him.

"I love you, Lacey," he whispered, and with a soft sigh, he was gone.

Lacey had known that his death was imminent, had thought that she was ready for it, but now that it was a fact, she was overwhelmed with grief.

But she did not have the luxury of indulging her grief. She must decide what in the world was she going to do. She had two dollars and some change in the little box. Not nearly enough to bury her father. She didn't know where to go for help.

She climbed up on the wagon seat to think. As the late October sun shone on her tawny head, she let her tears fall.

Chapter Two

The chuck wagon full of food and bedding reached the center of the river. The water lapped at the mules' bellies, but they moved forward steadily. The hoodlum wagon carrying wood and water barrels stood on the bank waiting its turn to hit the river.

Trey Saunders had worried about this crossing. Sometimes after a hard rain, the river ran wild and deep, hiding the uneven bottom that was filled with numerous deep holes. However, there had been no rain for three weeks, and today the river was quite tame.

He was ready to breathe a sigh of relief when the wagon hit one of the holes he had fretted about. It tipped precariously to the right, and the rear end began taking in water.

Swearing a string of oaths, Trey snapped a long whip over the backs of the mules, threatening them with death if they didn't drag the wagon the hell out of there. The team leaned into the traces, and step by straining step, the heavy vehicle was righted.

However, when it rolled ashore Jiggers, the cook, discovered that dirty river water had seeped into a barrel of flour and fifty pounds of sugar.

"The men will shoot me if I don't have biscuits for their supper tonight," Jiggers muttered as Trey helped him roll the wet barrel off the wagon.

Trey looked out across the prairie, where the herd of one thousand steers were grazing peacefully on lush green grass. Before long that forage would be covered with a foot of snow. They were into the last week of October, and winter would be upon them any day. He hoped it wouldn't snow until they got the herd to Dodge City, Kansas.

"The cattle have settled down from their swim across the river, and the cowhands can handle them without my help," Trey responded to the cook's complaint. "I'll ride ahead to Julesburg and buy enough flour and sugar to get us through tonight's supper and tomorrow's breakfast. You can drive the wagon into town tomorrow and buy enough for the rest of the trip."

Jiggers nodded, and Trey, covered with fine

dust from the crown of his hat to his scuffed boots, swung into the saddle. He kicked his heels into his mount's rump and rode off.

A slow fire began to smolder inside him. He wasn't fuming at having to ride a few extra miles; it was good to get off by himself for a while.

No, his anger was directed at his father. He had gone on this long cattle drive just to get away from the old tyrant.

For over a year, his father had been at him to get married; he claimed he wanted grandchildren. He had even chosen the daughter-in-law he wanted—a woman who had intimately known half the men in Marengo, Wyoming.

As for giving Bull Saunders grandchildren, never in this world would Trey let the man around any child of his. He remembered his own childhood. He had never received a kind word or look from the mean devil. On the contrary, his father had whaled him at least three times a week, usually for no reason at all. When his mother tried to intervene on his behalf, she was told gruffly that the beatings were making him tough.

They had toughened him all right, Trey thought, and had put a bitter hatred inside him for the man who was nominally his father.

As Trey's thoughts went back over the years, his eyes grew hard and his face became like stone. He would have hated Bull Saunders even if he'd never lifted a hand to his son. The bastard had spent years brutalizing the gentle, delicate woman who had given Trey life.

For the first eight years of her married life, Martha Saunders had uncomplainingly lived in a grass soddy. She had kept silent when her husband boasted to the ranchers who lived in frame homes that his place was better than theirs.

"It's made of sod three inches thick. It's sturdy enough to withstand any weather. A fire won't burn it down. It's cool in the summer and warm in the winter."

What the old bastard hadn't said, Trey thought angrily, was that when it rained, the roof dripped water for days, and it was not unusual for snakes to drop through the roof of mud and grass.

And if the beatings handed out to Martha weren't bad enough, she also had to bear the shame of her husband bringing women to the soddy. Trey remembered how at such times his mother would share his straw pallet while Bull and his whore took over the bed. His father never blew the lamp out, and his mother made Trey face the wall so that they wouldn't see her husband using the whore.

Trey and his mother had often wondered what Bull did with all the money he made from the sale of his cattle. Over the years, the small herd he had started out with had grown to well over a thousand head. Every fall more than five hundred were driven to Dodge, where they were loaded into box cars and shipped to Chicago. But Trey and Martha never knew what happened to the money from their sole.

One spring day when Trey and his mother were riding into Marengo to pick up some supplies, they discovered why Bull had hoarded his money all these years.

On a knoll overlooking the basin, they saw the framework of a house going up. Trey had given his mother an excited smile, exclaiming, "Ma, finally you are going to get out of that mud pile."

Martha had only given a wan little smile, and Trey said no more. His mother would still have to live with her husband. It really didn't matter to her where she lived.

Two months later, the house was finished. Bull had made sure that it outshone his neighbors' homes. The building was two stories high, with tall windows throughout, and was painted white. It had a wide porch where Bull could sit and gloat over his land and thousands of cattle.

He had furnished the place with fine pieces crafted by a cabinet maker in Julesburg. The day they moved into the place, he threatened Martha that she had better take good care of her new home or she'd feel the weight of his hand.

Trey had given him a hate-filled look. As if the old bully wouldn't beat her anyway.

When everything met with Bull's satisfaction, he announced that he was going to have a party. He would show those who had looked down their noses at him all these years that he now had a house that outshone theirs.

He sent a cowhand out to deliver his invitations to his neighbors. Every last one of them gave a lame excuse for not attending.

In a rage, he beat Trey and his mother so badly that Martha had two black eyes and two broken ribs. Trey bound his mother's ribs with strips of cloth, then bathed her face. With tears of hatred running down his cheeks, he swore to himself that someday he would beat Bull Saunders half to death.

That day arrived when Trey was fifteen. Bull had come at him with a bullwhip because a horse he was trying to break had thrown him twice.

"I'll learn you how to stick to the back of a horse," Bull growled, snapping the long whip on the ground, making it pop like a gunshot.

Trey was big for his age and strong from working like a slave since he was very young. He made up his mind that he'd had his last beating.

Bull gasped his surprise and pain when the whip was jerked out of his hand and a fist, hard as a rock, landed on his chin. He went down in the dust, his son on top of him. His arms driving like pistons, Trey rained punishing blows on the hated face until it was a bloody mess. The fat lips were cut, two front teeth were missing, and both eyes were swollen shut when Trey got off Bull.

He stood looking down at the moaning man, panting from his exertion. He still had enough breath left in him to grind out, "If you ever lay a hand on me or my mother again, I'll beat you to death."

He kicked Bull in the side for good measure before striding off to the stables.

Two grinning cowboys lifted Bull to his feet and led him into the house.

Trey and his mother were never beaten again by his father, but the mental abuse continued. Trey was continually called bastard and Martha a useless whore. As before, there was always some woman moving into the house, staying until Bull grew tired of her or she left because of his rough lovemaking.

It was to one of those women that Trey lost his innocence when he was seventeen. He gloried in the fact that he now had a way of striking back at his father. Every female Bull brought into the home after that ended up in the son's bed.

That ceased, however, when the wily Bull began bringing Indian women to the ranch. He purposely chose women who were so unattractive, Trey couldn't bring himself to sleep with them.

A shadow of sadness passed over Trey's face. When he was eighteen, his mother passed away from a mysterious illness. The doctor he called in could find nothing wrong with her.

"It's like she's willing herself to die," he told Trey. "I think she's worn out and wants to leave this world."

Trey could understand that. What did his mother have to live for? Her son was able to take care of himself now, and she probably was tired of living.

The night Martha passed quietly away, her son holding her hand, Bull was in the bedroom next to hers, making the bed springs squeak with his latest Indian woman.

All the people who had refused to come to Bull's party showed up for Martha's funeral. She was well liked and pitied by her neighbors. They expressed their sympathy to Martha's son but stayed clear of her sullen-faced husband.

Everyone had thought, including Bull, that Trey would leave the ranch now that his mother was gone.

Trey remembered with grim pleasure the scene that had taken place between him and his father when they returned home from the cemetery. Bull had lost no time asking in his blustery way, "Are you leaving tonight or tomorrow?"

Trey looked at him in pretended surprise. "Leaving? I'm not leaving, tonight or tomorrow or ever. This is my home. Why should I leave it?"

"This is no longer your home." Bull brought his fist down on the table. "Your mother is dead now, so that makes the ranch all mine." He glared at Trey. "I'll expect you off my property by noon tomorrow."

"Will you now?" Trey asked with dry amusement, reaching into his vest pocket. He pulled out a folded sheet of paper and opened it. "Lawyer Davis gave me this just before I left the cemetery. It's Ma's will. She left her half of everything to me."

Trey grinned wickedly. "It seems we're partners, old man."

Trey had thought, had hoped, that his father was going to have a stroke; his face had turned purple in his rage.

"Let me see that thing." He held out a hand that trembled slightly.

His eyes scanned the will, then he made a motion to toss it into the fireplace. Trey had expected he would try that, however, and he grabbed his arm and wrenched the paper out of his hand.

For twelve years after that day, they had existed together, each wary of the other. Days would pass when no word was spoken between them. An occasional flare of temper from either one would set off a heated argument.

Bull continued to have his Indian women, and Trey sometimes brought a woman home for the night. But more often he went into Marengo and visited the whorehouse there.

As the little mount galloped along, Trey wondered why his father wanted grandchildren. He evidently didn't like children or he'd have had more of his own.

It occurred to him suddenly to wonder why

his mother hadn't had a dozen babies over the years. God knew the old bastard had spilled enough seed inside her.

Slowly Trey's lips spread in an amused grin. By hell, for some reason Bull Saunders had become as sterile as the neutered steers out on the range. What a blow it must have been to his pride that he had only been able to sire one child—one he hated so much.

Julesburg loomed ahead, and Trey put the past behind him. He noted a faded, decrepit-looking medicine wagon pulled to one side as he entered town and rode past the livery. He felt sorry for the old mule that was hitched to the vehicle; his head drooped and his short, stubby tail only half-heartedly switched at the flies buzzing around his rump. The old fellow could use a bag of oats, Trey thought.

It didn't take Trey long to purchase the flour and sugar, adding to his order some chewing tobbaco for Jiggers and a box of cheroots for his friend Matt Carlton.

Matt Carlton, a bachelor, was a neighbor of the Saunders men, running a spread almost as large as theirs. He had felt sorry for the young, abused Trey and had become the boy's idol by giving him the attention he should have received from his father.

It had been the tall, quiet man with the sad eyes who had taught him how to bridle and saddle a horse and who had taken him hunting and fishing when Trey could slip away from Bull.

When Matt thought he was old enough, he taught Trey how to handle a gun and rifle.

His pupil became an expert with the Colt 45, eventually drawing and shooting faster than his teacher.

Matt, along with a Mexican couple—Lupe, his housekeeper, and José, his handyman—lived in a modest house situated in the foothills of the Rocky Mountains in the Wind River area.

He had chosen his land well. It included a river as well as many creeks. The grass grew tall and lush, ample for the twenty-five hundred head of cattle he ran. His friends all thought it a shame that he didn't have any children to leave his holdings to after his death.

Trey strapped his purchases onto his horse's back and swung into the saddle. Lifting the reins, he headed the animal back in the direction he'd come. He had one more stop to make, one that he looked forward to with anticipation. He hadn't had a woman lately, and there was a whorehouse at the edge of town, a short distance from the livery.

He was about to ride past the faded medicine wagon when he pulled the horse in. The prettiest little filly he'd ever seen sat on the wagon seat, mopping at her tear-wet cheeks. Her low-cut red dress and face paint marked her clearly as a soiled dove. Amusement curved his lips. That was a trick the women of the night often pulled: get a man's sympathy so he would give her more money before they went to bed.

He wondered what this one's excuse would be for her tears. A sick mother or baby? She needed money to buy a different mule? He could believe that. The old fellow looked as if he was on his last legs.

Trey asked himself how much she would charge for a quick tumble in the back of the wagon.

He rode up beside the wagon and asked, "Why are you crying, pretty little lady?"

Trey wasn't prepared for the grief-filled eyes that were lifted to him or the small choked voice that sobbed, "My father has just died and I don't know what to do."

Certainly that wasn't what Trey had expected to hear. But from her swollen eyes and lips, he judged that her grief was genuine and she had been crying for some time.

Trey moved uneasily in the saddle. He had never dealt with a young woman's tears before. He remembered how he had felt when he lost his mother and had no one to turn to except for Matt.

After the grave had been filled in and everybody had left the cemetery, Matt had come up to him and said, "Trey, get on your stallion and ride up the mountain. Find a secluded spot where you can howl your grief to the sky. There's no shame in a man shedding tears if he has good cause to."

Of course, this young girl couldn't do that, Trey thought, pushing the black hat off his forehead. He cleared his throat and said, "Well, I guess what you do is go to the funeral home down the street and make arrangements with the undertaker. He'll take care of everything."

He knew his words sounded cold and uncaring as they left his lips, but he didn't know what else to say.

The girl looked at him helplessly and then blurted out, "I only have two dollars and some change."

Ah, hell, Trey thought. Why did he have to stop? Why didn't he just ride on and stop at the whorehouse as he'd planned? He could have paid for a half hour's pleasure and gone on about his business. Now he felt it was his responsibility to see that this girl's father was buried.

Suddenly a thought popped into Trey's mind, a thought so wild that it almost knocked him out of the saddle. He had an idea that would enrage his father. He was going to ask this little whore to marry him. The old goat had been after him to marry Ruby Dalton so he could get his hands on her inheritance someday. It would gripe the hell out of him to be presented with a soiled dove for a daughter-in-law.

Would the girl agree to such an outlandish proposal? He thought that under the circumstances she might jump at the chance. After all, how many whores had offers of marriage?

"Look, miss," he said, leaning forward in the saddle so that only a couple of feet separated

them. "I've been thinking that you have a problem and I have a problem. We can help each
other if you're willing to do it."

Lacey looked closely into the cowboy's eyes.
He was a stranger to her, and for all she knew
his plan might involve robbing Julesburg's
bank. He knew that she needed money, and
from his scruffy appearance, he was in need of
some too.

But his face was strong-looking, and his
brown eyes were frank and open. He did not
have the look of an outlaw.

Finally she said, "I'll help you in any way I
can if it's honest."

"It's honest enough, but it's something you
may not want to do."

"Tell me what it is and I'll let you know if it's
agreeable to me."

Trey hesitated. He looked down at the
ground, trying to form in his mind the right
words to use. For some reason he couldn't figure out yet, it was important to him that the girl
with the lost look in her eyes accepted his proposal.

He took a long breath, lifted his head, and
looked into her green eyes as he said, "Let me
finish what I have to say before you give me an
answer, all right?" When Lacey nodded, he continued. "I'm in need of a wife, and you're in need
of a respectable burial for your father. If you'll
marry me, I'll see to his burial and give you a
comfortable home."

Lacey

This was the last thing Lacey had expected to hear. She stared open-mouthed at the stranger's lean, bronzed face. Had he recently fallen off his horse and addled his brains, or was he just plain loco?

"Look," she pointed out, "we don't know each other. What if we don't match?"

Trey ran a fast glance over Lacey's body. Her hips were gently curved, and he thought that her breasts were just big enough to fill a man's hands.

There was a hot glint in his eyes when he looked back at Lacey and said, "We'll match."

Lacey wasn't sure she liked the look in his eyes or the tone of his voice. But God knew she needed his help, and the thought of living in a house again was a great inducement.

He looked like an honorable man, she thought, one who wouldn't beat his wife. She scrutinized Trey closely. His clothes were wrinkled and dusty but were in good shape. He didn't look like a drifter or one of those cowhands who rode from ranch to ranch looking for a handout. Her eyes lingered a moment on the Colt strapped around his narrow waist. But that wasn't unusual. Most men wore a gun of some kind, if for no other reason than to kill rattlesnakes.

Of course, there wasn't any love between them, but what choice did she really have? Without the protection of a man, anything could happen to her.

Lacey lifted her eyes to Trey's anxious face and nodded. "If you're willing to take me as your wife, I'm willing to take you as a husband. I will be faithful to you and work hard for you."

Trey grinned. "That's all any man could ask," he said. "I'll go see to things now—and find a preacher."

Lacey noted that he hadn't said anything about being faithful to her. As she watched him ride away, she wondered if she had just made the biggest mistake of her life.

Chapter Three

Lacey felt like a bystander, a stranger who stood to one side watching events take shape that would change her life forever.

First a black-frocked, long-faced man had come and carried her father's body from the wagon and deposited it in a black, horse-drawn coach with heavy drapes at the side windows. The cowboy had then unhitched the old mule and taken him to the livery for a well-deserved bag of oats and a rest.

And now, half an hour later, she was standing in front of a preacher, marrying a man she had met only an hour ago. She was promising to love and obey a stranger. He had told her that his name was Trey Saunders.

Lacey came back to reality when a cold, thin

band of gold was slipped on her finger and the reverend said, "I now pronounce you man and wife." When he added, "You may kiss your wife now, Trey," she blinked in confusion, but dutifully lifted her face to receive her husband's kiss.

It was the first time her lips would touch those of any man other than her father.

Her new husband's kiss was tender, yet beneath the softness there was a heat that scorched her lips and sent a tingling from her breast to the inner core of her. When he lifted his head, she looked up at him, bewilderment in her eyes.

Trey laughed softly. Rubbing a thumb across her lower lip, he teased, "You look like you've never kissed a man before."

While she blushed and fumbled for an answer, the preacher called Trey's attention to the signing of the marriage certificate. He signed his name on the stiff square of paper; then Lacey wrote her name beneath his signature.

A sigh feathered through Lacey's lips. She was now Mrs. Trey Saunders. What did the future hold for Lacey Saunders? she wondered.

Good-byes were exchanged with the reverend and his wife and the handyman who had witnessed the ceremony. When Lacey and Trey stepped outside into the autumn sunshine, he handed Lacey the proof of their marriage.

"This is what I want you to do," he said. "After your father's burial, drive your wagon to Ma-

rengo, a town in Wyoming Territory. Ask anyone you see on the street there how to get to the
Saunders ranch. I'm sorry I can't go with you,
but I have to help drive a herd of cattle to Dodge
City."

Stunned, Lacey stared up at her husband. All
through the wedding ceremony, she had been
dreading the consummation of their wedding
vows tonight. And now she discovered that instead of spending the night with her, he was
going to ride off, leaving her to find her own
way to her new home. She was both relieved
and worried.

How far away was this Marengo? She had
been protected all her life, and now suddenly
she was expected to travel alone, her only safe-
guard a rifle and a pocket revolver.

Trey broke in on her thoughts by pressing
some money into her hand. "There's a grocer
down the street. Go there and buy three days'
worth of trail grub. Before you start out, have
the wheels on that old wagon checked. A couple
are ready to fall off. Don't forget to fill your water barrel," he added.

"How long will you be gone?" Lacey asked
anxiously as Trey prepared to mount.

"About two months," he answered, "but don't
you worry about it. You'll be fine at the ranch
until I get back."

Before she could question him further, Trey
had swung into the saddle. With a smile and a
lift of his hand, he rode off down the street.

She watched the easy play of his hips as he moved with the gait of the mount. She looked at his broad back and thought of how much power it displayed. He was undeniably handsome, with his shoulder-length brown hair that curled slightly, his dark eyes that sometimes teased, sometimes glinted with a light she didn't quite understand.

But what kind of husband would he be? Lacey asked herself.

A moment later she had a pretty good idea that he wouldn't be a perfect mate.

When Trey was just a few feet past the livery, he turned his mount's head to the right and disappeared from sight. She had noted as she and Papa rode into Julesburg that the last house on the street was a brothel. Surely her husband wasn't going to visit one of those women?

"I've got to know," she told herself and hurried down the half block to where the house of prostitution was situated. She peeked around the livery barn and gave a little choked cry.

Trey's mount was tied to the hitching post in front of the place. She stood a moment staring at the red-painted door, then turned and walked back toward her wagon. A grimace of distaste was on her lips and her skirt swished angrily. She had married a whoremonger. Although she hadn't looked forward to her husband's love-making because she was afraid of the unknown, she felt humilated that he preferred a prostitute to his wife.

But otherwise he's been very good to you, Lacey's conscience pointed out as she stamped along. He had made all the arrangements for her father's burial, even hired two men to dig the grave. *And don't forget, he went to the trouble of buying you a ring.*

"Twiddle-twaddle," Lacey muttered, climbing into the wagon. It was part of the deal that he'd take care of everything. As for the ring, she could bet he had some reason for that—a reason to his benifit.

As Lacey sat on the wagon seat staring gloomily ahead, she became aware of the money she still clutched in her hand. She unfolded the bills and counted them. The amount would have fed her and Papa for a month. Her husband might be a womanizer, but he was very generous with his wife.

The sun set and twilight arrived. Lacey climbed into the back of the wagon and stretched out on her narrow pallet. She looked across at her father's empty bed and cried herself to sleep.

An hour later, Trey rolled off the whore he had chosen to bed. He had picked a curvaceous blonde with big breasts. She wasn't his usual preference in women. He liked them slender and fine-boned . . . like the one he had married.

His dalliance with the plump blonde had been disappointing. Every time he thought he would achieve a release, a pair of sad green eyes swam before him and he lost his firm hardness. The whore, anxious to please, had called upon all her expertise to satisfy him. To Trey's embarrassment, nothing she did was successful.

Stuffing his shirt tail into his trousers, he gave the woman a crooked grin and said, "We'll try again on my way back from Dodge." He left the whore a good-sized tip for her eagerness to please him and hurried out of the pleasure house. He swung into the saddle, and before heading out, he looked back at the weather-beaten wagon with its peeling paint. His wife was not in evidence. Was she asleep or was she sitting in the privacy of the wagon crying out her grief?

He felt a pang of guilt as he rode out of Julesburg.

"It's about time you got back," Jiggers complained as Trey came galloping up to the chuck wagon. "The men will be coming in for supper anytime now. What took you so long? Some whore, I expect."

"Naw. I was getting married." Trey grinned at the old man as he carried the flour and sugar to the wagon and placed it on the tailgate.

"Yeah, and I'm gonna become a preacher," Jiggers snorted.

"You'd make a dandy one." Trey's smile widened as he filled a battered wash basin with water from the barrel attached to the hoodlum wagon, which pulled up behind the chuck wagon.

As he dried his face on a coarse towel, he ran his gaze over the thousand head of cattle grazing peacefully along the river they had crossed a few hours ago. The cowhands were lounging in their saddles as they rode slowly around the herd. An Easterner seeing them for the first time would think they had an easy time of it, herding the longhorns.

What they wouldn't know were the many dangers of tending the half-wild cattle. There was violent weather to contend with, rivers at flood to cross, and always the threat of a stampede. The wild ones could suddenly erupt in mass hysteria, particularly during a lightning storm. They could be set off by the flare of a match at night or the snap of a twig.

It was a fearful thing, riding at a dead run in the dark in an area filled with prairie-dog holes, knowing that the next jump could see you lying on the ground with a broken neck.

Trey dashed his wash water onto a patch of brush and then settled down in front of the cookfire to watch Jiggers stir up a batch of skillet-bread dough. Had it been preordained that the flour and sugar would be ruined and that he would make the trip to purchase more? he wondered. Had it been in the cards that he, in a moment of insanity, would marry a woman he'd known less than an hour? And that woman a young whore to boot?

His lips twisted wryly. He'd get a lot of ribbing for that, but it would be worth it just to rile

Bull Saunders. Anyway, when his free and easy ways didn't change, everyone would realize that his marriage meant only one thing—a way to antagonize his sire.

Darkness had settled in when Jiggers had the sourdough batter frying over a bed of live coals. He had lit two lanterns and placed them on the tailgate alongside a stack of tin plates, cups, and flatware.

He was slicing a beef roast when half the riders came loping in. After these men had eaten, they'd relieve the other half so that they could eat. The second group of men would roll up in their blankets when their bellies were full and sleep until midnight. The first bunch would come in then and sleep until just before dawn, when Jiggers would roust them out of their bedrolls. He would then serve all the hands a breakfast of bacon and beans and strong black coffee.

Camp settled down with only Trey and Jiggers still awake. The sky darkened and a million stars came out. Trey sat gazing into the fire while Jiggers washed the tinware, pots, and skillet and set out what he'd need in the morning. The handsome rancher was feeling guilty again about his new wife. He shouldn't have sent the little whore to the ranch without warning her about Bull Saunders. It was possible the old bastard wouldn't let her in the house.

If he'd been thinking straight, he'd have sent her to Matt until Trey got home. All he'd had on his mind at the time was the jolt the old man would get on learning that he had a painted-up little whore for a daughter-in-law.

"You gonna set there all night like a fly on a horse's rump?" Jiggers asked, breaking into Trey's thoughts. "Daybreak comes awfully fast," he said, stripping down to his long-legged red underwear. He shivered and hurried into his bedroll.

Before Trey could make a response, the old cook was snoring.

Trey came awake several times that night, a pair of clear green eyes looking at him reproachfully. When Jiggers banged on a pan a few hours later, announcing that breakfast was ready, Trey was tempted to leave the herd and ride with Lacey to the ranch.

More thought on the subject, however, made him change his mind. If he suddenly showed up at the ranch, Lacey would wonder why he'd altered his plans. He didn't want her to think she was going to change the way he lived his life.

There was nothing to do but stay with the herd and hope that his new wife would manage somehow.

Lacey had thought there were no more tears left in her. But when she awakened and opened her trunk to put on one of her modest, though worn dresses, she found the storage unit empty. Sometime yesterday while she was getting married, someone had slipped into the wagon and stolen all her clothes.

Her tears flowed freely as she realized she'd have to attend her father's funeral in the shameful red dress that Papa had so hated.

She scrubbed her face clean of all the paint and brushed the tawny curls that hung past her shoulders. Had Trey seen her now, he wouldn't have recognized her. When she had smoothed most of the wrinkles out of the dress, she went to the livery and brought the mule back to the wagon. She thought he looked a little more perky as she hitched him up.

The Reverend was waiting for Lacey at the grave site, and as he helped her out of the wagon he looked at her curiously. It was hard to believe that this lovely young girl was the same painted-up hussy he had married to Trey Saunders yesterday. If it wasn't for the red dress and tawny hair, he wouldn't have recognized her.

Lacey shivered in the late October wind that swept across the cemetery. The preacher's wife who had accompanied him took the brown shawl off her plump shoulders and wrapped it around Lacey's narrow shoulders.

"You'll catch your death in that skimpy little dress, dear," she said kindly.

"But you'll be cold," Lacey objected.

"Honey, I've got enough fat on me to keep me warm in a blinding blizzard, whereas the slightest breeze would go straight through you. You must get more meat on your bones. Consider the shawl a gift."

Lacey thanked the genial woman and was about to say that no matter how much she ate, she always remained slender, when the preacher opened his bible and began to read from it.

Lacey felt sure that the kindly man was reading encouraging words for her benefit, but none of them penetrated her mind. All she could think was that she'd never see her father again.

The reverend was leading her away from the grave then, saying, "Your husband arranged for a headstone. It should be in place in a couple of weeks. I'll need a few details to be etched in the stone: your father's full name and date of birth, your mother's name, and your name."

Lacey gave the information, thinking what a contradictory man she had married. He had done everything a loving husband should do for a wife, then turned around and taken a whore to bed on his wedding day.

When she had finished her business with the preacher, she glanced up to see the two men who had stood silently at a distance now come forward, each carrying a shovel. As clods of dirt rattled against the coffin, she became so choked up that she barely managed to say good-bye to the preacher and his wife.

With the pair calling blessings to her, Lacey climbed into the wagon and prodded the old mule with the handle of her whip, one that had never been used on him. The old fellow stirred into motion and headed back toward town.

Lacey pulled him up in front of the grocery store that Trey had mentioned and jumped to the ground. Inside the store, she gave the sour-faced grocer her order of flour, sugar, coffee, lard, bacon and beans, and a gallon of kerosene. The other supplies she'd need she already had in the wagon.

While her purchases were being gathered by the shopkeeper, Lacey glanced around the store, her attention caught by a few cotton dresses hanging in the window. She was tempted to buy one to replace the short red dress.

She immediately dismissed the thought. She had been told to buy three days' worth of grub, and that was all she was going to spend her husband's money on. He had already spent enough on poor Papa.

"Ain't you the girl what married that there wild Trey Saunders?" the grocer asked as he handed Lacey her change.

Lacey gave him a hard look and answered coldly, "Yes, Trey and I were married yesterday."

"You headin' for his ranch now? Talk is that he went on with his cattle drive."

"It appears that a lot of talk goes on in Julesburg," Lacey answered brusquely as she picked up the grub sack.

"You look mighty young to come up against Bull Saunders."

"What do you mean?" Lacey frowned.

"Nothin' much. He's got the reputation of bein' meaner than a sidewinder. Him and his son don't get along at all. I don't imagine he'd treat a daughter-in-law any better than he does his son."

Ten minutes later, as Lacey drove the mule out of town, she wondered what she was in for when she reached the Saunders ranch. Was there also a mother, sisters, and brothers? she wondered. Would they be as mean-tempered as the father sounded?

At any rate, it didn't sound as if she'd receive the warmest of welcomes.

Lacey sighed. In the passing of a day, her life was changed forever. She wondered again what the future held for her. At the moment it didn't look very rosy.

As the old mule ambled along, Lacey looked out over a wide, shallow valley. Low swells of green grass sloped up to the west. Stands of cottonwood, few and far between, stood out strikingly against a distant line of red rocks. Over it all crept the lengthening afternoon shadows.

It was a wild and ruthless land, Lacey thought, but glorious also. She could be happy here if she were allowed to be. She would just have to develop a thick skin and somehow get along with the Saunders family. The son, however, had to mend his ways drastically before she'd have anything to do with him.

The sun was almost down when Lacey brought the mule, Jocko, to a halt within one of the cottonwood groves. She unhitched the tired old fellow and gave him an affectionate pat on the rump before hobbling him in a patch of grass. She then filled a pail with water from the barrel attached to the back of the wagon and carried it to her old friend.

While Jocko chomped his supper, Lacey hurried about beneath the big cottonwoods gathering up dry limbs that had fallen to the ground. As she built a fire, a cool breeze sprang up. It was not a strong wind, but it was enough to stir the remaining leaves on the trees, casting eerie shadows on the ground.

She looked often over her shoulder as she fried some bacon and heated a can of beans.

Lacey ate her supper quickly and hungrily, giving an alarmed cry once when an owl swooped down from the tree under which she had camped.

Darkness was coming on when she made a trip to the bushes before climbing into the wagon and barring the door. She pulled the red dress over her head and curled up on her pallet. She had barely pulled the blanket up over her shoulders when she fell into a sleep so sound that she could have been carried away by a gang of outlaws and wouldn't have awakened.

The next morning Lacey was up early, and the day passed much like the one before. However, that evening when she sought her bed, she wasn't as tired as she had been the night before and didn't fall asleep immediately.

She heard every night sound, magnified by her awareness of being so alone. When a distant wolf yowl drifted on the night air, she prayed that by this time tomorrow she would have reached her destination and would be sleeping under a roof.

The skies were overcast when Lacey stepped out of the wagon the next morning. "I hope it doesn't rain," she muttered as she fried bacon and heated beans.

According to the pale sun trying to penetrate the dark clouds, Lacey thought it was around four o'clock when she heard the first distant rumble of thunder. To her relief, at the same time she saw a small town in the distance.

"Marengo. Thank God," she breathed and urged the old mule to go a little faster.

It was indeed a small town, Lacey discovered as she guided the mule down its one dusty street. On one side there was a grocery store, a cafe, and a doctor's office with a plaque on the door stating the doctor's name, Jonah Carson. On the other side of the deeply rutted street was a tavern, a mercantile, a Chinese laundry, and a bath house. At the very end of town was a blacksmith and then a brothel.

Lacey grimaced. How many trips had her husband made there? she wondered.

She kept the mule at a slow pace as she looked anxiously for someone she could ask for directions to the Saunders ranch. Trey had said that anyone could tell her where it was.

She kept her face averted and ignored the invitations called out to her from some men standing in front of the tavern. Certainly she wouldn't ask any of them.

When she saw an older man, tall and slender, come from the cafe, she felt that she could talk to him without getting any crude remarks. From the gray threading his dark hair, she guessed he was in his late fifties or early sixties. He was probably a grandfather.

She pulled up in front of the cafe and, leaning forward, said, "Excuse me, please, but could you tell me the way to the Saunders ranch?"

Ready to mount his horse, the man looked up at her, his eyes cool. Matt Carlton would never have taken this one for a whore if it weren't for that short red dress. Old Bull was picking them younger and younger. This one must not be aware of his mean and cruel nature.

"Look, young lady," he said, "are you sure you want to go to the Saunders ranch?"

"I'm quite sure, sir. My husband told me to go there."

Relief washed through Matt. The girl wasn't another of Bull's conquests. "Who is your husband?" he asked, the coldness leaving his eyes. "Maybe I know him. Does he work for Saunders?"

Lacey dimpled. "I guess you could say he works for Mr. Saunders. I'm Trey Saunders's wife."

After sixty-two years of living, there wasn't

much that could surprise Matt Carlton. But this piece of news left him speechless for several moments. That damn fool Trey had married this girl just to rile his father, Matt realized. He hadn't given any thought to the consequences of such a rash act. It hadn't entered his head how Bull would treat his wife. And he didn't know that marriage without love was a hell on earth.

When he noted the girl looking at him with worried eyes, Matt's teeth flashed in a wide smile. "Congratulations, Mrs. Saunders," he said. "You've got yourself a fine husband."

"I guess time will tell about that," Lacey answered, a little sharply. "We were married three days ago, and he left immediately to continue with a cattle drive to Dodge City. He said he'd be gone a couple of months."

Matt looked at the rickety wagon and the faded sign on its sides. "Did you and Trey meet during a medicine show?"

"No. We met before a show."

Lacey didn't add to her statement. It would be too embarrassing to relate the true details of her marriage.

When Matt realized there was no explanation coming after that flat answer, he said, "Follow the street out of town. You'll come to the ranch after a couple of miles." He smiled up at her. "Good luck to you, girl. Don't let Bull scare you. He'll not be too hard on you for fear that Trey will climb all over him when he gets back."

What had she gotten herself into? Lacey thought as she thanked the man and prodded the mule into motion. This was the second person to speak badly of Bull Saunders. She wished she'd remembered to ask the kindly stranger if there were other relatives of Trey's at the ranch. A friendly mother perhaps.

Matt watched the wagon roll across the range, a frown creasing his forehead. Would Bull dare turn the girl away?

He looked up at the lowering sky. It was going to start raining any minute, he thought as he swung into the saddle. The girl would be soaked in that skimpy dress and light shawl. He touched spurs to the stallion and galloped out of town.

Lacey figured she had traveled about a mile when thunder began to roll and lightning pierced the early darkness. Half a mile later the rain came, cold and slashing against her face and body.

She was soaked to the skin when the many buildings of the Saunders ranch came into view. It was quite a spread, she thought, her teeth chattering as she peered through the curtain of rain.

"Can't you go a little faster, Jocko?" she called. "I'm chilled to the bone and hungry as a hound dog."

The old mule plodded on at the same slow pace, and it was close to ten minutes later that

Lacey pulled him up in front of a large white house.

Added uneasiness swept through Lacey as she wound the lines around the whip stock and jumped to the puddle-filled yard. "What a mess I must look," she thought out loud, climbing the two steps to the wide porch. Her hair was a mass of wet curls clinging to her face, and the red dress was plastered to her body.

Shivering, she pulled the shawl tighter around her shoulders and rapped her knuckles against the heavy door.

The laughter she heard from inside the house came to an abrupt halt. It was a full two minutes before the door opened. A sharp-faced woman in her early thirties stood there, giving her a hard, cold look.

I wonder if she knows her shirt is buttoned up crooked, Lacey thought as she returned the unfriendly smile, wondering if the woman was Trey's sister.

Finally the woman asked rudely, "Who are you and what do you want?"

Before Lacey could answer, a rough male voice called out, "Who is it, Ruby?"

The woman's lips lifted in a sneer as she called back, "It's one of the whores from town. She's probably lookin' for Trey."

As Lacey glared indignantly at Ruby, a stockily built man in his mid-sixties appeared behind the woman. He ran a hot gaze over her body in the wet, clinging dress.

57

He lifted his eyes to her face and barked, "What in the hell are you doing out here? If you're lookin' for Trey, he's on his way to Dodge City."

Lacey tried to smile as she answered, "I know that, Mr. Saunders. Trey and I were married three days ago in Julesburg. He told me to come here."

A spasm of rage gripped Bull's face. "The hell you were!" he roared furiously. "This is one of Trey's gags to rile me."

"I have a marriage certificate." Lacey's voice trembled as she dug into her wrist bag.

Bull snatched the paper from her hand, skimmed it, and then shoved it back at her. "That whelp of Satan, I'll get him back for this." He swore an ugly oath. "He thinks he's put one over on me, but I'll show him."

When it looked as if he was going to let Lacey enter the house, Ruby slid him a warning look and said, "Shouldn't she go on to Trey's place up in the foothills?"

Bull looked confused for a split second, then said hurriedly, "Yes, that would be best." He stepped out on the porch and pointed in a westerly direction. "Ride beyond the corrals down there by the barn and you'll see the road leading up toward the mountains. If you hurry, you can reach his place before dark."

Lacey couldn't believe that she wasn't going to be invited to come in and have something to eat, or at least a cup of coffee before riding on.

But the door was being closed in her face and there was nothing to do but climb back in the wagon and drive on. She was miserably cold, and hunger gnawed at her stomach. She was beginning to believe all the bad things she'd heard about Bull Saunders.

The rain continued to fall as the wagon bumped along on the muddy road. It wasn't truly a road. It was only a set of wagon tracks cutting through the sod.

A gray twilight was coming on when, just above a line of trees, Lacey saw a small, rude building erected from scraps of lumber. It had no chimney, just a rusty stovepipe sticking out beside the one small window.

She gazed at the building, thinking that the wagon would be more comfortable.

Chapter Four

The storm that Lacey had traveled through was making its way south of the Wyoming border.

Trey pushed back his hat and wiped the dust and sweat off his face with his bandana as he studied the gray clouds gathering in the north.

He swore under his breath. They were in for a thunderstorm, and if the thick humidity meant anything, it was going to be a hellish one—one that was sure to spook the temperamental longhorns.

He gazed thoughtfully ahead. Should he tell Jiggers to make camp now? It was a little early, but it would be easier to handle a grazing herd if a storm did break. He looked back at the clouds. They had grown larger and darker and were moving closer. He nodded, as though coming to a decision.

Trey touched spurs to the little mustang he always rode during roundup and trail drives. The Indian pony was a hardy breed, tough and fast. They never wore iron shoes but could travel over the roughest ground.

He rode up alongside the chuck wagon. "Make camp, Jiggers," he said when the cook gave him a questioning look. "I think we're in for a storm."

"I've been thinkin' the same thing." Jiggers nodded and pulled the team of mules to a halt. He jumped to the ground and started pulling kindling and pieces of wood from the hoodlum wagon. Part of its use was to carry wood in case they had to camp where none could be found.

Trey next rode back to where a teenager tended the remuda. "Tim, make sure the horses are tightly tethered. There's a storm brewing." The boy nodded, and Trey rode back to the herd and reined the mustang alongside his drover, Cole Stringer. Ordinarily Cole would be in charge of the drive. He would collect the money when the cattle were sold and pay off the cowboys.

"Cole, start milling the herd. Let them graze. I don't like the looks of those clouds."

"I don't either." Cole shook his head, a worried look on his face.

"You'd better tell the men to get fresh horses in case them ornery critters decide to run."

The word was passed from cowboy to cowboy that camp was to be made. Trey watched the cattle slowly beginning to mill, coming closer together as they circled. They looked nervous, stamping and pawing loose dirt and tossing it over their backs to deter the flies biting them.

"The devils know there's a storm coming," Trey muttered darkly as he rode back to the chuck wagon.

All the riders had saddled fresh horses, and the first half of the group was eating the beef-steaks Jiggers had prepared for them when lightning lit up the area, followed by a deafening roll of thunder. The men were immediately on their feet and running for their mounts.

The cattle were running also. As Trey had feared, they were in for a stampede.

In minutes the clouds opened up and the rain came down in torrents. Drenched and blinded by the slashing rain, the men were trying desperately to turn the frightened cattle away from the chuck wagon, where Jiggers was hanging on to the frantic mules, and the horses in the remuda were squealing their terror as the thundering herd swept toward them.

With shouting and popping whips and gunshots, the cattle were turned just yards short of the chuck wagon and remuda. Their eyes wild, they raced across the range, bellowing their panic.

"Let the devils run," Trey yelled. "Let them run until they wear themselves out."

It was hours before the cattle became so tired that they couldn't run any farther. The men were just beginning to breathe a little easier when three shots, evenly spaced, rang out.

A distress signal. A man was down.

The men tore off through the rain, which had slowed to a drizzle, Trey in the lead. This was what everyone dreaded in a stampede.

Trey's heart sank when they came upon a cowboy kneeling beside a crumpled form. He dismounted and hurried to hunker down beside the fallen man. "It's Smitty," the cowboy said, his voice choked. "He's been trampled to death."

Trey gazed down at the broken body. This hard-working man, nearly thirty years old, was known only as Smitty. In this harsh land, a man's past and real name were a private matter. It was possible that he was running from the law. If Smitty had any relatives, no one knew about them.

Trey wondered if there were a mother and father somewhere who would mourn their son's death if they knew of his passing.

He stood up. Looking at the driver of the hoodlum wagon, he said, "Seth, as soon as you've eaten breakfast in the morning, take Smitty back to Julesburg and see to his burial."

Jiggers had managed to keep a small fire going under the wagon tailgate, and a mouth-watering aroma drifted over the area. It was a quiet, sober group of men who lined up with tin plates in hand. In their wet black slickers, they looked like so many black crows as they squatted around the wagon wolfing down stew and skillet bread. The big, battered coffee pot was soon emptied and another pot put on the fire.

As Trey had predicted, the herd was worn out and it was doubtful if a blast of dynamite would start them running again. He stood up, stretching stiff and sore muscles, and said, "I think it's safe enough for all of us to grab a few hours' sleep."

The words were barely out of his mouth before the bone-tired men were digging their tarps and bedrolls out of the hoodlum wagon. They were careful not to disturb the blanket-wrapped body of their fallen friend.

Trey spread his tarp and blankets beneath the chuck wagon, leaving room for Jiggers. The wet darkness weighed upon him as he gazed into the dying campfire. In the curling smoke he saw the image of a tall, slender girl with clear green eyes and full red lips. He wondered if it was raining back home. Had she reached the ranch yet? How would that devil of a father of his treat her?

Damn, he thought as he drifted off to sleep, he shouldn't have sent her to face the old bastard alone.

Lacey snapped the reins over the mule's back and they rolled up to what was to be her new home. She climbed to the ground, stepping into a puddle of water that rose to her ankles. She sloshed through the water and pushed open a sagging door hung with leather hinges. She stepped inside and came to a halt, her eyes growing wide. The friendly man who had directed her to the ranch had started a fire in the rusty stove.

He smiled at her and said, "Close the door, girl. You don't want this mansion to get wet, do you?"

When Lacey had struggled the door shut, he said, "I suspected that old heathen would send you here, so I came on ahead to get a fire started. My name's Matt Carlton, by the way."

Lacey held out her hand to shake his, but she was still soaked and shivering, so instead she held her hands out to the stove, where the fire burned fitfully. "What do you mean, you suspected I'd be sent here? Isn't this Trey's home?"

Matt Carlton shook his head. "Trey lives at the ranch. This place is a line shack. Cowboys use it sometimes when they're herding a bunch of cattle."

Lacey shook her head in confusion. "Why would my father-in-law send me here?"

"To get back at Trey for marrying you. The thing is, he had a woman in mind that he wanted his son to marry."

A thin smile lifted the corners of Lacey's lips. "Is this woman called Ruby?"

"That's the one. Did you meet her at the ranch?"

"I wasn't introduced to her, if that's what you

mean. But Mr Saunders called her Ruby. She's the one who opened the door to me and later suggested that I come here. Trey's house, she called it."

"That one," Matt said contemptuously. "She's as mean as Bull. Watch out for her, girl. She'll do you harm if she can. She wanted a marriage between her and Trey as badly as old Bull did."

Lacey smiled wryly at Matt. "I see I'm going to have a merry time of it."

"Things will change when Trey gets home," Matt assured her. "He'll bring you back to the ranch and see to it that Bull keeps a civil tongue in his mouth."

Lacey had her doubts about that. Matt didn't know the circumstances under which she and Trey had married. Nor did he know that she had no intention of living with Trey until he showed her that he was going to give up visiting loose women. Maybe they didn't love each other, but she intended to live up to her marriage vows and she expected her husband to do the same. She didn't want to be the laughing stock of the area because her husband whored around, nor did she want anyone's pity.

Matt shoved more wood into the stove, but though it glowed red from the roaring flames inside, its heat didn't reach more than two or three feet into the room. There were too many cracks in the walls where the bitter cold was seeping through.

"Look—" He paused and asked, "What is your

name?" Lacey grinned and told him. "Look, Lacey," he started all over again, "you can't possibly stay here. It will get colder later and we might even get some snow. There's not even a blanket on that poor excuse of a bed, and you could very well freeze to death."

When Lacey only looked at him helplessly, he said, "Here's what I've been thinking. An old cowhand of mine who retired a few years back died last week. He left a nice warm cabin and a horse and a cow and a few chickens. I've been taking care of them, but I really don't have the time for it. I'd appreciate it if you'd move in there and take care of the cabin and the animals until Trey gets back."

Lacey wanted to jump at the offer, but she didn't want to appear too forward. She looked around at the deplorable condition of the shack and suddenly she didn't care how she might appear to Matt. The offer of a warm place to live was too good to refuse.

"If you're sure you don't mind, Mr. Carlton."

"I'm Matt. Just call me Matt."

Lacey smiled and nodded. "I'll gladly take care of your friend's home and animals. I've never milked a cow, but I'm sure I can learn how." She grinned.

"Let's get out of here then. I believe it's warmer outside."

When Matt later pulled his stallion up beside a neat, sturdy-looking cabin nestled in a grove of cottonwoods, Lacey couldn't believe the difference between this building and the shack she'd left half an hour ago.

Matt swung out of the saddle and helped Lacey to climb out of the wagon. "Go on inside," he said, "while I put the mule in the barn and take care of the animals."

Lacey stepped up onto a wide porch that overlooked a shallow valley and a distant mountain. She visualized the old cowboy taking his rest in the chair pushed up against the wall, drinking in the beauty before him as he rocked.

She entered the cabin, and a pleased smile curved her lips when the floor squeaked beneath her feet. A wooden floor.

Lacey closed the door and pulled the wet shawl off her shoulders. In the shadowy room she walked to a fireplace and spread the shawl on the wide hearth. She noticed that the makings of a fire had been laid, needing only a match to be put to it.

She looked around and spotted a tightly capped jar of matches sitting on the mantel beside a clock. It was ticking, so evidently Matt had kept it wound. In a minute's time, she had flames leaping up the chimney.

Lacey was crouched in front of the fire, the red dress beginning to steam, when Matt stepped inside. In his hand he carried a pail of warm milk.

"We've got to get you out of those wet clothes." He frowned as he placed the milk on the table. "Old Jasper was a small man, and I think his clothes would fit you for the time be-ing. Until you can get into town and buy some feminine clothing."

"I had other dresses, respectable-looking ones, but they were stolen from the wagon," La-cey explained. "I had nothing left but what I'm wearing."

"We'll take care of that tomorrow," Matt said, pretending not to see Lacey's embarrassment. "I'll take you to the emporium and you can pick out everything you need."

"I don't know if I have enough money for that, Matt," Lacey said in a small voice. "I have some left over from what Trey gave me to buy trail grub, but it's his money and I don't know if he'd want me to spend it or not."

Matt looked at Lacey curiously. "Just what kind of marriage do you and Trey have?" he asked. "I'm beginning to think that it's a little unusual."

Lacey heaved a long sigh and sat down on the hearth. Matt Carlton had been so good to her, he deserved to know the whole story behind her and Trey's marriage.

Clasping her hands in her lap and gazing down at them, she said, "It wasn't a love match, Matt." She paused a second, then told him her story from start to finish, including Trey's stop at the brothel on his way out of town. "I felt really humiliated about that, Matt—preferring a whore over me."

Matt shook his head. This was one of the craziest stunts Trey had ever pulled. He hadn't taken into account that a wife was a big responsibility. He hoped that Trey was too honorable to just drop Lacey when he felt he had antagonized Bull enough. And since he hadn't slept with his wife, he might just have that in mind.

Lacey picked at the red dress. "I'm pretty sure Trey thinks I'm a loose woman because of this dress and the face paint I was wearing when we met."

Matt smiled wryly. This young woman certainly didn't look like a whore to him. Pure innocence looked out of her green eyes.

"Look, Lacey," he said soberly, "whatever the reason you and Trey married, you are his responsibility. Tomorrow you buy whatever you need and charge it to the Saunders's account. I promise you that Trey won't fault you for it.

"Now, light a lamp and go into Jasper's bedroom and see what you can find to wear. In the meantime I'll start a fire in the cookstove and make us some supper. I don't know about you, but my stomach is kicking up a ruckus."

"Mine too." Lacey gave him a wide smile, then went to search through the old cowboy's clothing.

The bedroom was smaller than the main room, but large enough to hold a full-sized bed, a small table beside it, a dresser, and a chair. The floor was bare except for a colorful Mexican rug spread beside the bed. The room was neat and clean and very masculine.

Lacey carried the lamp over to the dresser and opened the top drawer.

She didn't like going through another person's belongings, but the red dress was still wet and she was shivering so much, her teeth were chattering.

She finally chose a pair of twill trousers, a blue flannel shirt, a set of long johns, and a pair of woolen socks. The wet clothing was quickly exchanged for dry. The clothes were almost a perfect fit except for the seat of the pants. As she carried the wet clothes into the main room, she had a feeling that she filled that portion of the trousers more than the old cowboy had.

As Lacey spread her wet garments in front of the hearth to dry, her mouth watered at the delicious aromas coming from the kitchen.

"How do these steaks smell?" Matt asked when she walked into the kitchen. She crossed the floor to the stove and looked down at the two big pieces of meat sizzling in a skillet.

"I've never smelled anything better in my life," she answered Matt, who was stirring a pan of thinly sliced potatoes in another skillet. "Papa and I didn't have steak very often."

"Well, from now on you can have steak every day if you want it. God knows there's enough beef roaming around these parts. I run about a thousand head, and Trey and Bull have just as many, if not more out on the range.

"By the way, my place is only a couple of miles away. You can see my house and outbuildings from your porch."

Lacey was still trying to imagine so many cattle when Matt said, "Grab your plate and fill it up."

Matt and Lacey didn't talk much as they ate the tender steaks and lightly browned potatoes. They were both too hungry to waste their time on idle chit-chat.

Her stomach finally replete, Lacey was thinking of old Jasper's bed as Matt rolled a cigarette and lit it. She would clean up the kitchen, and as soon as Matt left, she would retire.

She stood up and started to clear the table. "Before you do the dishes, Lacey," Matt said, "let me show you what you must do with the milk I brought in."

He walked over to the dry sink and pulled open a shallow drawer. Out of it he brought a big square piece of white cloth. He held it for Lacey to see. "This is what Jasper strained the milk through. It must be washed after you use it, then boiled for ten minutes."

He opened a cupboard door and took out a large brown crock. He spread the cloth over it, and as he slowly poured the milk over it, he explained, "The milk has to be strained to catch all the dirt and other particles."

Lacey watched Matt carefully, thinking, *I can do that*.

"Now," Matt said when the milk pail was empty, "we put a big platter over the crock and store it in the little room off the kitchen."

73

Lacey followed him into the storage room and watched him place the covered crock on a shelf a few feet off the dirt floor. He looked at her and said, "The cream will rise to the top overnight, and tomorrow morning you can skim it off and keep it in a glass jar you'll find in one of the cupboards. When it's almost full, I'll show you how to shake it into butter.

"Of course, you'll need some for your coffee."

She followed Matt back into the kitchen, thinking, *I can do all that too.*

When she went back to clearing the table, Matt said, "There's a farmer woman, name of Annie Stump, who Jasper made a deal with. She'll come by a couple of times a week to collect the milk you haven't used. She feeds it to her hogs. In exchange for the milk, she supplied Jasper with pork and vegetables from her garden. She's a rough character but a good soul. She'll do anything for someone she likes."

Matt reached for his slicker. "I've got to get home now. I see the woodbox is full. Do you know how to keep a fire going all night?"

Lacey nodded. "You cover it lightly with ashes."

"That's right." Matt put his hat on and walked toward the door. Before he stepped outside, he said, "Tomorrow morning I'll teach you how to milk the cow."

When he closed the door behind him, Lacey thought, *I don't know if I can do that.*

74

Chapter Five

Trey came awake and stared up at the floor boards of the wagon. It was no longer raining, but in the approaching dawn the sky was cloudy and gloomy looking.

He shivered under his single blanket and muttered, "It's cold enough to freeze a man's rump off."

He could see Jiggers hobbling around the campfire, starting breakfast. This cold dampness was making the old fellow's rheumatism act up, he thought, feeling sorry for the elderly man he'd known and admired all his life.

The cowboys were still snoring away when Trey rolled out from beneath his shelter. He slipped his feet into his boots and grabbed their floppy "mule ears" to pull them on. His work boots were scuffed and worn down at the heels, unlike his dress boots, which were made of soft, fine leather with decorative stitching. They were handmade and cost more than a cow-hand's monthly wage.

Standing up, he tucked his still damp trousers into the boot tops so they wouldn't snag on brush or tangle in the stirrups. He joined Jiggers, who was pouring himself a cup of coffee.

"You're up early," the cook said, reaching for another cup. When he had filled it from a black-ened coffee pot and handed it to Trey, he added, "I figured everybody would sleep until I yelled for them to come eat. Couldn't you sleep?"

"I was too cold. I guess it's time to start using two blankets."

Slicing strips of bacon from a long slab, Jiggers said, "It seems to me that you've got more than rain and cold on your mind. Somethin' is botherin' you. You want to chaw about it?"

Trey started to shake his head, then reconsid-ered. Why not tell his long-time friend about what was worrying the hell out of him? Maybe talking about it would relieve his mind some.

He refilled his cup with the strong, hot brew. Staring into the fire he, asked, "Do you remem-ber me saying that I got married in Julesburg?"

"Yeah, I remember that wild tale."

"It wasn't a wild tale, Jiggers. It was the truth. I did get married."

The old man stared at him a moment, then

laughingly said, "Go on, you're joshin' me . . . ain't you?"

Trey shook his head. "It's the gospel truth."

"Who in the hell did you marry?" Jiggers spat a stream of tobacco juice into the fire. "I didn't think you knew any women in Julesburg exceptin' for the whores. I'm sure you didn't marry one of them."

Trey looked away from the confused cook as he said, "That's exactly what I did. I married a pretty little whore."

"Good Lord, Trey!" Jiggers exploded. "What in the hell did you go and do that for?"

Trey's firm jaw tightened. "I did it to give Bull Saunders a gouge he'll never forget, to make up a little bit for the torture he put my mother through. He pesters the hell out of me to marry that slut Ruby. To have a real whore for a daughter-in-law will give him a taste of his own medicine.

"Besides, I felt sorry for the girl."

Jiggers remembered the gentle Martha, who usually went around with a bruise on her face. He thought of how Bull had shamed her by bringing women to the house and sleeping with them.

He spat into the fire again and said in a hard voice, "I guess having a whore for a daughter-in-law would help to take the starch out of him, but he's not going to pay full price for his sins until he dies and burns in hell. What did you do with the woman? Leave her in the whore-house?"

"I didn't meet her in a brothel, and she's really not a woman yet. She looked to be around seventeen or eighteen. She and her father traveled around in an old worn-out wagon putting on medicine shows. He died from lung disease shortly before I rode into town.

"She looked so pathetic, crying out her grief, worrying about how she could get her father buried with two dollars and some change. The next thing I knew the idea of giving Bull the daughter-in-law he'd been yammering about hit me. I'd install a pretty little whore in his grand house.

"I struck a deal with her. If she'd marry me, I'd take care of her father's burial. She didn't like the idea, but she was desperate and finally agreed.

"After the ceremony I gave her some money and told her to go to the ranch and wait there for me."

"Good Lord, Trey, that's the damnedest fool thing you've ever done." Jiggers sent another stream of tobacco juice into the fire. "Even a whore don't deserve to meet that old devil all by herself. He'll chew her up and spit her out."

"I've been thinking about that, and it bothers the hell out of me. Lacey's not like the usual whore, brassy and forward. She's quiet and shy-like. Ruby and the old man will make mince-meat out of her. I should have sent her to Matt."

"Yeah, you should have. Matt would treat her decent and take care of her until you got back." After a short pause, Jiggers asked, "By the way, what *are* you gonna do with her when you get back?"

"Dammed if I know." Trey frowned into the fire, remembering the soft curves under the red dress. He'd like to sample them, but on the other hand he didn't like the idea of the folks back home knowing that he had married a whore.

The cowhands were beginning to stir, and the subject was dropped. "You've got a lot of thinkin' to do, son," Jiggers said and got busy around the campfire again.

The men were in a good mood despite the fact that their clothes were still damp and they'd been in the saddle for sixteen hours before rolling up in their bedrolls. With bantering and horseplay between them, the men took turns at the wash basin. Breakfast was ready then, and they lined up to have Jiggers fill their tin plates with flapjacks and bacon.

The sun was coming up and the cattle were struggling to their feet when the morning meal was eaten. The men straggled off to pick a horse from the remuda. Ten minutes later, astride the little mustang, Trey signaled the men to start the herd moving.

The herd would be halted around noon so the cattle could graze and the men could eat in shifts. The drive would resume then, completing ten to fifteen miles before the cattle were bedded down for the night.

As the mustang clomped along, Trey's thoughts were on the young girl he had married. Had Bull dared to refuse her entrance to the ranch house? A frown furrowed his brow. The old bastard was capable of anything.

He should go back to the ranch, Trey thought. Lacey was his responsibility until he decided what to do about her. He couldn't see himself remaining in such a marriage, but he couldn't just tell her to leave because he had changed his mind about wanting a wife.

"Maybe I'll give her enough money to go to another town and open up her own bawdy house," he mused out loud. "With her looks, she'd make a fine madam."

Lacey came awake to the crowing of a rooster. She lay a moment in a warm comfort she was unused to. Was a pleasant dream still lingering in her mind? she wondered. She tentatively stretched out a leg, sure that it would find the hard straw mattress she had slept on for ten years. But as her foot found the same downy softness, full awareness came to her.

She was in old Jasper's bed, in his cabin where that nice Matt Carlton had brought her.

Matt in all probability had saved her life. There was no doubt in her mind that in that drafty shack she would have caught pneumonia and died. No one would even have known she was there.

Lacey worried her lower lip with her teeth. Was that what her husband's father and the woman Ruby wanted? If so, it would have been a clever way of committing murder and getting away with it.

She must take Matt's advice and be more careful of those two, she thought as the sun rose and poured its light through the curtainless window. She put aside the disquieting thoughts of her two enemies for the time being and left her warm cocoon. Matt would probably be here any minute to teach her how to milk a cow.

Lacey quickly made up the bed, a habit she had acquired from living on the road. The wagon was so small, everything had to be kept neat and in place.

She hurried into the main room, and shivering in her borrowed long johns, she crouched in front of the fireplace and scraped away the ashes she'd spread over the coals before retiring. After she added some short pieces of wood to the glowing embers, she soon had a crackling fire sending its warmth into the room.

Lacey darted back into the bedroom and pulled on the trousers and shirt and woolen socks. She hadn't tried on the old man's boots yet.

Lacey liked the freedom of movement the masculine attire gave her as she strode into the kitchen and started a fire in the cookstove. If it was up to her, she'd continue to wear the old man's clothes. If she let the shirt tail hang free, it would hide the curves that men were in the habit of staring at.

She was sick to death of being ogled by hungry male eyes.

As she closed the lid on the firebox, she remembered the feel of her husband's smoldering eyes moving over her. Strangely, and to her discomfort, her body had responded to his hot gaze. Her breasts had tingled and her nipples had hardened. She had folded her arms across her chest so that he couldn't see how he affected her.

"And I'm glad that I did," Lacey said to the empty room as she placed a skillet on the stove and laid strips of bacon in it. "He's used to visiting whores, and I'll not have him thinking I'm that kind of woman."

She ignored the little voice that whispered, "He already thinks you're a whore," as she continued to think out loud.

"If he ever wants to get in my bed, he's going to have to stay away from such women. And not only that, he's going to court me, give us time to get to know each other."

That decision made, Lacey set a pot of coffee to brewing and went into the storage room carrying a spoon and a glass jar.

As Matt had promised, rich yellow cream had risen to the top of the milk. She skimmed off enough to fill the glass jar, and then replaced the cloth.

While the bacon was frying, Lacey found a bag of flour in one one of the cupboards and the ingredients to stir up a bread batter she would fry in the bacon grease later.

Fifteen minutes later, she was eating her breakfast and drinking a cup of invigorating coffee when Matt stepped up onto the porch and rapped on the door.

"Come in, Matt," she called cheerily. "The door is unbarred."

Her smile died when Matt stepped inside and she saw his angry face. "What's wrong?" She started to stand up.

"You foolish girl," he barked at her. "Did you sleep all night with the door unbarred?"

"Yes," Lacey answered in a small voice. "I'm not used to taking care of such things. Papa always saw to everything."

Matt's voice softened but his face remained stern. "Lacey," he began, "when word gets out that a pretty young woman is living here alone, there are some men who will start sneaking around the house at night. They'll not come around in the daytime for fear of what Trey would do to them if he found out. But there are some who do their meanness under cover of darkness so that the women can't name them.

"Now listen carefully to what I'm going to tell you. You must take care of all outside chores before darkness sets in. That also means bringing in enough wood to last you through the night. When all that's done, you bar the door and don't open it to anybody but me. Especially Bull or that bitch, Ruby. I trust them less than any man in Marengo."

Lacey's face had paled as Matt spoke, and he said gently, "I'm sorry if I've frightened you, honey, but I had to impress upon you the dangers that a woman alone has to face if she's not careful. If you keep the door barred at all times, you'll not come to any harm."

"Thank you for telling me, Matt. I'm afraid I'm pretty much a greenhorn with a lot to learn about living alone." A wistful look came into her eyes. "I imagine it will be a little lonesome sometimes."

"Not after you meet some of the womenfolk. They'll visit you, and you'll visit them." Matt smiled at her as he poured himself the cup of coffee she had forgotten to offer him. "In fact," he said as he sat down at the table, "you're going to meet Annie Stump sometime this morning. She'll be here to pick up your extra milk and will probably bring you a loaf of bread or a pie."

"That will be awfully nice of her," Lacey said.

"Around here it's what we call being neighborly."

Matt finished his coffee and asked with a twinkle in his eyes, "Are you ready for your first lesson in milking a cow?"

Lacey nodded. "But I'm a little nervous about it. I've never been around a cow before."

"Don't be nervous. Daisy is a gentle cow. All you have to worry about is getting whacked across the face with her tail. For some reason, cows have a habit of swinging their tails when being milked."

He picked up a pail, different from the one he'd used last night, and said, "These two pails are used only for milking. After every use they must be washed out with soapy water and rinsed well."

He picked up a small wooden pail then, and after filling it half full with warm water from the tea kettle on the stove, he dropped a piece of cloth in it. "The udder has to be washed before you start milking," he explained. "Cows aren't always careful where they lie down." He grinned. "If you get my meaning."

"I think I do." Lacey's eyes twinkled as she took from a peg in the wall an old jacket of Jasper's. Matt waited until she had pulled it on, then they left the cabin to begin Lacey's big adventure.

After three attempts, Lacey got the hang of squeezing and pulling on the milk-filled teats. When a stream of milk hit the bottom of the pail, she looked up at Matt with a wide smile.

"I can do it!"

"I knew you could." Matt's eyes crinkled with amusement at her glad cry.

When the pail was almost full and Daisy couldn't, or wouldn't, let down more milk, Matt took the pail from under her and placed it on a

Norah Hess

bale of hay. "Now I'll show you where the chicken feed is and how much you should feed them twice a day. About gathering their eggs— I should have taken them from the nests last night, but I was in a hurry to get home. When winter sets in, you must gather them every day by noon. Otherwise they will freeze and crack."

Matt also showed Lacey where the corn and oats for the cow and horse were kept. He pointed up to the half-loft and said, "Give them each a fork of hay along with the grain."

When they left the barn, Lacey was wondering if she could keep everything straight in her mind. Just then she saw a wagon bumping over the frozen ruts of the road leading to the cabin.

"Here comes Annie Stump," Matt said and waved a greeting to the amply proportioned woman handling the reins of a plow horse. "I see she has Franklin and Glory with her. They're nice kids."

Lacey wasn't listening to Matt. Her attention was on Annie Stump.

From the black floppy hat on her head down to her worn boots, the woman was dressed in male attire.

"Don't stare, Lacey," Matt said sotto voce. "Except when she goes to church, that's the way Annie dresses."

"Why does she do that?"

Matt chuckled. "I guess because she figures she's the man of her home. Her husband, Tollie, is a gentle man, but I don't think God ever cre-

86

ated a lazier one. Annie has to keep after him every minute of the day to get any work out of him. She and the children do most of it."

The wagon was entering the yard area, and Annie was sawing on the reins as she yelled, "Whoa!" She gave Lacey a curious look as she and the children climbed off the wagon.

"Who's the pretty young lady, Matt?" she asked. "Don't tell me an old buck like you finally went and got married?" Her eyes were teasing.

Matt's lips twisted in a half smile. "Annie, meet Lacey Saunders, Trey's new wife."

"You don't say?" Annie's mouth gaped open. "I never thought that wild hellion would settle down and get married."

Matt laughed. "I think that's everybody's opinion."

"Where you from, honey?" Annie looked at Lacey. "I don't remember ever seein' you in these parts before."

While Lacey was deciding what to answer and how much to tell the woman, Matt spoke.

"Lacey's from Julesburg. Matt's been courting her every time he drives a herd through there."

"My land, he sure has been close-mouthed about it. I ain't noticed he's changed his ways any."

"I'm sure he will now," Matt said, frowning at Annie.

"Of course he will," Annie said hurriedly, realizing she should have been more careful of what she said. After all, the girl probably didn't know about her husband's wild past.

Lacey held her breath when Annie said, "I'll bet ole Bull and beanpole Ruby didn't take kindly to Trey's gettin' married. It's well known that Bull had Ruby picked out to be his daughter-in-law."

Matt wasn't about to save face for Bull Saunders. He told the neighbor woman exactly what had happened when Lacey showed up at the Saunders ranch.

"Why, that's criminal," Annie exclaimed when Matt finished. "I wouldn't let my hogs sleep in that shack. They'd freeze to death."

"Exactly." Matt nodded. "And since Lacey would have known the same fate, I brought her here to old Jaspar's place until Trey gets back from the cattle drive. He'll straighten that old buzzard out, you can bet on that."

He abruptly dropped the subject. "Annie, you and Glory go on into the cabin and have some coffee with Lacey while Franklin and I load the milk on the wagon." He smiled at the fourteen-year-old, who had just hopped from the wagon, then turned to help his sister climb over the wagon wheel.

Lacey led the Stumps into the kitchen and was embarrassed at the state the room was in. The table still held her breakfast dishes, the stove was splattered with grease, and they could see through to the main room, where her red dress still lay on the hearth spread out to dry. She prayed Annie wouldn't see it and get the wrong impression of her.

"Please have a seat." She pulled out a chair that would put Annie's back to the fireplace. "I'll just clear the table before I pour us some coffee."

If Annie noticed the messy table, she made no mention of it as Lacey picked up her plate and cup and flatware. She was too busy firing questions. "How old are you, Lacey? You don't look much older than my twelve-year-old Glory."

"I'm eighteen, soon to be nineteen."

"Have you always lived in Julesburg? Are your parents alive?"

Matt, where are you? Lacey thought in near panic, not knowing how to answer Annie's questions. People would think badly of her if they knew she had spent most of her life traveling from town to town peddling her father's herbal tonics. Women who did things like that had a bad name.

Matt was suddenly beside her, an affectionate arm around her shoulders. "I'm afraid Trey has married an orphan town girl, Annie. She doesn't know a thing about ranching or farming. I guess we'll have to teach her about cattle and turnips."

They all laughed, and as Lacey poured coffee, Annie said, "I'll be right glad to help you in any way I can, girl."

"Thank you, Annie." Lacey smiled at the big woman as she put cream and sugar on the table.

"I expect I'll be calling on you quite a bit."

"Lacey and I are going into town later to buy her some heavier dresses and a warm coat," Matt said. "The clothes she brought with her are too lightweight for cattle country."

"I've been thinking, Matt," Lacey said as she stirred sugar into her coffee, "I like the feel of Jaspar's pants and shirt. I'd just as soon continue to wear them."

Matt looked startled and Annie looked pleased. "You've got the right idea, girl," she said. "They're more comfortable than wimmen's clothing and a whole lot warmer when it's thirty below and the wind insists on gettin' up under your skirt.

"Now the thing to do is buy a heavy jacket, strong boots, a wide-brimmed hat, a woolen scarf, and leather gloves." Annie paused a moment, then added as an afterthought, "Get yourself a church-goin' dress. A person has to show respect in God's house.

" 'Course you won't be goin' to church much when winter sets in and the snow is up to your butt."

A short time later, when Annie had taken her children and left, Matt looked at Lacey and asked, "Are you sure you want to wear men's clothing? Annie is the only woman around here who does. She gets away with it for two reasons—one, she doesn't care what people think, and two, she does outside work all the time."

"I'll be doing outside work too, Matt. And I

don't care to have the wind whistling up my skirts either." Lacey grinned at him. "Of course I don't want people talking about me. I wouldn't want to shame Trey."

Matt gave a snort of laughter. "You wouldn't shame Trey. He'd get a big laugh out of it because he doesn't give a damn what people think either. And if it makes old Bull mad, he'll like it all the more that you're running around in britches."

"Good. Then that's settled. When do you want to go to town?"

"Just as soon as you've strained the milk and put it in the storage room."

The sun was trying to break through the cloudy sky when Lacey and Matt started out for Marengo. Matt rode his black stallion, Midnight, and Lacey rode Jasper's sorrel.

Red was a spirited horse, but he was gentle and very intelligent. The old man had trained him to respond to different whistles.

"Where exactly are we situated in Wyoming?" Lacey asked as they cantered along.

"We're in the Powder River basin. It runs northeast through Wyoming and up into Montana. The basin lies between the Black Hills on the east and the Big Horn Mountains on the west. In between it's flat—fine grazing range."

"It's a beautiful land," Lacey said, wondering how long she'd be allowed to live in its splendor. It was possible that Trey could send her packing once he returned from Dodge City. There was

91

no telling where she might be two months from now.

The small town loomed ahead, and Lacey's mind swung to a new worry. Would they see some of her neighbors, and if so, would they be friendly like Annie, or cool and aloof like Ruby?

It was Saturday, and the women from the surrounding area had come to town to shop and to catch up on the current gossip as Lacey and Matt rode into Marengo. When he and Lacey dismounted in front of the mercantile, they received curious looks from three women across the street.

"Who is the teenager with Matt?" one of the women wondered out loud.

Their eyes widened when Lacey turned around and her very feminine rear end was outlined in Jasper's trousers.

"That ain't no boy," another woman whispered. "That's a grown woman."

"Are you sure, Tilda? The jacket is awfully flat in front."

"It's too big for her. It's hidin' her breasts."

The three women watched Lacey step up onto the wooden sidewalk. "I wonder who she is," the third woman said. "A relative of Matt's, do you think? I never heard that he has any kin."

"Let's go across the street and say howdy. He'll tell us who she is," Tilda said and led the way to where Matt and Lacey were engaged in serious conversation.

"Ladies." Matt touched his hat brim, finding

it hard not to laugh out loud. He knew the women were curious about Lacey.

When pleasantries had been exchanged he said, "Ladies, I want you to meet a new neighbor. This young lady is Lacey Saunders, Trey's new wife. She's living in old Jasper's place until Trey gets home from the cattle drive."

There was dead silence for a moment as the ranch women stared at Matt, dumbfounded. Then in unison they swung their gazes at Lacey.

"My goodness," the outspoken Tilda said, "she don't look much older than my fifteen-year-old at home." She stuck out her hand to Lacey. "Welcome to our community, Lacey." She smiled and added, "It's always nice to have a new face around. We get tired of having to look at each other."

The other two women laughingly agreed and then shook hands with Lacey also. "I can imagine why you don't want to live with that overbearing Bull," a woman called Loretta said.

As Lacey wondered what to reply to that, Bull himself came stomping up to them. Ignoring her, not even recognizing her in the male clothing with her hair tucked up under her hat, he started right in on Matt.

"What's this I hear about you taking that little whore in? I'd like to know why in the hell she went to you."

The cold look Matt bent on the furious Bull was deadly. "You've got both things wrong, you miserable bastard," Matt ground out. "One, Lacey is not a whore, and two, she didn't come to me. Now, do you want me to come right out and tell these ladies why Lacey is living in old Jasper's place? Are you sure you want them to know the truth?"

All the bluster went out of Bull. However, the hatred he felt for Matt Carlton was hot in his eyes. He stood a moment, trying to stare Matt down. When Matt's threatening gaze never faltered for a moment, he wheeled around and stamped off, muttering to himself.

Matt looked at Lacey, saw her pale, stricken face, and took her arm. Turning her toward the store's door, he said, "If you'll excuse us, ladies, we've got some shopping to do."

The ladies said a friendly good-bye to Lacey, with invitations to come visit them.

Lacey smiled shyly at them, her spirits lifted somewhat. Evidently her neighbors didn't believe her father-in-law's description of her.

"That low-life bastard," Matt gritted between his teeth as he pushed the door open and stood aside for Lacey to enter, "I should have put a bullet through his heart years ago."

Lacey wanted to ask about the hostility between Matt and Bull, but the shopkeeper was greeting Matt.

"What can I do for you and your friend, Matt?" Erwin Doolittle asked. He glanced at Lacey, started to look away, then returned for a sharper look. "I guess I should have said young lady."

Matt repeated the same information he'd given Annie Stump and the ladies outside. He received the same reaction from the storekeeper as he had from them.

It seemed to Lacey that no one had a good word for her father-in-law.

"Lacey is a town girl, Erwin, and needs warmer clothes for ranch life," Matt said when Erwin finished imparting his opinion of Bull Saunders. "We need to buy some two-piece ladies' long johns, woolen socks, trousers and shirts, a hat, boots, and a sheepskin jacket. And—oh yes, she'll need a go-to-church dress."

Lacey tugged at Matt's elbow. "That's too much," she whispered. "Trey won't like it. He'll think he's married a gold-digger."

"Hell, Lacey, it's not like you're spending his money on fripperies. You're only buying the clothing that is necessary if you insist on dressing like a man. Now get busy and choose whatever you need."

"Well, if you're sure," Lacey said, still doubtful. She walked over to a long table where shirts and trousers were stacked and started looking through them for the smallest size she could find.

"Why don't you look over the boys' clothing on the other table," Erwin suggested. "You'll more likely find your size there."

Lacey found that he was right, and in less than an hour she had chosen four shirts, three pairs of heavy trousers, a light-colored hat, boots, and a jacket.

She was looking through the rack of dresses when Matt walked over and stood beside her. "Take that red woolen one," he suggested. "You look good in red." His eyes teased her.

Lacey blushed, knowing that he was referring to the short red dress she'd been wearing the first time he saw her.

However, the red dress Matt suggested was altogether different from the other scanty one. It had a high, white lace collar and cuffs, with glass buttons going down the front of the close-fitting bodice. The full skirt would fall to her ankles. It was a very sedate, respectable dress.

"I like it," Lacey said and took the dress off the rack.

On their way to the counter where Lacey had piled the other clothing, Matt said, "I saw you eying that material over there. Would you like to sew yourself some other dresses?"

"Oh no. I was only thinking that the one bolt would make pretty curtains for the cabin windows."

"That's right—Jasper didn't have anything at his windows," Matt said. "Go get the cloth. A woman needs her privacy."

Lacey had no idea how many yards of material she'd need for two windows, nor did Matt. But Erwin did. He deftly measured out the necessary length of the blue-and-white flowered calico she had chosen.

"Do you have thread and needles?" he asked as he wrapped the cloth in a sheet of brown paper. Lacey shook her head, and he reached below the counter and brought up a packet of needles and a spool of white thread.

"Much obliged for your help, Erwin," Matt said when Lacey's purchases were wrapped. "You and Nellie will have to come out to the cabin and see what kind of job Lacey does on her curtains."

"We'll sure do that. Nellie will at any rate. I don't have much time to go visiting."

"He's awfully nice, isn't he?" Lacey said as they tied the packages on their mounts.

"Yes, he and Nellie are fine folks," Matt said as he boosted Lacey onto the sorrell. "You'll find that most of your neighbors around here are good, hard-working people."

As she and Matt rode homeward, Lacey prayed that she'd be around long enough to get to know those people.

Chapter Six

Stars were still shining coldly in the sky when Trey awoke. The white glow in the east, however, said that dawn was approaching.

As he lay waiting for Jiggers to build a fire and start a pot of coffee to brewing, he relived the dream that had awakened him. What had it meant, if anything? He'd had the same kind of dream before, in which Lacey was in some kind of danger. Did a feeling of guilt have anything to do with these dreams?

More and more he was feeling contrition at what he'd done. He should never have sent Lacey to face his father alone. So what if she was a little whore—she didn't deserve that. A cur didn't deserve that.

Trey pushed the worrisome thoughts from

his mind when he heard Jiggers making waking-up noises. He watched the the cook crawl from beneath the wagon, grunting in pain from aching and swollen joints.

The old fellow was getting too old to make these drives, he thought. Before the next drive he intended to hire a younger man to take over the chuck wagon. Jiggers would feel insulted and raise a ruckus, but he'd just have to get over it. He was getting too old to be out in this kind of weather for any length of time. Before they got back to the ranch, there would be snow on the ground and the temperature would be below freezing. Jiggers was going to become so stove-up, he wouldn't be able to get out of bed in the mornings, and that would kill his spirit.

When the aroma of coffee wafted to him, Trey crawled out of his blankets. He quickly rolled them up in the tarpaulin that had kept the damp coldness of the ground to a minimum. Yanking on his boots, he stamped over to the fire and grunted good morning to Jiggers.

"Looks like it's gonna be a fair day," Jiggers said as Trey helped himself to a cup of coffee.

"How in the hell do you know that?" Trey grunted, hunkering down beside the fire and sipping at the hot coffee. "The sun isn't even up."

The old cook studied Trey's stony face a minute, then complained, "You're so damn grouchy lately, Trey. I never see you smile or laugh anymore."

100

"I haven't seen anything to laugh or smile about lately," Trey answered sourly.

"The other fellers always find somethin' to laugh about."

"Will you stop your jawing at me and start breakfast. I'd like to get the herd moving before lunch time."

"Yes, sir, right away, sir," Jiggers said indignantly and began banging pots and pans around.

"Will you stop that racket," Trey growled. "you're gonna start them ornery critters to stampeding."

Jiggers knew what Trey said was true and went about frying bacon and mixing a bowl of flapjack batter in a quieter fashion. Sometimes it took only the snapping of a twig to start the longhorns running.

He was still irked with Trey, though, and his stiffly held back and jerky actions showed it.

Trey was instantly sorry for having spoken so sharply to his old friend. As he poured himself another cup of coffee, he asked in a genial voice, "What's the date, Jiggers?"

Jiggers looked at the calendar tacked inside the chuck wagon and said, "The twenty-ninth of November."

Another month to go before he got back home. Trey stared moodily into the fire. He looked up at Jiggers, who was adding more wood to the fire, and asked, "Do you think Cole could take the herd on into Dodge without me?"

" 'Course he could. I don't know why you even come along on this drive. Cole Stringer is the best trail boss in all of Wyoming. Are you longin' to see your little bride, or are you afraid of what Bull might have done to her?"

Trey ignored the first question and answered the last one. "There's no telling what he might have done to her. I guess it's expecting too much that she might have come to know Matt."

"Yeah, it's a little too far-fetched to think that." Jiggers's tone softened a little. "You'd have nothin' to worry about if she was with him. He'd look after her as if she was his own."

Trey nodded and went back to staring into the fire, his thoughts on Matt Carlton.

It had been Matt to whom he'd taken his troubles as a youngster, and it had been the same kind friend who said it was all right for a fellow to cry if he was hurting. Trey sighed. He'd have had a hard time growing up if it hadn't been for his friend Matt.

The cowboys were beginning to rise, grunting and groaning from sore muscles. But after a bracing cup of Jiggers's strong coffee, they were up to their usual tricks as they lined up for breakfast.

Trey waited until Cole Stringer took his place in the line, then stepped up beside him. "Cole," he said, "I'm going to leave you to take the herd on in alone. I have a feeling I should get back to the ranch."

"Sure, boss." Stringer gave Trey an amused

look. "That's my job, isn't it?"

"Yes, it is, Cole. I only used the trip as an excuse to get away from the place for a while."

"I can't fault you for that. I always look forward to gettin' away from Bull for a while myself."

Nothing more was said between the two men, and as soon as breakfast was eaten, the cowboys went to select their horses from the remuda. They were saddled and ready to ride out just as the herd was struggling to their feet and looking for grass.

Trey watched the cowboys move out the herd, thinking that in a few weeks they would be in Dodge City if everything went well. He smiled to himself. The men's first stop would be for a shave, haircut, and bath. They'd stop next at a mercantile for new clothes to replace their filthy tatters.

Then, decked out in new duds, the men would head for the nearest saloon. After a couple of drinks to cut the dust in their throats, they'd move on to a house of prostitution. After they'd enjoyed a few days of carousing, they'd head back to the ranch . . . to start all over again.

Jiggers looked down at Trey from the chuck wagon seat. "I'm glad you're going back, Trey. I'm sure that girl married you in good faith, and she's your responsibility as long as you're married to each other."

"Yeah, I know," Trey said, and when the

wagon started to roll he turned the little mustang in the direction of home.

The early afternoon was cold and still as Lacey rode along, her thoughts on the warmth awaiting her in Jasper's little cabin.

There had been one light covering of snow in late November, which had not been unexpected for that time of year. What had been surprising was the small amount of it. Usually the first snow dumped six to eight inches on the ground. It was now the second week in December, and there had been no more. Everyone said that they were in for a blizzard before long.

Lacey nudged the sorrel with her heels. "Step it up, fellow. I've got to get the chores done before dark."

She had ridden into Marengo to purchase kerosene. This morning when she filled the lamps and two lanterns, she had used the last of the oil. Having no desire to be left in the dark when night came on, she had left for town right after lunch.

After living in near poverty the last ten years, it was a comfortable feeling to be able to buy what she needed without counting pennies.

I mustn't get too used to it, Lacey reminded herself. She could be right back to those near-starving days when Trey returned home. She had no idea what kind of man he really was. He looked and acted like a man who would do right by a wife, though. And Matt claimed that he was a fine man.

Lacey hoped that the life she knew now could continue. She enjoyed not only this new-found comfort but also the women friends she had found for the first time in her life. She would hate to lose them.

The sorrel topped a small knoll, and Lacey looked down at the sturdy little cabin. It was a welcome sight with the smoke curling up from its chimney. The temperature had dropped several degrees since she started out at noon. It would be cozy and warm inside.

But that warmth would have to wait a little longer, Lacey thought, riding to the barn. She had to take care of Red first.

The old mule brayed her a welcome when she led the sorrel into the stall next to his. "You're getting fat, Jocko," she said as she removed the saddle from the horse, then removed the bit from his mouth. "You appreciate your new life, too, don't you?"

When Lacey left the barn, she went straight to the long cords of wood stacked behind the cabin. She knew the woodbox was empty and Matt had said not to go out after dark. So fuel for both the fireplace and the cook stove had to be brought in before the sun went down.

She carried in six armloads of short split logs, enough to fill the woodbox and extra, which she stacked beside the raised hearth. It would see her through the night and part of tomorrow.

Lacey brushed off her arms and glanced up at the clock on the mantel. It was a little early to milk the cow, but since she was already bundled up, she might as well get it done.

Half an hour later, as she was returning to the house, a pail of milk swinging from her hand, she saw Matt riding toward the cabin. She hadn't seen him in a couple of days, and she returned his wide smile as he dismounted.

"Why don't you put the stallion in the barn and have supper with me?" she invited him. "It's sugar-cured ham. Annie brought it to me yesterday."

"I'll take you up on that, Lacey. I can't remember when I last had ham." He took a loop of rope off the saddle horn. "I'll be in as soon as I string this rope from the cabin to the barn. We're going to have a blinding blizzard any day now, and you'll have to use this guide rope to move from the cabin to the barn. A few years back, a man was caught in a snowstorm, became lost, and froze to death six feet from his house. It appeared the wind had torn loose the rope tied to his barn door and he had nothing to guide him."

For the first time, Lacey became fully aware of how alone she was most of the time. What if she got sick, or fell and broke a bone? Days might pass before anyone came along.

Matt saw her worried frown and suspected what was on her mind. He took a square of red material from his pocket and said as he shook it out, "I'm going to rig this up to a rope and pulley. If you should ever need help, just hoist it to the top of the cabin. Someone will see it and come hurrying over. It's a signal we ranchers have. We always watch for a red flag."

"I hope I never have to use it," Lacey said soberly.

Matt's dog came up to them, his tail wagging a greeting to Lacey. "Why don't I leave my hound with you until Trey gets back," Matt said. "He'll be company for you, and you'll feel better knowing that he will protect you."

"I appreciate that, Matt." Lacey patted the big dog on the head. "I hear so many noises at night. I've never lived alone before."

"Well, you won't be alone anymore. Cy will be with you." Matt grinned. "He's a real good listener if you want to talk. Oh, and one other thing—make sure you let him out for a few minutes before you retire. You don't want him to have any accidents in the cabin."

"I hope he likes staying with me," Lacey said, her hand on the doorknob.

"He'll like it fine. Stretched out in front of a fireplace beats burrowing in the hay in the barn. Lupe, my housekeeper, doesn't like dogs underfoot."

Lacey had supper on the table when Matt returned from the barn. He had two helpings of ham and sweet potatoes, declaring it was the finest meal he'd had in a long time. "The only pork I get at the ranch is either bacon or salt pork.

They took their coffee into the main room to drink in front of the fireplace. With their stockinged feet propped on the hearth, they sipped the strong brew, conversation unnecessary between them.

Then Matt, in the act of rolling a cigarette, suddenly lifted his head, listening. "Hear the hound tuning up, Lacey?" The corners of his eyes wrinkled with his wide grin. "He's chasing a bobcat. What do you say we follow him, see if he trees it?"

Lacey jumped to her feet, readily agreeing. She and Matt had done this twice before and she enjoyed tramping through the woods at night, Matt carrying a lantern.

She slid her arms into Jasper's old worn jacket, stuffed her hair up under her hat, and said as she pulled on her leather gloves, "I'm ready. Let's go."

"Aren't you forgetting something?" Matt raised an amused eyebrow.

"I don't think so. Should I take my rifle?"

Matt looked down at her feet. "What about your boots?"

Lacey gave an embarrassed giggle, then slipped her feet into the fur-lined boots sitting on the hearth.

A full moon and the lantern swinging from Matt's hand made it easy to follow the hound's prints in the light snowfall. Although they ran as fast as they could to keep him in sight, the young dog soon out-distanced them. His baying yowl finally became so muted, they could barely hear him.

Matt and Lacey stopped for minute to catch their breath and to decide whether to go on or return to the house. Matt had just said that they might as well go back home when the long, drawn-out howl of a wolf rent the stillness of the cold night.

It was a lonely call that chilled Lacey to the bone and made Matt swear under his breath.

He was checking the loading of his rifle when, as if from thin air, a shaggy gray wolf stood in front of them. The hair on his back was bristled, and his fangs were bared in a deep snarl. When his long body went rigid, a warning that he was ready to spring, Matt raised the rifle to his shoulder and squeezed the trigger.

The gun misfired, and the next instant the beast was at Matt's throat, his sharp teeth ripping at his jacket collar. Screaming at the top of her lungs, Lacey picked up a thick stick protruding from the snow and brought it down on the wolf's head. The club was rotten and cracked in half. It served only to enrage the animal more.

As Matt wrestled with the wolf, trying to break its grip, Lacey, still screaming for help, grabbed the useless rifle and began beating the wolf over the head.

The hammering on his head didn't deter the

animal for a moment, and Matt was growing tired. Lacey became desperate and was about to grab the wolf by the scruff of his neck to try to pull him off Matt. Then a shot rang out, and with a frightened yelp, the wolf turned Matt loose and took off through the cottonwoods.

Lacey spun around to see who their rescuer was. She could only stare, not believing her eyes.

Chapter Seven

Trey awakened with a bad case of morning desire. It was six weeks since he'd been with a woman—a month on the cattle drive and two weeks on his way home. The whore he'd visited in Julesburg didn't count. He'd been unable to achieve a release.

But he'd be pulling into the ranch today or tomorrow and would be able to take care of his condition.

He planned to stop at the house long enough to clean up, see how his wife was faring with Bull, then ride into Marengo. There he'd go to the tavern, Whiskey Pete's, and spend the night with Sally Jo.

Sally Jo was the singer at the tavern, and ever since she came to town two years ago, he had visited her about three times a week. Although she wasn't known as a whore, she was an expert in bed, and he couldn't wait to get between the sheets with her.

An idea hit Trey that brought a smile of startled surprise to his face. He had a wife at the ranch, a pretty little whore. He'd be a damn fool not to try her out. She might be real good. If she didn't suit him, she was young enough to be taught what pleased him.

Trey rolled out of the blankets and went through the same routine he'd followed since turning the herd over to Cole. As he built a fire and started a pot of coffee to brewing, he thought to himself that he'd be glad to get a decent meal inside him again. His suppers had consisted mostly of sage hens he'd shot from the saddle and roasted over his campfire. His breakfasts had been fried salt pork, hard tack, and coffee.

Trey had been riding half the day when he began to spot familiar sights—a grove of cottonwoods, the skeleton of a steer's head nailed to a tree, a pile of buffalo bones bleached white by the sun. He decided that he could make it home today, although darkness would probably have set in.

It was around six o'clock when Trey spotted the dim kerosene light shining from the kitchen window in the ranch house. A strange eagerness gripped him. Suddenly he was looking forward to seeing his wife. He remembered how the red

Lacey

dress had revealed her soft, feminine curves, and he smiled with anticipation.

His smile turned sour when he rode up to the house and Bull spoke from the shadows of the porch.

"I guess you've come lookin' for that whore you married."

"Sure have." Trey slid out of the saddle and stepped upon the porch. "How do you like her? Isn't she a beauty? I'll bet you're real proud to have such a looker for a daughter-in-law."

Bull sniffed contemptuously. "There ain't a man alive who wouldn't be proud to welcome a whore as a family member."

"I knew you'd feel that way," Trey said, pretending not to hear the sarcasm in Bull's voice. He stepped up onto the porch. "I'll just go in and give her a loving howdy."

"You won't find her here."

"Why in the hell won't I?" Trey swung around to face Bull, his eyes narrowed dangerously. "This is her home. Where else would she be?" He took a threatening step toward the man he reluctantly called father. "Did you refuse to let her in the house?"

"Not exactly. She didn't want to stay here." Bull's fat lips lifted in a sneer. "I hear that she's took up with your old friend, Matt."

"I don't know if I believe that, but thank God Matt has befriended her." Trey stepped off the porch and climbed back into the saddle. As he picked up the reins, he said, "I'm sure I'll have more to say to you after I've found Lacey and got the truth from her. There's a lot more you're not telling me, old man."

Bull looked uneasy as Trey put the mustang to a hard gallop. Trey in a rage was something he didn't look forward to confronting.

Trey raced the little mount across the range. If Lacey hadn't wanted to stay at the ranch, she had been made to feel unwelcome. He'd find out the truth of it, and if it was as he suspected, all hell was going to break loose when he returned home.

His resentment grew as he remembered the many whores his father had brought into their home over the years, shaming his mother. And there was the Indian woman he kept permanently at the house for his lust and abuse.

Trey felt sorry for the woman and had often wondered why she hadn't killed him in his sleep a long time ago, or at least left him. He imagined that she stayed on because she had nowhere to go, and that was the reason she continued to take his beatings and degrading use of her.

Within half an hour, Trey was knocking on Matt's door. José Perez, Lupe's husband, opened it. He smiled widely and said, "You're back early, Trey. Did you run your cattle all the way to Dodge?"

"Not hardly." Trey laughed. "There wouldn't be much meat left on them if I did that. I left the herd a couple of weeks back. I had a feeling

I should get back home."

José slid him a sly grin. "I don't blame you for hurrying home. Your wife is a beautiful young woman. And, I might add, too good for a wild hombre like you."

Trey hid his surprise at the Mexican's praise of Lacey. He knew she was beautiful—but too good for him? Didn't the man know he was talking about a whore?

"Is Matt here?" he switched the subject.

"No, he's not, Trey. I think he probably had supper with your wife. He does that a lot. I heard his hound baying before, and they are most likely running him. They do that once in a while."

"Isn't my wife living here with Matt?" Trey looked at José curiously.

"Oh, no. She's living in old Jasper's place. He passed away shortly after you left with the herd."

Trey stood a moment trying to make sense out of everything. Nothing was going the way he had planned it. "Well," he said, turning and walking off the porch, "I'll ride over there and chase them down if necessary."

Trey was dead tired and gut-hungry as he approached old Jasper's neat little cabin. When no one answered his knock, he pushed the door open and walked inside.

The burning lamp in the table revealed that two people had recently eaten a meal there. His mouth watering, he touched the back of his hand to the ham shank lying on a platter and smiled. It was still warm, as would be the coffee pot sitting on the back of the stove. He cut himself a thick slice of the meat, laid it on one of the used plates, then spooned the two remaining sweet potatoes alongside the ham. He sat down and pulled the small woven basket of biscuits up to his plate.

Trey forgot the table manners his mother had taught him as he tore into his supper like a starving dog. When his hunger was sated and he had a cup of coffee under his belt, he let his gaze wander over the kitchen and into the part of the main room he could see from his spot at the table.

Everything was vastly changed from the last time he visited Jasper. Beneath the dirty dishes there was a flowered tablecloth, and lifting his gaze he discovered matching curtains at the window. Jasper hadn't had anything at the window except dirt and grime.

Trey's eyes glinted with amusement. It appeared that his little whore was quite a homemaker.

Satisfied that Matt and Lacey were running the hound, he went back outside and climbed onto the tired little mustang. "I promise that you will get a bag of oats soon." He patted the little pony's neck.

Matt's big footprints and Lacey's small ones were easy to follow in the moon-lighted snow. He hadn't ridden far when shrill screams split the air. He urged the little mount to run again. That yell was a distress call if ever he had heard one.

Trey arrived on a scene that made his blood run cold. Matt was on his back wrestling with the biggest wolf he'd ever seen, while a young teenager was beating the animal on the head with a rifle butt. A hound bayed at the edge of the clearing. Trey snatched his Colt from its holster and fired into the air, wondering where Lacey was and scared to death that the wolf had killed her. With a yelp of surprise, the wolf turned Matt loose and sped off toward the mountain, the hound in pursuit.

Matt sat up, and the teenager stared at Trey in surprise and something else he couldn't put a name to. Was it a mixture of shock and uneasiness?

"Howdy, Matt," he said, looking around for Lacey. When he saw no sign of a sprawled body, he decided that she wasn't with Matt. She could have been in bed asleep all the time he was in the cabin.

As he blew the smoke from his gun barrel and reached into his vest pocket for a cartridge to refill the empty cylinder, he grinned at Matt and said, "Ole Lobo almost got you, didn't he?"

"He sure as hell did." Matt fingered the frayed and mangled collar of his jacket, which was all that had kept the sharp fangs from piercing his throat. "I'd have been a goner if you hadn't come along.

"You're home early," he added, climbing to his feet. You didn't have any trouble with the herd, did you?"

"Naw, I just got tired of punching cattle." Trey grinned.

"That little bride of yours wouldn't have anything to do with your early arrival, now would it?" Matt asked slyly as he brushed the snow and leaves off his legs and thighs.

"Speaking of my bride, where in the hell is she? Perez said she was with you."

"Well, dammit, she is." Matt snorted. "You nit-wit, she's standing right in front of you."

Trey turned a disbelieving gaze on Lacey. This fresh-faced innocent boy—girl—couldn't be the whore he had married.

"There's something fishy going on here, Matt," he said, keeping a suspicious gaze on Lacey. "This is definitely not the person I married."

A bitter smile twitched the corners of Lacey's lips. So this was how he intended to get out of the marriage he had rushed into. She didn't blame him for changing his mind. She had suspected that he would once he thought everything over. But to pretend that he didn't know her was a yellow-bellied cur's way of getting out of a predicament. She had thought better of him.

Well, there was one thing he had forgotten. She had a marriage certificate, and when they got back to the house she'd wave it under his nose and see if it didn't refresh his memory.

Lacey snatched Jasper's old hat off her head and the loosened tawny hair fell around her shoulders. Her stormy green eyes glaring at him, she said sharply, "It won't work, Trey Saunders. You know damn well that I'm your wife.

"I'd have agreed to an annulment if you'd been man enough to ask for one, but since you want to act like a cur, I'll never agree to it. Nor will I give you a divorce. Now what do you think about that?" She continued to glare at Trey, her fists on her slender hips.

Trey tried to speak but couldn't utter a word as he stared at the angry, spitting little kitten he now recognized. Who wouldn't remember that hair and those rich red lips?

A slow smile crept across his face. To bed this fiery little miss might be worth being tied to her for a long time.

He swallowed, regained his speech, and said with a grin, "I sure married myself a wildcat, didn't I, Matt?"

"Wild enough to hold her own with you, I'd say," Matt chuckled. "What made you decide she was Lacey after all?"

"Her hair and eyes. What threw me at first is that she doesn't have her face all painted up like she did when I married her."

He gave Lacey a rakish grin. "Let's get on to the ranch, and after I've chewed Bull out good and proper, you and me will get better acquainted."

Lacey's face clouded indignantly. "I will never live under the same roof with that awful old man."

Trey's eyes narrowed. "What did the old bastard say to you?"

"It wasn't so much what he said," Matt answered Trey's question, "it was what he done."

A savage look came into Trey's eyes. "Are you saying that old no-good tried to get Lacey in bed with him?"

"No, he didn't do that, but he tried something that could have turned out worse. He and that Ruby told her that your place was a couple of miles from the ranch house. They sent her to that line shack up in the foothills. She was soaking wet from the rain storm we'd had. If she'd stayed in that shack, she would have died from pneumonia.

"I had directed Lacey to the ranch, and I knew damn well she wouldn't be welcomed. I suspected what Bull might do, so I was at the shack when she arrived there. I took her to Jasper's place, and that's where she's been ever since."

"And that's where I intend to stay," Lacey said defiantly.

"I'll kill that son-of-a-bitch for that," Trey grated. "He meant for Lacey to die."

"I think that too, Trey, but calm down. He's not worth hanging for."

"It was that Ruby woman's idea," Lacey interjected.

"I'll take care of her too," Trey said grimly as he took Lacey's arm and boosted her onto the mustang's back. As he swung up behind her, he picked up the reins and said to Matt, "Thanks for looking out for her, Matt. I'll see you sometime tomorrow."

Matt's lips lifted in amusement as he watched them ride away, thinking that Trey couldn't wait to get his bride in bed. They'd had a rocky start, but he felt sure that in time the rough places would be smoothed out and they would have a very happy marriage.

"Well, Cy," he said, stroking the panting hound's head, "I guess she won't be needing you after all."

Matt was right about Trey being impatient to make love to his wife. Feeling the softness of her in his arms had his blood simmering by the time they arrived at the small cabin. He took Lacey's arm and helped her to dismount, then rode on to the barn.

A horse was never unsaddled and fed as fast as the little mustang was that night.

Lacey was clearing the table when Trey walked into the kitchen and closed the door behind him. In one motion, he jerked off his jacket and pulled Lacey into his arms. As she gazed up at him, startled, his hand came up to cup her breast and his lips came down to cover hers.

Norah Hess

"Let's go to bed," he whispered huskily against her mouth.

Lacey stiffened and, giving him an unexpected shove, freed herself from his embrace. "You're not sleeping here," she said sharply.

"Of course I'm sleeping here." Trey frowned at her. "Where else would I sleep? I'm your husband."

Lacey moved until the table was between them. "I'm not going to sleep with you until I get to know you. Also, not until you stop visiting bawdy houses."

Trey gave a bark of laughter, then jeered, "Did you get to know all the other men you slept with? Why the innocent act now?"

Lacey gave a disbelieving cry, and darting around the table, she slapped him across the face with all the force she could put behind it. "Get out before I shoot you," she said through clenched teeth.

Trey looked at her, his expression one of astonishment. Then, slowly, a dark flush of anger spread over his face. "You little bitch," he bit out, "if you were a man, I'd knock you flat on your ass for that."

"If I were a man, you wouldn't have insulted me in the worst kind of way." Lacey's glinting eyes dared him to lay a hand on her.

Trey snatched up his jacket, and jerking it on, he sneered, "I'm sure you've been insulted worse than being called a whore."

While Lacey sought for some cutting words

122

that would slice into him as his had into her, he left the house, slamming the door behind him. Minutes later, she heard the little mustang tearing past the cabin.

Lacey ran to the window and peered out. She could barely make out the shape of horse and rider. While she and Trey were having their bitter words, it had started snowing—big heavy flakes accompanied by a vicious wind whipping across the range.

Winter had arrived in earnest.

Still shaking with rage, Lacey pulled the curtains together and started clearing the table. When she had set the kitchen to rights, she walked into the main room and sat down before the fire. As she rocked slowly, some of her anger began to die.

She leaned her head back and let her gaze wander around the cozy room. She had sewn curtains for the window and made cushions for the two chairs from the same material. They were quite comfortable, lightly filled with hay from the barn. Her gaze dropped to the brightly colored rug before the fire. Matt had visited an Indian village and bought it from the old woman who wove rugs to sell to the white people.

Lacey sighed. She loved this little cabin, the first real home she'd had in years, almost in her memory. How much longer could she live in it? she wondered. Not long, more than likely. Trey would have their marriage annuled as soon as possible now, and she'd have to leave. And as angry as he was when he left, he wouldn't care what happened to her. There would be no monetary aid from him.

There was Matt, Lacey remembered, He'd help her get settled in some kind of job or position, but she couldn't live in the same community with Trey knowing what he thought of her.

The tears she had withheld while battling with Trey were set free. As they ran down her cheeks, she thought how foolish she had been to marry a man she didn't know and didn't love.

The snow and wind stinging his face and bringing tears to eyes, Trey urged the little mount on. His anger at Lacey had abated, leaving him confused. Why was it that his father and Ruby recognized his wife as a whore while José Perez and Matt spoke of her with respect and affection?

The ranch house lights came in view through the swirling snow, and Trey put everything from his mind, preparing himself to face Bull and not to strike him in his anger.

Chapter Eight

As Trey rode past the ranch house on his way to the barn, he saw the wide shape of his father peering at him through the kitchen window. "Take a good look, you old devil," he muttered, "and pray that I don't beat the living hell out of you."

In the barn he wiped the little mustang down with a burlap bag, then gave him a good helping of oats. He draped a blanket over the tired little animal for extra warmth before going to his stallion's stall. He scratched the handsome horse behind the ears as he said, "I've missed you, fellow. Have they been taking good care of you while I was gone?"

Trey had raised the five-year-old stallion from a colt he had roped from a herd of wild horses.

Somewhere back in his bloodline there had been a palomino. It showed in his coloring and slender legs that indicated speed.

Prince had come up to his expectations. He had won the last three races the community put on every Fourth of July. He intended to win in this coming July's celebration also.

Giving Prince a pat on his magnificent head, Trey left the barn ready to do battle with his parent.

Unleashed anger was in his eyes and in the swiftness of his movements as he flung open the kitchen door, then slammed it behind him.

"Dammit, Trey, you didn't clean the snow off your boots," was Bull's greeting when Trey walked into the parlor.

Trey looked down at the heavily encrusted snow on his boots. "I must have forgotten," he said and deliberately stamped one foot and then the other. He looked up at the furious Bull and drawled, "There, My boots are clean now."

His father stared with furious eyes at the dirty melting snow that was forming puddles on the carpet in which he took such pride. He took a threatening step toward his son, but Trey had turned his attention to Ruby, who slouched lazily in a chair, smiling up at him.

Trey jerked a thumb over his shoulder and ordered coldly, "Get your coat on, Ruby, and get the hell out of here."

"Now just a damn minute," Bull thundered.

"I invited Ruby here, and she can leave when she's ready."

"No, she can't." Trey sent the older man a warning look. "She's leaving right now."

He took Ruby by the arm and jerked her to her feet. As he walked her into the kitchen, where her coat and hat hung on a peg, Bull hurried after them, protesting loudly.

"Damn you, Trey. There's a howlin' blizzard goin' on out there. You can't send her out in that. If she doesn't get lost, she's bound to catch pneumonia."

"I'm sure she can make it to the line shack the same way my wife did when you directed her there in a driving rain storm." Trey's icy eyes bored into Bull.

"It was her wish to go there." Bull glared back. "And I was just as glad. I don't want no whore in my house anyway."

Trey gave a short, harsh laugh, totally lacking in mirth. "You don't want a whore in your house? You mealy-mouthed old bastard, I can't count the times you've brought whores home with you, shaming my mother while you carried on with them in your bedroom. And what about Ruby here? She's been your whore for years, and you wanted me to marry *her*."

Ruby, who had kept silent during the heated argument between father and son, now began to protest. "That's not true, Trey. Me and your father have never—"

"Bullshit." Trey pushed her toward the

kitchen. "I've seen the two of you going at it out in the barn at least a half-dozen times. The first time was six years ago. I had climbed up in the loft to pitch some hay down to the horses when the pair of you came sneaking into the barn.

"I was stuck up there for over an hour. Do you want me to refresh your memory of what went on between you? The whores in the bawdy house could take lessons from you, Ruby. The old man could hardly walk when you finished with him."

Her face beet-red, Ruby pulled on her coat and, jerking open the door, flounced outside. Trey grinned and slammed the door shut behind her.

"Now," Trey said, turning on Bull. "I've talked to Lacey and Matt. They both tell me the same story. You deliberately sent that young girl to the line shack knowing that she would die there. And she would have if not for Matt. So far, she refuses to live in the same house with you. So until she comes here on her own, where she belongs, you will not be bringing any more women to the house. That includes that tramp, Ruby."

Trey gave a short, sneering laugh. "Of course, that won't bother Ruby. She'll spread her legs for any man who comes along. But it's going to be hard on you, you rutting old buffalo, because tomorrow I'm taking that poor Sky to Big Josy's bawdy house. She'll be paid for the use of her body there. She's still young, and after a week or two of rest, and when her bruises are gone, she'll be pretty again. After all, she was only thirteen years old when you brought her to the house and started using and abusing her. Josy's customers will line up to spend ten minutes with her because I'm sure there's not much you haven't taught her."

By the time Trey finished his hot tirade, Bull was beside himself with rage. "You can't do that!" he yelled, his fists clenched. "She's a servant—the housekeeper and cook. Who's gonna keep the house clean and put food on the table?"

"And warm your bed when no other female is around," Trey jeered.

"Bah! that won't bother me," Bull blustered. "I can visit the whores in Marengo."

Trey paused at his bedroom door. "That's good, because Sky begins her rest tonight. I'll know if you go sneaking into her room later." He closed the door on a black-faced Bull.

As Trey shucked off his clothes and climbed naked into bed, the wind howled around the house, rattling the windows and pounding at the heavy front and back door. He thought of Lacey and hoped she was all right. Was she afraid of the storm as she lay alone in the little cabin?

He fell asleep remembering how soft she had felt in his arms and how sweet her lips had tasted . . . and how hard she had slapped his face.

* * *

Lacey was frightened of the storm. It worsened as time passed, rattling the shutters and whipping at the door. When a wolf's distant howl drifted across the range, she began to sing as loudly as she could. If she was silent, the wind roared so loudly, she couldn't bear it.

Finally, her voice gave out and she was huddled on the hearth when a knock sounded on the door. Her heart raced with hope. Trey had returned. She would welcome even him.

She jumped to her feet and was halfway to the door when she remembered Matt's cautioning words—never open the door until she knew who stood on the other side of it. She rushed back to the fireplace and took down the rifle hanging above the mantel. Hurrying back to the window, she parted the curtains.

Lacey saw a heavy-set man standing on the porch, a stranger to her. That didn't say much, though, considering she only knew Matt and the storekeeper—and of course her hateful father-in-law.

She knew, however, that she wouldn't trust this man in her home even if she had been acquainted with him for a long time. In the lamplight, she saw a face heavy with beard stubble, and the eyes that stared back at her were small and mean-looking.

"Go away!" she called loudly over the howling wind.

"It's cold out here, miss. Surely you wouldn't

refuse a man a warm spot in front of your fire."

"Yes, I would," Lacey answered back and lifted the rifle so that he could see it. "If you ride a mile straight down the basin, you'll come to a ranch. Matt Carlton will take you in."

The stranger continued to stand on the porch, wondering if the pretty little woman would actually shoot him if he burst through the door. He could see that she was alone in the cabin. He looked back at Lacey, saw the determined look in her eyes, and decided that she likely would shoot him.

He left the porch and, climbing on his mount, headed down the basin.

Lacey sighed her relief, but when she went to bed half an hour later, she took the revolver from her bag and slipped it under her pillow. The man might decide to come back. She knew how to use the small firearm. Papa had made sure she could handle it expertly. She seldom missed what she was shooting at. She was equally good with the rifle.

As the storm raged on, Lacey, the covers pulled over her head, finally fell asleep to dream of hard, yet tender lips on hers.

Seven hours later, she awakened to silence. The wind no longer howled. She jumped out of bed and rushed to the window. Jerking the curtains apart, she looked outside and smiled. It was no longer snowing either. She figured it must have stopped shortly after she fell asleep, for she could still faintly make out the man's footprints on the porch and those of his horse going in the direction of Matt's place.

"Oh dear," she whispered, looking out at the white world. There were at least two feet of snow on the ground, and in some places the wind had piled drifts as high as four feet. Thank goodness it hadn't piled up against the barn door.

"I've got to get dressed and start shoveling a path to the barn and the outhouse," she thought out loud. "The cow has to be milked and fed as well as the chickens and horse and old Jocko."

It was seven o'clock when, bundled to her eyes, Lacey started shoveling. It was past ten when she reached the barn door. She was leaning on the shovel handle, her breath escaping her lips and nose in small clouds, when she saw Trey's stallion come lunging through the snow that rose above his fetlocks.

Her eyes narrowed angrily as she saw a blanket-wrapped Indian woman sitting behind Trey. What arrogance the man had, flaunting the woman he had slept with last night. He was telling her that if she wouldn't sleep with him, he could find one who would.

When the beautiful animal was pulled to a halt in front of her, Trey slipped out of the saddle with lazy grace. He walked toward her. The dark eyes in his lean, tanned face, smoldered as they ran over her.

Her expression cool and aloof, Lacey asked flatly, "Why have you come here?"

"To see how my wife fared during the storm, naturally." He smiled down at her. "I intended doing the shoveling for you."

"As you can see, I've already done it."

Trey nodded, then asked abruptly, "Who was here last night?"

So he had seen the footprints on the porch. Lacey lifted her chin and said defiantly "It's none of your business who comes to visit me."

"Like hell it's none of my business." Trey took a step toward her. "Maybe we're not living together, but as long as you're my wife you're going to behave in a decent way. I'll not have my friends and neighbors thinking of you the same way they do Josy's girls."

And though Lacey was as angry as Trey appeared to be, she thought it best to tell him the truth. "I don't know who he was. I didn't let him in."

Trey looked into her clear green eyes and knew she was telling the truth. "Good girl," he praised. "Never open the door to a stranger."

"Or to some you do know," Lacey answered drily.

There was amusement and irritation in Trey's eye when he asked, "Especially husbands?"

Lacey shrugged as though he might be right.

"Do you think you could trust me enough to invite me in for a cup of coffee?" Trey gave her one of his most charming smiles.

Lacey shook her head. "I have to milk the

cow. I'm at least three hours late doing it. She's bound to be in pain."

No more than I am, Trey thought wryly. "Look, Lacey," he said earnestly, "I'm trying to court you, and I don't know much about wooing a woman. I've never done it before."

Lacey gave him a withering look. "That doesn't surprise me, but what does puzzle me is why you want to court a whore. I didn't think they needed any sweet talk and coaxing."

Trey winced. "Don't call yourself that."

"Why not? That's what you call me."

"Look, Lacey." Trey took her arm. "I'm—"

Lacey jerked free of him. "The first thing you must learn when trying to impress a woman is to keep your hands to yourself. Second, you don't bring your latest bed partner along with you."

Trey looked startled a moment. He had forgotten that Sky was with him. He looked up at the Indian girl. "You mean Sky here? I've never slept with her. I got tired of the way Bull treats her and I took her away from him this morning. I'm taking her into Marengo to Big Josy."

Lacey raised a contemptuous eyebrow. "Do you think you're doing her a big favor turning her into one of the madam's girls?"

"I *am* doing her a favor, dammit." Trey barked. "You don't know the hell this girl has lived through since she was thirteen and Bull Saunders got hold of her. Can you think of any other kind of work she could find around here?

Josy will be good to her and see to it that her customers don't abuse her."

Lacey realized that everything Trey said was true. Where could an Indian maid find work in the small town of Marengo? And he looked sincere about never having slept with the girl.

She looked up at Sky, who smiled at her shyly. "Are you going with Trey willingly?" she asked. "You're not being forced to go?"

Sky shook her head vehemently. "I happy to go, to get away from evil man. That Bull, he beat me, made me do bad things to him."

"Do you believe me now?" Trey took Lacey's arm again.

She jerked free again. "I told you not to paw me."

"Hell, I only touched your arm," Trey replied testily.

"And I know how fast your hand can move to other places."

"You mean like this?" Trey said angrily and the breath whooshed out of Lacey as he grabbed her to his chest. When she opened her mouth to cry out, he dipped his head and crushed his lips to hers, his tongue darting between her parted lips.

Lacey tried to push him away, but she was locked securely in his embrace. Suddenly, as his mouth moved over hers and his tongue stroked her soft underlip, a weakness came over her. She was about to grasp his shoulders to stop from falling when he dropped his arms and lifted his flushed face, breathing hard.

He gazed down at her a moment, then turned and strode to the stallion. Her body trembling from a sensation she'd never experienced before, Lacey watched him swing into the saddle and head the mount in the direction of Marengo. Her shoulders drooped dispiritedly. When he took Sky to Josy, would he stay to visit one of her girls?

As Lacey walked back to the house to get the milk pail, she told herself she didn't care how many of Big Josy's girls Trey Saunders slept with.

But she knew that she lied to herself. She did care. She cared very deeply. She sighed raggedly. Marriage to a man like Trey would be a living hell if she let herself fall in love with him. She would never know who he was sleeping with, for she doubted he would ever change his womanizing ways. Hadn't he visited a house of prostitution within an hour after they were married? Vows of marriage meant nothing to him. It was true that theirs was not a love match, but he should have thought of that before he married her if he didn't mean to honor the promises he made in God's house. She knew now that he had only married her to anger and irritate his father.

There were four horses tied to the hitching rail in front of Josy's house of pleasure when

Trey pulled the stallion up in front of the gray, weathered building.

He recognized all the mounts. Two belonged to cowhands who worked for him, and the other two came from neighboring ranches.

In the winter when the temperatures plunged to well below freezing, cattle were left to fend for themselves. Consequently, with time on their hands, the men became bored. When they tired of playing cards in the bunkhouse, they braved the freezing weather and rode into town to have a few drinks or visit Josy's place.

Trey slid out of the saddle, then turned and helped Sky to dismount. The girl looked uneasy, and as he nudged her to walk ahead of him on the shoveled path, he said, "Don't be scared, Sky. No one is going to hurt you here. Josy won't let them."

The big waiting room, rank with the odor of spilled drinks on the worn carpet and the stale odor of unwashed bodies, was empty. Trey hadn't expected anything different. The men would be upstairs being entertained by the whore of their choice.

He motioned Sky to sit down in a chair, then knocked on a door that had *Private* printed on it. From inside came the tapping of heels; then the door opened.

The kindly, serene face of the woman who greeted him with a smile hid a fiery nature that could erupt into a frightening rage if one of her girls was handled roughly.

"Won't Sally Jo let you in her bed this early in the morning?" the madam asked, a slight sneer in her voice. The big woman had lost one of her best customers to the singer, and she still held a resentment toward the woman.

"I don't know if she would or not, but I expect she would." Trey grinned rakishly at the big-bosomed woman. "I've come to town on a different business."

He nodded his head in the direction where Sky sat, her hands gripped nervously in her lap. "Sky over there used to work at the ranch. I've brought her here to work for you if you'll have her."

"Yes, I've heard of the girl Bull treats like an animal." Josy walked across the room to a window and pulled aside the heavy drape. The pale winter sun shone on Sky's bruised face and one black eye.

The big woman's eyes grew hard, but her fingers were gentle as she explored Sky's battered face. When she had finished her examination, she looked up at Trey and said, "The old bastard hasn't broken any bones, and she's been eating well at least. The marks on her face will fade in a couple of weeks and then I'll put her to work."

"Thank you, Josy." Trey smiled at the big woman. In the way of saying good-bye to Sky, he gave her shoulder a quick squeeze, then left the bawdy house.

Trey rode on down the street to the tavern, where several horses were hitched. When he walked inside Whiskey Pete's, Matt made room for him at the bar. The other men who were lined up there called greetings to him, one man asking, "How does it feel to be an old married man now?"

Trey stiffened, waiting for the snide remarks that must follow—like why in the hell had he married a whore? Surprisingly, nothing of the sort was said. Instead, one man remarked, "I hear your wife is a real beauty. How did a wild man like you ever convince her to tie her life to you?"

Another rancher said, "Matt tells me she's a real lady. Do you think she'll tame you down a bit?"

Amused laughter followed that question. "Ain't no woman gonna put a ring in your nose, huh, Trey?" one of the men asked.

"You don't see one there, do you?" Trey answered as he picked up the glass of whiskey the bartender placed in front of him.

When he had downed half the glass's contents, Matt said for Trey's ears alone, "You didn't spend the night with Lacey, did you?"

"What makes you say that?" Trey frowned at his friend.

"When I rode past the cabin earlier, I saw Lacey shoveling a path to the barn. I knew that if you were there, you'd be doing it."

When Trey toyed with his glass without answering, Matt asked impatiently, "Well, Trey, where did you sleep? Not with Sally Jo, I hope."

Trey ignored the question and asked instead, "How do you court a woman, Matt?"

Matt stared at him a moment, then gazed down at the amber-colored liquid in his glass. *How do you court a woman?* he silently repeated Trey's question.

His thoughts went back to the young woman he had courted in his youth—the only woman he had ever loved. He thought of the long walks they had taken arm-in-arm. He remembered picking bouquets of wildflowers for her and giving her trinkets on her birthday and at Christmas.

He recalled their first kiss, how sweet and tender it had been. His blood stirred when he remembered the first time they made love, just before he went off to war.

"Well, Matt, can't you answer me? Didn't you ever woo a woman either?" Trey's impatient voice brought Matt back to the present time.

"Yes, Trey, I have courted a woman," he said, then told the younger man all the things he had been thinking about, omitting the time he and his sweetheart had made love.

"That seems like a lot of trouble to go through just so you can go to bed with your wife."

"You're wrong, Trey. It's no trouble at all if you love the woman. In fact, it can be very enjoyable."

Trey stared moodily into his drink. Number one, he didn't love his wife. She was a whore regardless of the fact that everybody else thought different. And number two, how in the hell could he take her on long walks when the snow almost reached her rear end? And number three, how was he to pick wildflowers when they were buried two feet under the snow?

"How come you rode into town so early?" Matt broke in on his gloomy thoughts. "Did you and Bull get into it?"

"Not this morning, we didn't. But we sure as hell had a row last night. I told him that until Lacey moves to the ranch house on her own, he's not to bring any more whores into our home."

He gave Matt a crooked grin. "I also took Sky away from him. She'll start working for Josy in a couple of weeks, as soon as her bruises fade."

Matt let loose a loud burst of laughter and slapped Trey on the back. "That's a worse punishment than a horse-whipping to that mean bastard."

Before Trey could agree with him, Sally Jo pushed her way in beside him. She looked at him with invitation in her eyes as she asked, "What do you two find so funny?"

"Oh, life, I guess," Trey answered as Matt turned his stiff, disapproving back on them. The action told him whose side he was on.

"I expected you to come to me last night," the dark-haired singer said, looking into his eyes as she stroked her fingers down the inside of his thighs.

He looked at her painted face and smelled the

overpowering perfume she used to sweeten her unwashed body. Trey remembered Lacey and how she had looked this morning. Her skin was smooth and fresh looking, and only the faint scent of rose soap teased his senses when he embraced her.

Sally Jo's hand had moved to his crotch and was gently massaging him there. Any other time, he would have been instantly aroused and would have hurried her upstairs to spend an hour or so with her.

To his mortifaction, however, he remained limp. He removed her stroking hand and said, not unkindly, "I've got no time to dally with you today, Sally Jo. I've got a bunch of business to attend to."

He finished his drink, slapped Matt on the back, and strode out of the tavern. As he climbed into the saddle, he cursed the day he ever laid eyes on Lacey Stewart, now Lacey Saunders. She had ruined him for other women, and he hadn't even slept with her yet.

Trey swore under his breath when he arrived at the ranch and entered the kitchen. He heard loud bumping and squeaking coming from his father's bedroom. How had he gotten hold of another woman so fast?

He left the kitchen and made his way through the parlor, knowing that he was leaving dirty wet tracks in his wake—tracks that the old man would have to clean, for there would be no woman to do it.

Bull, in the throes of lust, didn't even hear his door open. Trey stood and gazed at his father's bare rump and the Indian girl lying beneath his pounding body, and shook his head. The old bastard hadn't lost any time in going to the nearby Indian village and buying himself another body to vent his meanness and lust on.

This buying of Indian females happened every winter. The half-starving tribe up in the foothills would sell their daughters for as little as twenty-five dollars. He wondered if they knew, or even cared, what happened to the young maids once they left their village.

He looked at the girl who lay with her eyes closed and her hands clenched in fists at her sides. She was waiting for it to be over with the patience born of hopelessness.

That look of spiritlessness on the girl's face so enraged Trey that he wanted to draw his gun and shoot the man who was despoiling her. Instead he lifted his foot and, sorry that he wasn't wearing spurs, planted it squarely between the white, fat cheeks. He gave a hard shove, and Bull was tumbling off the girl.

"What the hell!" Bull came up fighting mad.

"I guess you didn't believe me when I said there would be no more females brought in here for your pleasure." Trey glared down at him.

"Now look here." Bull was scrambling into his trousers. "I've been thinkin' things over. You got no right to tell me I can't have a woman in the house to pleasure me once in a while. I'm not a castrated horse. I paid good money for this squaw and I'm keepin' her."

"You think that, do you? You'd better think things over again, for I'll see to it that you turn into a gelding if you ever sneak another woman into this house."

While Bull glared his hatred at his son, Trey looked at the girl huddled against the headboard, the sheet clutched to her naked breasts. "Get your clothes together, girl, and go back to your village."

The girl gave Bull a frightened look, then said uneasily, "My people will not give back money paid for me. They very hungry."

"Don't worry about that," Trey soothed her. "I suspect the old buffalo has already got his money's worth out of you."

"I'll get you for this!" Bull yelled as Trey left the room to wait for the girl in the kitchen.

Chapter Nine

Lacey hurried toward the cabin. As she stepped up onto the porch, gripping a basket with four eggs in it, she saw a rider approaching. She didn't recognize him until he pulled the mount in close to the steps.

What did Trey's father want? she wondered, waiting for her father-in-law to state his business.

Bull's fleshy lips smiled at her, but malevolence lay just below the surface. "I guess you're wonderin' what I'm doin' here," he said.

Lacey nodded and answered coolly, "That thought crossed my mind."

"The thing is, I've come to ask you to come live with Trey at the ranch. It's your duty to live with your husband."

Lacey looked at him suspiciously. The old devil couldn't care less about her duty to his son. It griped him no end that Trey had married her.

What was the real reason he wanted her at the ranch house?

"Trey and I have an understanding, Mr. Saunders. I won't be moving into your house soon, if ever. He has a lot of changing to do in his life before I'll be a wife to him."

"I admit that Trey is a little wild," Bull said, "but you can't fault him for that. Husbands like to cut loose once in a while, carouse with their friends, visit a—"

"A whore? Is that what you're saying, Mr. Saunders?"

"Well, there ain't no real harm in that. It's not like a man cares anything for the likes of them."

"What about his special whore, Sally Jo? I was told he'd never give her up."

"He will. Just give him a little time. If you keep him happy in your bed, he won't be goin' to hers."

Lacey couldn't believe the words coming from her father-in-law's mouth. Did he really think that marriage only meant keeping a husband happy in bed? Didn't faithfulness and caring for each other mean anything?

Did other husbands think the same way Bull Saunders did? Did their wives accept sharing their men with whores? She thought not. Annie Stump would take a whip to Tollie if he even looked at another woman with lust in his eyes.

Then there were Tilda and Loretta, the two ranch women she had met. They didn't strike her as being the sort who would turn a blind eye to a husband's philandering.

Lacey looked at Bull and said coolly, "You may think that it's all right to break your wedding vows, Mr. Saunders, but it's far from right with me. Until your son completely drops his old habits, he won't be sleeping with me."

Bull stared down at Lacey's lovely, defiant face and envied his son the pleasure he would get from bedding this one. She had a stormy nature and would be like a wildcat when gripped with passion. Unlike the whores he used to bring home. After a couple of good humps they whined that they were tired and wanted to sleep. Trey's mother had been the same way.

The trouble was, these days he had to go to the whorehouse like everyone else, pay his money and be allowed only fifteen minutes with the slut he had chosen. And he couldn't be rough with them.

"Look," Bull began, trying to speak softly but failing. Lacey suspected it wasn't his habit to speak gently to a woman. "Trey really wants you to move to the ranch house. He's all moody and don't have a decent word for anybody."

"I'm sorry to hear that, Mr. Saunders, but he'll just have to get over it. I'm not changing my mind."

Before Bull could add to his plea, Lacey entered the house and closed the door behind her. For good measure, she bolted it. She didn't trust Bull Saunders one bit. Hadn't he sent her off to die one stormy night?

As she put the eggs in a crock and carried them into the storage room, she wondered if Trey had sent his father ride over to coax her to become a proper wife.

She dismissed the thought. Trey Saunders would ask no man to plead a case for him. Especially the father he didn't seem to care for. Coming back into the kitchen, she breathed a sigh of relief when she looked through the window and saw that Bull was almost out of sight, riding in the direction of his ranch.

Minutes later, however, her nerves tightened. She heard the plodding sound of a horse approaching the cabin. She hurried to the window, thinking that Bull had returned. If he wanted to come in, she wasn't going to let him.

It wasn't Bull though. It was the same man who had knocked on her door the night of the blizzard.

She could see him more clearly now in the daylight, although he had his collar pulled up around his neck and wore his hat low on his forehead. He still hadn't shaved his brutish face, and his clothes were dirt-stained and wrinkled as though he had been sleeping in them.

She watched him swing from the saddle and step up onto the porch. He walked over to the window and gave her a smile that just missed being a leer.

"It's me again, pretty lady. Do you think you could spare a feller a cup of coffee? It's mighty cold this mornin'."

"If you don't get on your horse and ride away, I'll spare you a bullet in your rear end," Lacey said tightly.

"But I won't harm you, missy," the man cajoled. "I swear it. I only want a cup of coffee to warm me up."

Lacey pulled the little revolver out of her pocket and aimed it at the stranger's head. "If you're not off the porch and gone in two seconds, I'll give you something that will warm you up fast."

"Keep your coffee, you uppity bitch," the man ground out before jumping off the porch and hurrying to his horse.

Lacey shook her head as he rode away. If she hadn't met Matt, she would think that all the men around here were scoundrels.

Trey had ordered his second glass of whiskey when the saloon door banged open and a stranger came lumbering into the barroom. He walked to the end of the bar and growled for whiskey.

Trey and the other men ran a scanning eye over him, then turned back to the conversations his noisy entrance had interrupted. Strangers weren't unusual this time of year. There were

Norah Hess

always out-of-work cowboys riding the grub line.

The regulars who were lined up at the bar paid no more attention to the outsider until a feminine squeal of pain rang out. Heads turned and foreheads furrowed. The man had grabbed one of the prostitutes and had her arm twisted behind her back, holding it with one hand while he shoved the other down the front of her dress.

"What in the hell do you think you're doin', man?" big burly Pete demanded, walking down the length of the bar.

"I'm teachin' her not to tease a man. She's been rubbin' up against me ever since I come in. I'm gonna rub her for a while now."

"That's a damnable lie about her teasin' you. She just now came into the barroom." Pete picked up the club he kept hidden out of sight and laid it on the bar. "Turn her loose before I bust your head open."

The stranger flung the woman away from him and sneered, "I don't want any of your whores anyway. I've got my eye on a little beauty that's young and firm. She's a spitfire and I can't wait to bed her. She's chased me away with a gun twice, but I'll catch her unarmed one day and teach her a thing or two. If you get my meanin'."

A dead silence came over the room. Whoever the woman he spoke of was, she was from the area. She was somebody's wife, sister, or daughter.

Trey knew immediately who the scruffy-looking individiual was referring to. Lacey. He had been to her house the night of the blizzard and had probably just come from there now.

Trey stepped away from the bar, his right arm hanging loosely, his thumb hooked in the car-tride belt wrapped low on his hips.

"Mister," his cold voice rang out, "we don't take kindly to having our womenfolk discussed in a saloon."

His face surly, the man turned around to face Trey. "Is that so?" he snarled. "What are you gonna do about it, cowboy?" he added, sweeping aside the right side of his jacket and revealing the pistol on his hip.

"I'll do whatever I have to do," Trey said, his eyes cold and steady on the hostile man. "You'd better draw your horns in and get out of here. In fact, get out of our area."

"Nobody tells Frank Norton when to leave a place." Norton dropped his hand to rest on his gun handle.

"Don't draw your gun, mister," Trey warned.

"You're just full of advice, ain't you?" Norton growled, and in the next instant he was snatching at his gun.

The firearm had barely cleared leather when it was spinning across the floor. "Damn you!" Norton cried out, clutching his bleeding hand. "You've shot off my trigger finger."

The acrid smell of gunfire hung in the air as Trey sheathed his Colt and said, "That's just as well. You'll probably live longer without that finger. There's nothing a Westerner hates worse that a swaggering desperado, a make-believe gunman like you. Now get the hell out of here and ride off."

"I'm hurt, man. I'm gonna bleed to death. I need to see a doctor."

"You'll not bleed to death, but if you want to I'll allow you the time to stop at Doc Carson's to put a bandage on it."

With one last venomous look at Trey, Norton picked his gun off the floor and slammed out of the saloon.

"Drinks are on the house," Pete the bartender called out as Trey's friends gathered round him, slapping him on the back, praising his swift draw.

"Man, I never saw a faster draw," one of the men said. "It was like a blur the way you palmed the Colt and squeezed the trigger."

When everyone had settled down to their drinks, Matt, standing next to Trey, said quietly, "I'm glad you didn't kill the bastard, Trey. Taking a man's life is a hard thing to live with."

"I wanted to for a minute. I knew he was talking about Lacey. He was at the cabin the night of the blizzard trying to talk her into letting him in. I figure he tried the same thing today."

"She's not safe out there alone, Trey. I watch after her as much as I can, but I can't be nearby all the time."

"I know." Trey nodded. "I've got to do something about her. I don't know what, though. She won't live at the ranch, and she won't let me move into the cabin with her. Hell, she doesn't even want to talk to me."

"You've got to change the way you act around her. Don't let her see that you can't wait to get her in bed."

Trey gave a short laugh. "Do you know how hard that's gonna be? I only have to think of her and the picture of a bed pops into my mind."

"When that happens, just remember that Lacey's a decent young woman and you must treat her as such if you're ever to be her husband in every sense of the word."

"Hell, Matt, I don't think I want to be like all the other husbands around here; staying home all the time, a bunch of kids underfoot."

"What have you got against youngsters?" Matt looked at him, amused.

"I haven't got anything against them. Actually, I kinda like them. They're honest little buggers, tell it to you straight. I just don't want any of my own. What if I turned out to be a father like the one I have?"

"You wouldn't. Believe me when I say that, Trey. You have too much of your mother in you."

Trey finished his drink and pushed away from the bar. "I'm going to stop by Jasper's place and tell the little witch that she doesn't have to worry about Norton anymore."

"You do that. And don't act like a rutting bull while you're there." Matt grinned.

As his stallion clomped along through the woods, Trey wondered where Matt had gotten the idea that Lacey was a decent, innocent young woman. If he'd seen her in that red dress with her face all painted up, he'd know different, Trey thought as the stallion entered a patch of pines.

When a snow-laden branch dropped its burden on Trey's head and shoulders, he looked up through the branches. The dark green pine needles and the light brown cones were quite eye-catching, he thought.

A crooked grin curved his lips. Matt had said to pick Lacey bouquets of wildflowers, which was out of the question now, but he could break off a few of the pine branches and take them to her. They would look right nice in a tall jelly jar.

Lacey had just settled down in front of the fire and picked up a shirt of Matt's she was mending when she heard the approaching sound of a horse.

"Now who?" she muttered, laying aside the flannel garment and standing up. If it was that seedy-looking man again, she was going to take a shot at him—put a hole in the crown of his hat, maybe part his hair a little.

Walking toward the window, she heard footsteps accompanied by clinking spurs on the porch. She looked outside just as Trey knocked on the door.

Her heart began to pound with slow, deep

beats. Should she ask him in? She was sick to death of his taunts and his sarcasm.

She decided that she was strong enough to take his insults as long as he kept his hands to himself. She had to give him a chance to be nice. She unbarred the door and opened it.

"What do you want?" She scowled at Trey when he stepped inside.

Trey brought the spray of pine boughs from behind his back. "I thought these would pretty up the room some." He smiled as he handed them to her.

Lacey couldn't hide the surprise from her eyes. The greenery with the cones on the branches was very pretty and would brighten the kitchen. "Thank you," she said in a small voice. "I'll put them in the jar that Jasper used to keep his pipe and tobacco in. They will look lovely in the center of the table."

Trey's eyes raked hungrily over Lacey as she placed his gift in the clay jar, then added some water. His stolid face didn't show what he was thinking, however. He remembered Matt's warning.

"Don't tell me you came out in the cold just to bring me these." Lacey turned from the table and gave him a suspicious look.

"No, I came to tell you that you don't have to worry about that stranger coming around anymore."

"Oh?" Lacey raised a questioning eyebrow. "How do you know that?"

"I told him to leave the area."

"And just like that, he left?" Doubt was in Lacey's voice.

"It wasn't that simple," Trey admitted. "I had to shoot him up a little."

Lacey looked horrified. "What does a little mean?"

"He drew on me and I shot the gun out of his hand. His trigger finger went with it."

"Oh," Lacey said with relief. "I wouldn't want you doing real harm to anybody on my account."

Trey made no response, but he was thinking that he would kill any man who would harm his wife in any manner.

"Do you think you could give me a cup of coffee before I head home? It's god-awful cold out there."

Lacey hesitated. So far he had behaved himself, and he had scared that dreadful man away. "Sit down," she said. "I'll give you a slice of pumpkin pie to go with it."

Trey removed his jacket as he watched Lacey go to a cuboard and take out two cups. His eyes fastened on her small rear in the tight trousers, and he wondered how long he could control himself.

As Lacey poured the coffee and placed a wedge of pie before him, Trey asked, "Why do you always dress in men's clothing?"

"Because it's practical. Unlike dresses that let the wind and cold air in, trousers keep my legs warm when I go to the barn to do my chores and bring in wood. Annie Stump wears men's attire all the time."

But she doesn't look like you do in trousers, Trey thought as he forked pie into his mouth.

"Say, this is the best pumpkin pie I've ever tasted," Trey said, looking at Lacey with admiration. "How did you learn to cook like this? Did your father teach you?"

"Not likely." Lacey's gay laughter rang out, making Trey look a little stunned. He had never seen Lacey smile or heard her laugh. It was delightful. "Poor Papa couldn't so much as brew a pot of coffee."

She paused, thinking back over the years. "You wouldn't believe the stack of recipes I have in my trunk. They're the only things the thief left in it when he stole my clothes. It seemed that every town Papa and I stopped in, some kind woman gave me her favorite recipe."

A shadow came over her lovely green eyes. "I guess they didn't stop to think that I could only cook over a campfire. But I kept their carefully written-out instructions, and now that I have a stove and an oven, I've been trying my hand at some of them."

Trey studied the delicately boned face of his wife and for the first time realized that she hadn't had an easy time of it, always on the road.

"Before your father died, how long had the

two of you traveled along in the medicine wagon?"

"A week short of ten years."

Trey wanted to ask at what age had she started to prostitute herself, but knew that if he asked her such a question he could forget about ever getting into her bed. She was very touchy about that subject.

"How old are you, Lacey?" he asked instead.

"I turned eighteen a month ago."

"You look about sixteen." Trey smiled at her.

"How old are you?"

"Thirty."

Lacey's gaze skimmed over his lean face, making note of the strong lines around his mouth. His dark eyes gleamed with serene confidence, along with the mockery lurking far back in their depths.

She decided that he was the handsomest man she'd ever seen. Also the hardest. Trey burst out laughing when she said, "You look older. Probably from the kind of life you've lived."

"You mean whiskey and wild women?" Trey joked.

"Yes."

His wife wasn't averse to speaking her mind, Trey thought with a wry smile. When she didn't add to her single word, he asked for a second piece of pie. As she placed it before him, he said, "I wish you'd reconsider about moving to the ranch."

"No." Lacey's answer was short and clipped again.

"Even if you had your own room and I kept my hands to myself?"

"I'm not dumb enough to believe that last promise, and I don't trust that father of yours. I haven't forgotten how he sent me to that shack to die."

"I'm ashamed he did that to you, Lacey, and I swear to you he won't bother you if you move in with us. It's not safe for you out here alone. Besides the men who might come around, there are so many other things that could harm you."

Trey realized with some shock that he was truly concerned about his wife's welfare and that for once he wasn't thinking about taking her to bed.

When Lacey answered, "Matt is looking after me," he was gripped with irritation and some jealousy. It was *his* right to look after his wife.

"Matt has a big ranch to run," he said shortly. "He doesn't have time to be looking after you."

"Look!" Lacey slapped her hand on the table. "I don't need anyone to look after me. I'm quite able to look after myself."

"As long as you're in the cabin, maybe you can." Trey's voice rose also. "But what about when you're in the barn, for instance, or bringing in wood?"

"I never leave the cabin after dark, and never without my revolver," Lacey said, jumping to her feet. "Are you about ready to leave?"

"Hell, yes!" Trey shoved his half-eaten pie away. "I feel like a damn fool for worrying about you. You probably want men coming out here. For a minute I forgot your trade."

He was out of the house, slamming the door behind him before Lacey could hotly deny his charge.

She looked at the pine bouquet that had pleased her so a short time ago and laid her head on her folded arms. Great sobs shook her body. She told herself that she shouldn't care, but it hurt her that her husband had such a poor opinion of her.

Chapter Ten

The dark days of winter settled over the range, and the cold white hours passed slowly.

Although most of the ranch women complained of the solitude and monotony of those days, Lacey welcomed them. She loved the warm little cabin, where she could putter about trying out her recipes and keeping the three rooms neat and clean. It was a new way of life for her, and she delighted in every minute of it.

She was always happy to see Matt and Annie Stump, however. She was at ease with them—Matt with his Southern drawl, telling stories of his youth in Virginia, and Annie catching her up on the gossip coming out of Marengo.

Lacey liked the neighboring ranch women. They were very friendly to her and made her feel welcome. If only she knew what to talk about when she was in their company. They had little in common. Most of the ladies' conversation had to do with horses and cattle, and she knew little about either one. Had they talked about herbs, roots, and barks, she would have been right at home with them, talking as much as anybody.

But she would learn about horses and cattle, she thought as she changed the linens on her bed. If she was allowed to stay in the neighborhood, that was to say. She didn't know what Trey had in mind. If he had their marriage annuled, she would have to leave her comfortable little home.

And where would you go? What would you do for money? she asked herself.

Her inner voice answered, *You could go back on the road come spring. Sell your father's herbal medicine.*

She could do that, Lacey mused as she carried the bed linens to the storage room, where she did her washing every Monday. As much as she hated that kind of life, it would pay enough to keep body and soul together. Jocko was rested up now and getting quite fat from his two good meals a day. The wagon needed some fixing up. There was that one spot in the roof that leaked when it rained.

Closing the storage room door behind her, Lacey decided to have a cup of coffee and some of the oatmeal cookies she had baked the day before.

She had just filled a cup and was about to sit down when she heard the sound of wagon wheels. "Now who could that be?" she wondered out loud, glancing out the window.

To her surprise, she saw her friend Annie handling the reins of the mule that pulled the wagon along. What was her friend doing here today? she asked herself. Annie had picked up the milk yesterday and wasn't due to come again for a couple of days. She hoped there was nothing wrong at the Stump farm.

She opened the door as Annie clambered to the ground, no easy feat because she was bundled up from head to toe. "Come on in, Annie," she called to her rosy-cheeked neighbor.

"Boy, it's a cold one today," Annie groused, stamping the snow off her boots before stepping into the kitchen. "I guess you're wonderin' what brought me out on such a day," she said, peeling off layers of sweaters and a jacket.

"Well, yes, but I'm happy to see you again," Lacey smiled, pouring another cup of coffee and placing it on the table. "Is everything all right at your house?"

"Oh yes, we're all fine. I forgot to tell you somethin' yesterday." Annie pulled a chair away from the table and sat down. "When winter sets in, we women don't get to see much of one another, so it's our practice to get together twice a month and have a dance social. It's held in the grange hall next to the saloon. The men enjoy the dancin', and we women have a chance to get together and chat."

She grinned, " 'Course, we women like the dancin' too. Especially the young, unmarried girls."

Annie paused to sip at her coffee, then said, "The first one this season takes place Saturday night. Do you want me and Tollie to pick you up in the wagon, or will you be ridin' with . . . somebody?"

Lacey knew why Annie had hesitated over Trey's name. She, like everyone else, was confused as to the relationship between her and Trey. It was known in and around Marengo that she didn't live at the ranch, but no one knew for sure whether Trey stayed with her at the cabin. Matt had told her that some claimed he did, while others were sure he still lived with Bull.

She imagined that gossip ran rampant about her and Trey. She had wanted to ask Matt if Trey was still seeing the singer, Sally Jo, but she was too proud to inquire. Matt would think that she cared about what her husband did, and she didn't want anyone thinking that.

Lacey wanted to answer Annie that she wouldn't be going, but the way the farm woman had put it, it was expected that she'd attend. She answered that she would be riding.

"Well, however you want to travel, just be sure that you come," Annie said.

Half an hour later, when she was preparing

to leave, Annie said, "By the way, I always wear a dress at the dances."

"I suppose I should too." Lacey was amused that her friend was hinting that she too wear a dress.

When Annie had left, the wagon bumping over the snow-covered frozen ruts, Lacey sat back down at the table and picked up a cookie. Saturday was two days away, she thought, nibbling at the sweet. It would be the first social event she had ever attended. Would she know how to act? If a man, other than her husband, asked her to dance, would it be proper to do so? And would her husband be there? Would he ask her to dance? It would look strange if she refused. People would talk all the more.

Lacey half wished that Trey wouldn't be there. She always became rattled in his presence. Against her will, she was drawn to Trey Saunders and was very much afraid that she would give in to his advances some day. She would hate herself if that happened, knowing what he thought of her.

It was just getting dark and Lacey was coming from the barn when when Matt rode up. "The days are getting shorter, Lacey." He frowned as he dismounted and took the pail of milk from her. "You've got to start your chores earlier from now on."

Lacey patted her jacket pocket. "I've got my little 'peacemaker.' " She smiled at him.

"Hah!" Matt snorted. "A lot of good your revolver would do you if a man slipped up behind you and pinned your arms to your sides."

"You're right of course," Lacey agreed as they stepped into the kitchen. "I promise to be more careful from now on." She unwound the scarf from around her head and throat, then shrugged out of her jacket.

Matt still had on his long coat and she asked, "Aren't you going to stay a while, have a cup of coffee?"

"No, I've got to get back to the ranch. I have a mare ready to foal and she's having a hard time of it. I just stopped by to see if Trey has said anything to you about the dance Saturday night."

Lacey shook her head. "Annie told me, though."

"Do you want to go?"

"Yes, I think I'd like to. I'm a little nervous about it, though. I've never been to a social."

"Do you know how to dance?" When Lacey nodded and explained that her father had taught her, Matt said, "There's nothing to be uneasy about then. Everybody is friendly and is there to have a good time.

"I'll be here around six o'clock, and we'll ride in together."

"Thank you, Matt, if it's not too much trouble."

Matt smiled and tweaked a tawny curl. "Too much trouble to escort the prettiest girl in all of

Wyoming Territory to a dance? You must be joshin', girl."

Lacey smiled back at the man she was rapidly coming to look upon as a father. "I'll be ready," she said, following him to the door.

When Matt rode away with a wave of his hand, he wore a dark frown. What kind of game was that damn fool Trey playing? If he wanted to make things right between him and his wife, why hadn't he invited her to the social?

When he arrived home and put the stallion in the barn, he was surprised, yet pleased, to see Trey's Prince standing in one of the stalls. Since the horse was still saddled, he assumed he wouldn't be having company for supper.

He stripped the saddle off his own mount, covered him with a blanket, and gave him a helping of oats. Then, as he walked to the far end of the barn, he could hear the mare's deep cries and Trey talking soothingly to her, telling her to hang on, that it would soon be over. Matt looked over the stall door and saw Trey, his sleeves rolled up to his elbows, his hands thrust inside the laboring mare.

"I'm trying to turn the foal." Trey looked up at him. "It wants to come out backwards."

Matt hunkered down beside Trey and gently stroked the animal between her pain-filled eyes. This was his favorite mare. She was high-spirited, but gentle in manner.

About five minutes later, sweat pouring off his face, Trey said, "I think I've got it turned."

He stood up, and a few minutes later a small, perfectly shaped little head appeared from between its mother's hind legs.

Matt and Trey looked at each other with pleased smiles when a wobbly little body followed. "Another filly, Matt. Are you disappointed?"

"Naw, I'm just as glad," Matt said, thinking that he was going to give Lacey the little animal when it was weaned from its mother.

When Trey began scrubbing his hands and nails in a pail of soapy water, Matt said, "Come on up to the house and have supper when you've finished washing up."

"Thanks, Matt, but I promised the men I'd ride into town with them, kick up our heels a bit."

Matt bent disapproving eyes on his young friend. Trey was married now and had no right to go carousing with his friends, even if he and Lacey were going through a rough patch right now. Besides, people were talking enough about him already.

Matt didn't voice his thoughts, but asked instead, "Are you going to the dance Saturday night?"

Trey shrugged indifferently. "I may drop in for a while. It depends if I'm in a heavy poker game or something. Are you going?"

"Yes. Lacey is going with me."

Trey's hands went still, the brush dropping into the pail. It hadn't occurred to him that his wife might attend the social. And though Matt was his oldest friend, and old enough to be Lacey's father, Trey didn't like the idea of his escorting Lacey anywhere. Not only that, if she showed up without her husband, it would give the young Romeos around there the idea that she was fair game.

He managed to keep the frustration out of his voice as he said, "That's right kind of you, Matt. Do you think she'll enjoy herself? She doesn't know anybody."

"Sure she does. You might not have noticed, but Lacey has met several people. As sweet and pretty as she is, she'll know everybody by the time the dance is over."

Matt chuckled to himself. Lacey would know all the cowboys and rancher's single sons, that was for sure. And Trey wouldn't like that one bit.

When Trey didn't make a response, only dried his hands, his face stony, Matt hid his mirth and said, "Thanks for helping the mare, Trey. I'm going to get on up to the house. Lupe probably has supper waiting. I hope you make it to the dance."

"You're damn well right I'll make it," Trey muttered to himself as Matt left the barn. He pulled on his jacket and led Prince out of the stable. "I'm not about to let that little witch make a fool out of me."

*   *   *

Lacey glanced at the clock. Another half hour before Matt arrived to take her to the dance.

She was almost ready. She had washed her hair this morning right after she had finished doing her chores and combed it dry in front of the fire. She had used melt-water, and her hair now lay on her shoulders in glossy, tawny curls.

Earlier she had bathed in the big wooden tub kept in the storage room for that purpose. She could still smell the rose scent of the soap on her skin as she donned her underclothing. All she had left to do was put on the red woolen dress and her shiny new shoes. They, like the dress, had not been worn before.

If Trey should be at the social, what he would think of the red dress with its demure little white collar? Would its color remind him of the daring red satin she had been wearing the first time he saw her? The one that prompted him to label her a whore.

I don't care if it does, she thought defiantly. He wasn't going to change his mind about her, and there was nothing she can do to change that—even if she wanted to.

As Lacey walked about the bedroom, pulling her hardly used shawl and matching gloves from the dresser, then taking her sheepskin jacket off its peg on the wall, her heavy petticoat swirled around her legs and ankles, almost tripping her. She longed for her trousers. She had such freedom of movement in them.

Lacey looked at the clock again. Matt would

be here any minute now. It was time to put on her dress.

Suddenly Lacey was excited about going to the dance. Her face glowed, and her green eyes sparkled as she buttoned up the glass beads on the bodice. She could only see her face and throat in the small mirror and had no idea how she looked in the party dress. The soft wool outlined her proud breasts and hugged her rib cage before flaring out at the waist and falling to the tips of her slippers.

When she opened the door to Matt's knock, he could hardly take his eyes off her. What a vision of loveliness she was. If he didn't stick close to her tonight, there would be fights started over her.

"Do I look all right, Matt?" Lacey looked at him anxiously.

"You look just fine, honey. You look like a bouquet of wildflowers."

Lacey blushed her pleasure but said, "I didn't mean how does my face look. I was referring to my dress."

"It looks fine too, Lacey," Matt answered gently, realizing that she was nervous, attending her first social event. "I'll go saddle Red while you bundle up."

Matt cursed Trey under his breath as he tramped to the barn. He should be the one looking out for Lacey, and telling her how pretty she looked.

* * *

Trey stood up in the wooden bathtub, soapy water sluicing down his muscular body. *I wish I'd thought to ask Matt what time he and Lacey are going to arrive at the dance,* he thought as he briskly dried himself off. He didn't want them to get there before he did.

He had a plan. One that had kept him awake half the night thinking it up.

The clock showed five-thirty as Trey leaned close to the mirror, taking extra care shaving his lean, handsome face. He wanted it to look as good as his pristine shirt and the black trousers tucked into the tops of his fine, handcrafted leather boots. After he had brushed his long, loosely curling hair, he took the Colt from the bedpost and strapped it around his waist.

He'd better get a move on, he thought, and pulled on the heavy jacket he wore only on special occasions. As he walked through the parlor, Bull gave him a sour look and sneered, "The way you're all decked out, I'd think you was goin' to get married. But since you're already harnessed to that little whore, I guess you're goin' to the dance."

Trey didn't bother to respond.

As he rode into Marengo and pulled up in front of the lean-to attached to the grange hall, he was relieved to see that Matt's stallion and Lacey's sorrel weren't there with the other horses tied to the hitching rail. He led Prince to a spot well away from the others, then spread a blanket over him. The thin walls only kept the wind off the animals while their owners were dancing.

A few minutes later, Trey walked into the saloon and sat down at a table that gave him a clear view of anyone who rode up to the grange hall.

After waiting for about twenty minutes, Trey was beginning to think that Matt and Lacey weren't coming to the dance after all. Almost all their neighbors had arrived, including the musicians—a banjo plunker, a fiddler, and a young man who played the harmonica. Then at last his wait was over.

At the far end of the street, he saw Matt and Lacey riding in. He hurried outside and waited in the shadows for them to reach the hall. As they came nearer, his eyes widened. Lacey was wearing a dress. It was a brilliant scarlet color, though it was longer than the one she'd been wearing the first time he saw her.

"She's still advertising her trade," he muttered, clenching his fists.

When Matt and Lacey had put their mounts in the lean-to and were about to enter the hall, where a rollicking tune was being played, he hurried up behind them and took Lacey's arm.

"I'll take over now, Matt," he said, his tone saying he would brook no argument.

"Sure, Trey," Matt managed to say over the fit of laughter that rose inside him. The handsome devil wanted everyone to think that he had brought his wife to the dance. Especially the bachelors.

But Lacey wasn't agreeable to entering the building with his possessive hand on her arm. Why hadn't Trey ridden in with her? He had his own reasons for this unexpected act, and she wasn't going to help him carry it out.

Her eyes snapping, she tried to jerk free of him. But Trey, knowing she would try just that, tightened his grip and marched her into the crowded room.

"Behave yourself tonight," he growled as Annie Stump and Nellie Doolittle came toward them, their faces beaming.

"What do you mean, behave myself?" Lacey asked stiffly as Trey removed her shawl.

"I mean don't cozy up to the men, hint that they would be welcome if they came calling. For a price, that is."

Lacey was too stunned and hurt to reply to his insult. Tears smarting her eyes, she stood numbly as he unbuttoned her jacket and removed it.

God, she's beautiful, Trey thought. He'd give his shooting arm if she was as innocent as she looked.

Two other women whom Lacey had met briefly joined Annie and Nellie, all expressing their delight that Trey had brought his wife to the social.

Annie's sharp eyes searched Lacey's downcast face. "Ain't you feelin' well, girl?" she asked.

"You're lookin' kinda pale." She turned to Trey and demanded, "You've been treatin' her right, ain't you?"

Trey stole a look at Lacey's white face and felt a pang of guilt. He shouldn't have made that last remark to her, and he didn't know what had driven him to say it.

He put an arm around Lacey's shoulders, and she wanted to kick him hard when he said, "Lacey has been a little under the weather. She caught a slight cold."

"Everybody gets sick this time of the year," Annie said. "Make sure you keep her warm and give her lots of beef broth to drink."

The musicians had taken a break and were headed for the keg of hard cider. Nothing stronger was ever served at the gathering. Lacey thought that now she would be free of Trey for a while, that he would join the men. But he stuck by her side.

"There's sweet cider for the ladies," Annie said. "Why don't you go fetch Lacey a cup, Trey?"

Trey looked down at Lacey. "Would you like some?" When she nodded, he said, "Well, we'll just mosey over there and get you some." While Lacey fumed inside, he took hold of her arm again.

As they walked away Annie exclaimed, "My goodness, he don't want to let her out of his sight, does he?"

"I'd say he's right smitten with her," Nellie agreed.

"Can you blame him?" one of the other women said. "The girl is downright beautiful. Look at the men ogling her. They don't know there's another female in the place."

"There's gonna be a lot of men gettin' the cold shoulder from their wives and girlfriends after they leave here tonight," Annie said laughingly.

"They can't blame Lacey, though," Nellie pointed out. "She hasn't even looked any other man's way."

"That's true," Annie said, "but have you noticed, she ain't looked at Trey either? I got a feelin' things ain't goin' too smooth for them. And I bet that Bull has somethin' to do with it. He wanted Trey to marry Ruby."

"Hah!" Nellie snorted. "Trey would have never married that slut."

"I wonder why she's not here tonight?" someone said. "She's usually the first one to arrive."

"She's probably got some man in her bed," another woman said scathingly. "The only reason she comes to our socials is to snag a man to spend the night with."

The music began again, and the ladies went searching for their husbands. This was a slow dance, which the females liked because there was less danger of getting their feet tramped on. Also the young, unattached women could snuggle up to their beaux.

Trey took Lacey's cup from her and placed it beside the keg. Before she knew what he was about, he had put an arm around her waist and danced her in among the others circling the floor.

He held her close, his cheek resting on her head, her small hand in his large one.

They moved well together to the music, and Lacey relaxed after a while and let her body move in rhythm to Trey's. It wasn't long, however, before she felt the hardness of an arousal pressing against her stomach. She lifted shocked eyes to Trey and hissed, "Stop it!"

"I can't help it." He gave her a crooked grin.

"Yes, you can. You're making yourself be like that on purpose. You just want to make me mad."

Trey looked at her in disbelief for a moment; then, when he saw that she was serious, he laughed so loud that people turned their heads to look at them.

"Lacey, Lacey." He shook his head. "You beat the hell out of me. I don't know what to think half the time." He pulled her tighter into him, so close she could feel the throb of his desire rubbing against her.

When the number ended and another began, Lacey flatly refused to dance with Trey again. "I'll make an awful scene if you try to keep me here."

"Are you gonna let me walk off this floor with

this bulge in my pants?" Trey gave her a rakish grin.

"You're the most vulgar man I've ever known," Lacey snapped. She made her way through the dancers to a bench placed against the wall. She looked up to see Trey coming toward her and she wished that all the buttons would pop off his fly.

They had sat through two numbers, Trey's black look warning off any man who started across the floor toward them, when the old swamper from the saloon burst into the hall.

"Listen up, folks," he yelled over the music, "A blue norther just blew in. It's a fierce one, and you all had better head for home right now."

The music came to an abrupt end, and everybody was hurrying into their coats and heading for the door. To be caught in a blinding blizzard was something to be feared.

Lacey jumped to her feet. "I'd better find Matt," she said, a tremor in her voice.

Trey stood up beside her and growled angrily, "You don't need Matt. I'm taking you home."

"I'm going with Matt!" Lacey insisted, trying to dig in her heels and not take another step as they fell in line with the rest of the people. But those behind them propelled her along.

"You're going with me," Trey said, dragging her along. "Why make Matt go two miles out of his way in a snowstorm?"

"I'm *not* going with you," Lacey insisted, her chin tilted belligerently.

"You're going to," Trey snarled. Putting his arm around her waist, he practically lifted her feet off the floor.

When they reached the door, Matt was there as though waiting for Lacey. "I'll see that she gets home, Matt," Trey said, and pushed Lacey out into a roaring white hell.

Chapter Eleven

Lacey stopped arguing when Trey pushed her outside. Every time she opened her mouth, the wind took her breath away.

Leaning against its force, Trey gripped her arm so that she could stay on her feet, and they made their way with the others to the lean-to. While he went to saddle their mounts, she huddled up against Annie, who stood outside with the other women.

When Trey led Prince and Red through the wide door, Lacey noted that he had tied his bandana across his mouth and pulled his hat low on his forehead. As he helped her to mount, he said, "Pull the ends of your shawl up across your mouth. Otherwise your lungs might freeze."

Trey swung onto his stallion and led the way through the blowing white curtain of snow. Their neighbors were doing the same, riding off in different directions, in such a hurry that no good-byes were called out. There was only one thing on everybody's mind—get home before the storm worsened.

Lacey kept Red's nose almost on Prince's rump. She didn't dare lose sight of Trey.

They had been riding for about half an hour when the wind reached gale force. It whipped across the range, howling like a banshee. Lacey was chilled to the bone and longed for her woolen trousers to keep the cold wind off her legs. She pulled the shawl tighter around her head and shoulders, leaving only enough room for her eyes to peer ahead at Trey's broad shoulders. She found it hard to see him, her eyes were tearing so from the wind and snow beating against her face.

Trey looked back often to see how Lacey was faring. He could tell by her hunched shoulders that she was tired and cold. He longed to give her some of his strength but knew that it would be a big burden for the stallion to carry both of them. Already the two horses had slowed to a plodding walk.

When another half hour had passed, Lacey, her feet and hands numb from the cold, called to Trey through chattering teeth, "Do you think we'll be able to find the cabin through all this snow?"

"All I can do is give Prince his head and hope that his homing instinct is working."

Lacey was thinking that she couldn't hold on much longer, that she was bound to fall off the horse any minute, when Red bumped into Prince, who had come to a full stop.

"We made it!" Trey's voice was jubilant as he dismounted and hurried to Lacey, who was desperately hanging on to the saddle horn. "Prince brought us in." He lifted his arms to her.

Lacey fell into them, muttering, "He's a good boy."

Trey smiled at her child-like expression as he half carried her into the barn and set her down on a bale of hay. "Sit there while I tend to the animals."

As Trey stripped the horses, then rubbed them down, Lacey gradually became aware that she wasn't sitting in her little barn. This one was large, with many stalls in it.

When Trey walked up to her minutes later, she turned on him, saying angrily, "This isn't my barn! You said that Prince would bring me home."

"I didn't say any such thing," Trey answered sharply. "I didn't say he would take us to Jasper's place. This barn is his home, and this is where he's brought us."

He grabbed her arm and jerked her to her feet. "You little fool, you should get down on your knees and thank God that the stallion was able to bring you safely through the storm, no matter where you ended up."

Lacey felt shame as Trey grabbed her hand and led her outside. She had sounded like a sullen, whining child. It wouldn't kill her to spend one night in the Saunders home. When Trey grabbed the guide line that would lead them to the house, she stumbled along behind him on feet that had no feeling.

A flow of warm air bathed Lacey as Trey led her into the parlor, where Bull Saunders was seated with Ruby. In a stupor, she heard Trey say in a harsh, worried voice, "Build up the fire. We're about frozen."

Bull stood up, sneering. "I knew that eventually you'd get your whore here."

"And I knew that against my order, you'd get *your* whore here," Trey snarled back. "Now move your asses and make room for us at the fire."

Trey led Lacey to the chair Ruby had occupied and gently pushed her into it. He knelt in front of her and speedily took off her shoes. She half-heartedly tried to stop him when he reached up under her skirts and pulled off her stockings.

Trey picked up her bare feet and closely examined them. Placing them back on the floor, he looked up at her with a relieved smile. "Thank God, they're pink. If they were white, it would mean that they were frozen and you might lose them. Now we've got to get the blood circulating. I'll tell you up front, Lacey, it's gonna hurt like hell when you start to warm up."

As Trey began to massage her calves and feet, Lacey thought that he had never spoken truer words. As her flesh began to warm, it felt as though a thousand hot needles were pricking her. She wanted to cry out her pain but wouldn't give her two enemies, who watched her closely to see if she suffered, the satisfaction of seeing it.

But Trey, glancing up at her face, saw the agony in her eyes. "Ruby," he ordered, "bring me half a glass of whiskey."

Ruby, a sullen look on her face, rose and went into the kitchen. When she returned with the liquor, Trey took it from her and pressed it into Lacey's hand. "Drink," he ordered.

She mechanically raised the glass to her lips and took a big swallow. Its fiery strength half choked her, making her cough and causing tears to run down her cheeks.

Trey gave her a puzzled look and asked, "Haven't you tasted whiskey before?"

"Not like this. When I used to catch a cold, Papa would give me hot toddies."

Trey shook his head. She was the first whore he'd ever known who didn't drink whiskey like it was water.

Gradually the pain went away, and Lacey began to feel uncomfortably warm beneath her sheepskin jacket. She was also feeling the effects of the whiskey she had drunk. She wished that she could go to bed, but didn't dare say so. Trey would undoubtedly want to sleep with her, and she wasn't about to let him. She would sleep in the chair first, she thought, her head nodding and her lids growing heavy.

"I think your *wife*"—Bull sneered the word— "is ready for bed."

Trey gave his father a hard look, then took Lacey's arm to help her stand.

"No," she protested, pulling away from him. "I'm going to sleep here in the chair."

"Don't be foolish," Trey snapped, reaching for her again. He grunted in surprise and a little pain when Lacey's small, hard fist caught him in the eye.

As Bull laughed loudly and Ruby giggled, he jerked Lacey out of the chair. Swearing under his breath, he guided her staggering feet down a short hall. He stopped in front of an open door at the end of it and pushed her inside.

"This was my mother's room." Trey's voice gentled as he spoke of his mother.

Lacey vaguely noticed that the room was totally feminine. The flowered bedspread matched the ruffled curtains at the window; the dresser, table, and chair were very dainty, and the small fireplace was constructed from white marble.

She was to learn much later that Trey had fought his father for this room, a safe haven for his mother. The door was heavy and the lock on it strong. From the day it was installed, Bull never again got at his wife.

Trey helped Lacey off with her jacket, then started undoing the buttons of her bodice. She slapped at his hands, missed, and he laughed at her feeble attempt.

"You're tipsy, my girl," he said, "so just stand still and let me get you out of your dress. Then you can go to bed."

Lacey swayed drunkenly as the room seemed to spin around her. Just as Trey pulled the dress over her head, she slumped up against him. With a soft chuckle, he picked her up and carried her to the bed, managing to pull the covers back with one hand. Before he pulled the blankets up over her, he stood a moment looking down at her.

His eyes stroked over her silken shoulders and the top half of her firm young breasts. Tawny curls spread over the pillow, framing her delicately boned face.

Her lips were slightly parted in sleep, and Trey wondered with a pang how many men had seen her like this.

With a ragged sigh, he pulled off his boots, then all his clothing. He slid slowly into bed, careful not to touch Lacey. He wasn't about to try to make love to her in her present state. When that happened, he wanted her fully awake and wanting him as desperately as he wanted her.

Trey was a long time falling asleep. The scented warmth of Lacey's body flowed over him, making him so hard he didn't think he could bear it. He heard the clock strike two before tiredness finally overtook him and he slept.

Half awake, Lacey pulled the covers up over her chilled shoulders. The rest of her body was cozy and warm, sunk in a thick feather mattress. Old Jasper's bed was very comfortable, but she didn't remember it being this soft before.

She slowly became aware of a scent she wasn't used to. It was the smell of clean, outdoors freshness. She frowned. What had happened to the smell of the dried rose petals she always sprinkled in her pillowcases?

Coming fully awake, Lacey sensed the presence of a body lying beside her. The events of the night before began gathering in her mind. Finally she remembered everything. There was the cold ride through the storm, then Trey rubbing the circulation back into her feet. There was the whiskey he had given her to drink and her overwhelming sleepiness.

Her eyes flew open and she gave a soft gasp as she vaguely recalled Trey taking off her dress and swinging her into his arms. After that she couldn't recall anything. Her body went completely still. What had happened after that? Had she and Trey made love? If so, wouldn't she feel different . . . down there? Everything felt the same as usual.

Lacey gave a startled jerk when a sleepy,

raspy voice said, "Good morning, Mrs. Saunders. How are you feeling this morning?" Trey laughed softly. "A little stiff and sore, I imagine."

Lacey flipped over on her side to face Trey. As she gazed into his lazy, smiling eyes, she demanded, "What do you mean, stiff and sore? Why should I feel that way?"

As Trey gazed back into Lacey's troubled and confused gaze, he realized that she was wondering what, if anything, had happened between them during the night.

Keeping the amusement off his face and out of his voice, he answered evasively, "You know. You had quite a bit of exercise last night."

The color drained from Lacey's face. They *had* made love.

Irritation built inside Trey when he saw Lacey's alarm. She probably couldn't count the times she had slept with strangers, and she was horrified that she and her husband had made love.

His mouth curled scornfully. "Don't try to make out that you've never been with a man before. Is it so terrible that you gave your husband the free use of your body? I'll pay you if that's what's bothering you. How much do you charge for a full night?"

Trey had raised himself on one elbow in his agiation, and the covers fell down to his waist. Lacey stared at his broad chest. The dark curly hair covering it narrowed to a thin line that disappeared beneath the quilt. She was so shocked that she didn't hear the insult Trey had just thrown at her.

"You haven't got any clothes on!" she accused him, scandalized. She moved closer to the edge of the bed.

Goaded almost beyond endurance, Trey grabbed her by the shoulders and dragged her back, rasping, "How dare you object to your husband's naked body, when you've seen many other men's nakedness?"

Lacey shook her head vehemently, but before she could tell Trey that he was mistaken, his mouth came down on hers and he was kissing her.

She tried to escape the moving lips, the thrusting tongue, but he cupped her face with his hands, holding her head still.

As the kiss went on and on, Lacey began to feel a weakness growing inside her. She knew she should object when he removed one hand and slid the strap of her petticoat down over her shoulder. She felt the cold air on her breast, but only for a moment. The marauding lips had left her mouth and settled on her chilled breast, sucking its nipple into the warmth of his mouth.

She moaned softly at the unfamilar sensations his drawing lips were causing to flow over her, reaching all the way down to her lower regions. When Trey freed her other breast, pushing the petticoat down to her waist, and settled his mouth over the other puckered nipple, she unconsciously cupped his head and pressed him closer to her breasts.

Their bodies were heated and they were breathing hard and fast when Trey began to rid Lacey of her clothing. Trey had built so much desire inside her that she could hardly wait for him to bring her relief.

Everything else escaped her mind—her dislike of him, that he didn't love her, that he thought her a whore. She only knew that she hurt and he could take it away. When he spread her legs apart and knelt between them, she looked down at his long, hard arousal, and her eyes widened. Were all men made that way? she wondered.

Trey bent over her, gently lifted her legs up around his waist, and took his arousal in his hand. Lacey let loose a pained gasp as he entered her. Gripped with aching bewilderment, she heard Trey swear under his breath and felt his body grow very still.

Trey made a remorseful sound and started moving slowly inside her. "I'm sorry, Lacey, I truly didn't know. I'll make it right for you now, I promise."

As Trey's warm virile body rose and fell, stroking, expertly stroking, Lacey suddenly realized that he was no longer hurting her. Actually, the slip and slide of his manhood felt very good.

Trey sensed this in the way she clutched his

shoulders, and he began to move a little faster, to thrust a little deeper.

"Take me, Lacey," he whispered huskily. "Take all of me."

Lacey tightened the walls of her femininity around his working maleness and began to thrust back. "Oh God, that feels good," Trey moaned.

He grasped her small rear and pulled her up tight into the well of his hips. Holding her securely, he stroked slow and deep until he felt the convulsing of her body. He began to move fast and hard then, until tremors shook her spasming body. With one last deep drive, they came to a shuddering release together.

Lacey, limp from the heights to which she'd been carried, lay sprawled on her back, supporting the weight of the body that had scaled the summit with her. Trey's sweat-damp head lay in the curve of her shoulder and throat, his breathing fast, his heart racing against hers.

What have I done? she asked herself silently and reproachfully.

You have given your innocence to a man who doesn't love you, her inner voice answered. *What are you going to do now?*

Get home as fast as she could and try to forget this ever happened, Lacey thought, dreading the moment when she would have to face Bull and Ruby. Trey had loudly moaned his pleasure, and the bed had squeaked and protested the hard treatment his body had given it. She had no doubt that the noise had been heard throughout the house.

And how would Trey react to her now? Would he be smug? Mocking? Was the taking of her innocence just another notch to cut in his belt?

While Lacey was wondering how soon she could go home, Trey raised himself on his elbows, taking most of his weight off her. He smoothed the damp hair off her brow and gazed down at her.

"Why didn't you tell me that you were still a virgin? Why did you let me go on saying those insulting things to you? Did you plan to punish me later for the cruel thoughts I spoke out loud?

"I never wanted to hurt you, Lacey."

"I didn't have revenge in mind," Lacey said quietly. "You were so cocksure that I was like Josy's girls, I didn't bother to correct you. You wouldn't have believed me anyhow. I hope you've learned to stop making snap decisions about people."

"I certainly won't where you're concerned." Trey smiled and gingerly touched his slightly swollen right eye. "I bet you've given me a shiner."

Lacey looked closely at his eye and burst out laughing. Her husband definitely had a black eye. She wondered how he'd explain it to his friends.

"That pleases you, doesn't it, you little vixen," Trey growled and lowered his head to kiss her.

Lacey felt him stiffen, and his manhood

jerked and grew hard inside her. And though she wanted to feel again the mindless magic it could bring her, she didn't want Trey to think that things had changed between them. She intened to wait and see if he changed his wild ways and stopped seeing the singer. He might not love her, but by God he was going to show her respect. She would not be one of those wives who turned a blind eye to her husband's whoring.

She gave Trey an unexpected push and rolled out from beneath him. Before he could stop her, she was out of the bed.

"Come back, honey," Trey cajoled huskily. "Just one more time. I'm hurting bad."

"So am I," Lacey retorted, "but not in the same way you are."

Trey looked at her naked, slender body hurrying into the underclothing he had feverishly stripped off her, then glanced down at the blood-stained sheet. Remorse for having hurt her made him lose his hardness.

"I'm sorry, Lacey," he said softly. "Do you hurt a lot?"

"Enough," Lacey answered tartly, holding up her dress and assessing its wrinkled condition in dismay. Bull Saunders and Ruby would think that she was so eager to get into bed with Trey, she hadn't bothered to undress.

Trey saw her distress and said, "My mother was small like you. Look in her wardrobe and pick out a dress."

Lacey looked at him in surprise. Matt had told her that Trey idolized his mother. "Are you sure?" she asked.

"You are my wife," Trey answered simply, his tone conveying that he wouldn't extend that offer to any other woman.

Lacey opened the double doors of the wardrobe. There weren't many dresses hanging there, but they were all quietly beautiful. The sort a lady would wear.

She chose a deep green gown with a white lace collar and cuffs. When she pulled it over her head, she found that it fit perfectly.

There was sadness in Trey's eyes when she turned around to face him, but he smiled and said, "You look beautiful."

"Thank you," Lacey answered. She went to the window and pushed aside the heavy drapes.

It was all white and silent outside. Sometime during the night, the wind had died down and the snow had ceased to fall. But it had left in its wake an additional foot of snow. It would be a laborious trek back to old Jasper's cabin.

"When are you going to get up?" She turned and looked at Trey, who lay on his back, his head resting on his crossed arms. She wished he'd cover himself up. His half-aroused manhood was making her feel uneasy.

"I don't know when I'll get up," Trey answered her. "It's a fine day for just lying around. What are you going to do all day?" She saw his male member jerk and swell a little larger. He didn't have to tell her what he thought she should do. He would like her to lie around with him.

Since she had no intention of doing that, she answered, "First, I'm going home. Then I'm going to do my chores and after that a little baking. Annie brought me over a bushel of apples last week. I intend to bake some pies for Matt and me. His housekeeper mainly makes Mexican dishes, and he misses having American pastries."

At first Trey looked blank; then he sat up in bed. "What do you mean, you're going home?" he demanded hotly. "You are home."

"Home? You call this place a home with all the hate that permeates its very walls? This place would stifle the life out of me."

Trey was silent for several moments, then he said quietly, "You're right. It's not a home. It never has been. It's only a showplace for Bull Saunders."

Trey abruptly changed the subject. "You like Matt a lot, don't you?"

"Yes, I'm very fond of him. I don't know what would have become of me if he hadn't been in that shack your father sent me to. I firmly believe that he saved my life that night."

Trey was silent again for a minute, then said, "He's old enough to be your grandfather, you know."

Lacey's laughter pealed out. "Hardly that. My father, yes." She gave him a searching look.

"Surely you don't think I have any romantic notions about him?"

Trey looked away from her, a little shamefaced. "I owe him a lot for looking after you."

"His looking after me didn't have anything to do with you, Trey. Matt is the sort of man who would look after stray dogs and helpless women no matter who they might be."

"And you don't think I'd do the same?" Trey lifted an angry eyebrow at her.

"I have no idea what you'd do. I don't know you."

"You could know me if you tried."

"It's not up to me to figure out what sort of man you are. It's up to you to show me."

"You're referring to the stipulation you set down before?"

"That's right."

"There's no give in you, is there, woman?"

"Not when I know I'm right."

"And of course you are always right," Trey grumbled.

Lacey gave him a wide smile. "Usually."

Trey swung his feet over the edge of the bed and stood up. Lacey gasped and turned her back as, naked and unabashed, he went about the room gathering up his clothes.

"Get used to seeing me in my natural state, wife," Trey grunted. "Before you die, you're going to see me like this many times. You'll get to know my body as well as you do your own."

Lacey answered with a sharp "Hah" as she

combed her fingers through her tangled curls.

Completely dressed now, Trey said, "Stay here while I go pack my clothes."

Lacey looked at him suspiciously. "Why are you doing that?"

"It should be obvious," Trey answered. "If you won't live with me, then I'll go live with you."

"You'll do no such thing." Lacey left off trying to smooth her hair. "I have no intention of living with you anywhere."

"Look, Lacey," Trey said, trying to be patient, "we are truly man and wife now, and as such we should live together." He gave her a coaxing smile. "If we live together, we'll get to know each other faster."

"You mean you'll get to know my body faster." Lacey gave him a chilling look. She hurriedly left the room before Trey could argue further.

But Trey was right behind her when she swept into the big parlor. She slowed her steps when she saw Bull and Ruby sitting before the fireplace. She had hoped to leave without seeing them.

Bull looked up and jeered, "I'm surprised either one of you can walk, the way you was carryin' on. I expect that sheet-shakin' went on all night."

As Trey took Lacey's arm and steered her toward the kitchen, he ignored his father's taunts until Bull said, "Remember your promise to me, Trey. You said when your whore moved in, I could bring my own whore back. Well, your woman's here now, so I'm goin' into town and find me one, too."

While Lacey gasped her outrage, Trey spun around to face his father. "Hold your jaw, old man," he said through clenched teeth. "Lacey is my wife, not my whore. If you ever refer to her again as one, I'll smash your face in."

He paused long enough to let his words sink in, then added, "She's not staying here, so you won't be moving any woman in."

As Bull almost choked on his spleen, Trey said to Lacey, "As soon as we have some breakfast, I'll take you home."

Trey fried them bacon and eggs, which they washed down with coffee. "While you get into your jacket, I'll go get our horses ready."

"Where are my jacket and shawl?" Lacey asked.

"They're in the parlor. I put them on the hearth to dry out last night."

When Trey left the house, bundled up to his nose, Lacey gathered her nerve to face Bull and Ruby alone. She knew that without Trey there to intercede for her, they would snap at her like hungry wolves.

Bull started in on her as soon as she entered the room. "Why ain't you stayin' here?" He looked at her with wintery eyes. "Don't try to tell me this place ain't good enough for the likes of you. I heard in town that you and your paw lived in that medicine wagon for years."

Before Lacey could answer, Ruby took over. "You ought to get down on your knees and kiss the Saunders men's feet for bein' willin' to take you in. If you had any sense, you'd take your nose out of the air and make friends with Bull. Trey will never be faithful to you. When he gets tired of you, he'll go back to Sally Jo. He's not going to give her up for a skinny little thing like you."

Again before Lacey could speak, Bull cut in. "It's true, what Ruby said. Trey likes to ride his women hard and long." He ran scornful eyes over Lacey's slender body. "You couldn't stand up to it more than a few nights. He'd wear you out real quick."

Lacey was finally allowed to give vent to her long-witheld anger. Pinning first Bull and then Ruby with stormy green eyes, she said, "I couldn't care less who Trey Saunders sleeps with." She looked at Ruby. "He can sleep with whores, or he can sleep with you. It's common knowledge that you've slept with both father and son."

She looked back at Bull. "Yes, I do think that I'm too good to live in this house of hate. It reeks of misery and pain. Old Jasper's three-room cabin is a palace compared to this cold mausoleum. Maybe my father and I did live in a wagon, but it was filled with love. This house has known little of that. I expect what little there was died when your wife passed away."

"I love this house!" Bull half rose from his

chair. "I planned it for years."

"Bah!" Lacey snapped. "You don't know the meaning of love. You built this house as a monument to yourself, to show off your wealth and power."

The three were unaware that Trey had returned to the house. He stood in the doorway, listening to their battle of words. Their heads swiveled to look at him when he said dryly, "She gave it to you good, didn't she, old man? Do you still want her to live with us?"

"I'd rather live with a rattlesnake." Bull glared at Lacey as Trey helped her on with her jacket.

"No doubt you would," Trey said with a grim smile. "I've always thought you kin to the diamondback."

When Lacey had buttoned up her jacket and wrapped the shawl over her head and around her shoulders, she and Trey walked out of the house, leaving behind a pair of sullen, simmering people.

Chapter Twelve

Trey had chosen to ride the tough little mustang. He could more easily break a path through the new snow than the high-strung stallion, who might balk at a high snowdrift. Lacey, astride Red, followed closely behind Trey, her teeth chattering from the cold.

The first time Trey had to dismount and help the little horse push through a three-foot wall of snow, she wondered if she had been selfish, insisting that she go home. But there was the stock to consider. They needed to be fed, and the cow had to be milked.

At last the little cabin came in sight, and Lacey thought she had never so relieved to arrive anyplace. The snow was drifted past the kitchen window, but miraculously the wind had swept it clear of the door.

The half-hour trip from the ranch house to the cabin had taken them close to two hours. They couldn't wait to get inside.

However, when they walked in they found the little place almost as cold as it was outside.

Lacey sat shivering in the rocking chair as Trey hurriedly built a fire in the fireplace, then lit the stove in the kitchen. She glanced through the open door of her bedroom, seeing her discarded shirt and trousers on the bed's footrail.

So much had happened in the hours since she had changed into the red party dress. She had became a wife in every sense of the word—a fact that made her cringe in shame every time she remembered how she had exalted in Trey's lovemaking. And more to her shame, she would have willingly experienced it a second time had her pride not stepped in and stopped her.

She watched Trey fan the glowing embers into flames with his hat. She was afraid that Ruby had spoken the truth about Trey and his women, especially Sally Jo. After all, he had overheard what Ruby said and hadn't bothered to correct her.

Lacey watched the play of Trey's waist, the movement in his thighs as he reached for more wood to feed the fire. She remembered that sleek, naked body lying on top of her, his male part thrusting slowly inside her, and a warm weakness flowed over her. Pray God he didn't ask her to go to bed before he left. She doubted very much that she could refuse him.

However, all Trey asked of her when he had both fires going was," "Could I have a cup of coffee before I start the cold ride home?"

Lacey repressed the derisive laughter that rose in her throat. Evidently he had lost interest in taking her back to bed. He probably planned to visit that Sally Jo tonight.

"I'll get a pot on right away," she said, standing up and removing her jacket. The garment wasn't necessary now. The little cabin had warmed up nicely.

While she poured water into the coffee pot and added fragrant grounds to it, Trey went out onto the porch, where a good supply of wood was stacked, and began carrying in logs to fill the woodbox.

When he had finished, he said, "I'll take the horses and break a path to the barn for you."

Later, as they sat at the table sipping coffee, Trey said, "I hate to leave you here alone. There's so much that could happen to you."

"Like what?" Lacey lowered her cup to the table.

"Like maybe slipping in the snow and breaking a leg. Like catching pneumonia and nobody knowing that you are sick. Like some grub-liner coming along and raping you."

Before Lacey could point out that everything he said was true, but not likely to happen, there came from outside the sound of champing bits and stamping hooves. A moment later they heard footsteps on the porch and then a knock on the door.

Lacey started to rise, but Trey pushed her back down. "I'll see who it is," he said. "It could be a stranger riding the grub line—one of the dangers I pointed out to you."

He swung open the door and said warmly, "Good morning, Matt."

"The same to you, Trey," Matt replied, obviously startled. "If I'd known you were here, I wouldn't have fought my way over to check on Lacey," he added, stamping the snow off his feet before stepping inside.

"We got here about half an hour ago," Trey said.

We? Matt thought, looking at Lacey, who blushed and didn't quite meet his eyes. Her embarrassment told him that Trey had finally slept with his wife. And about time, he added silently.

When Lacey rose and poured Matt a cup of coffee, he shrugged out of his jacket and sat down across from Trey. As he stirred sugar into his drink, he looked at the couple with a wide smile and said, "I guess I'll have to be mushing over here every day to attend to the stock and milk the cow."

Lacey gave him a puzzled look. "Why should you do that? I'll still be here to look after things."

Matt's confusion showed on his face as he stammered, "I thought that . . . well I got the

Ab

Lacey

notion that . . . that you had moved in with Trey."

Lacey gave a negative shake of her head. "I spent the night at the ranch because that's where Trey's stallion took us in the blizzard."

"I see." Matt nodded slowly. Then, looking at Trey, he said, "That sure was one hell of a blizzard, wasn't it? There was a time or two when I didn't know if I'd make it home. I finally did what you did. I gave my mount his head."

"Sometimes that's all you can do," Trey answered in a flat voice. A moment later he was standing up and taking his jacket from the back of his chair. Shrugging into it and picking his hat off the floor where he had laid it, he said gruffly, "I'll be leaving now. I've got some business to take care of in town."

He left then without any good-byes, not even looking at Lacey.

When the door snapped shut behind Trey, Matt looked at Lacey. Her face had grown pale. "What are you thinking, honey?" he asked gently.

"I'm not thinking," Lacey answered, a tremor in her voice. "I'm knowing. He's gone to that woman, Sally Jo."

"Who told you about her?" Matt put his empty cup down.

Lacey gave a bitter little laugh. "Ruby delighted in telling me all about her this morning."

"That one would," Matt growled. "And em-

207

broidered it considerably too, I'll wager. I warned you that Bull and that bitch would say or do anything they can to break you and Trey up."

"I know you did, but Trey was angry at me when he left. I'm sure he's on his way to visit that Sally Jo."

"He wasn't angry at you, Lacey. He was embarrassed that I found out that you still refuse to live with him. It's a big slap to a man's ego for his friends to find out his wife keeps him from her bed."

"But doesn't everybody know that already?"

"Not neccessarily. The main thought among our neighbors is that you just refuse to live in Bull's house. Seeing the two of you together at the dance will swing the others to that same belief."

Matt patted Lacey's hand. "It's true Trey still carouses with his friends, but ever since he came home he's left the whores strictly alone. And that includes Sally Jo."

"According to Ruby, Sally Jo is his favorite and he'll never give her up."

"Ruby said!" Matt snorted impatiently. "Did she bother to tell you that Sally Jo isn't a whore, that she's a singer?"

"No, she didn't," Lacey said in a low voice. She was very upset at this piece of news. She would rather have gone on thinking that the woman was a common saloon wench, that she meant nothing to Trey. But if she was an entertainer, a singer, he could be very serious about her. Which didn't explain, though, why he had chosen to marry Lacey Stewart.

She looked at Matt and said, "Tell me about this woman."

"Well," Matt began, chewing thoughtfully at his mustache. "She's around Trey's age, attractive in a hard way. Her hair is black and she has ample curves, if you know what I mean." He grinned at Lacey. "She sings well enough and doesn't fraternize with the customers."

"Except for Trey?"

"Well . . . yes," Matt answered grudgingly, looking away from Lacey. "I don't know how she feels about Trey, but he's not in love with her or anything like that."

"He's not in love with me either, but he married me. How do you account for that?"

Matt shook his head. "I stopped trying to figure Trey out a long time ago. He told me that he wanted to rile Bull."

"Wouldn't marrying a saloon singer made Mr. Saunders just as angry?"

"Not quite. As you know, Trey thought you were a woman of loose morals when he married you." He gave Lacey a sly, teasing grin. "I expect he knows better now."

Lacey choose to ignore the innuendo and said, "I guess I'd better get down to the barn and milk the cow and give the stock some food and water. The cow has been bawling ever since I got home."

Matt knew he was being dismissed and he knew why. Lacey didn't want to discuss her new relationship with Trey. He didn't blame her, the way Trey had walked out of the house like a sore-assed bear. If the dunderhead wanted to win over his wife, he was going about it in the wrong way.

He stood up and pulled on his jacket. "I guess I'll mosey on back to the ranch, seeing as how you're all right."

"Thanks for coming over, Matt." Lacey followed him to the door. "I hope it won't be an inconvenience to continue stopping by occasionally and checking to see if I've got the flag flying from the cabin top."

"I won't mind in the least, Lacey, you know that." Matt opened the door and said before stepping outside, "Don't fret about Trey going into town, Lacey. He'll go to the saloon and have some whiskey, probably more than he should, but he won't go around Sally Jo. Take my word for it."

Lacey lifted her small chin in the air and sniffed, "I'm sure I don't care if he does."

Matt kept a straight face, thinking to himself, *Like hell you don't.*

The mount of another early riser had already broken a path through the snow when Trey hit the trail leading into Marengo, and it didn't take him long to reach town. Nevertheless, the little mustang was blowing slightly

210

when he drew him to a halt in front of Whiskey Pete's.

There were two other horses tied to the hitching post as Trey swung from the saddle and looped his mount's reins around the worn hitching rail. He recognized one as belonging to Tollie Stumps, but the other, a claybank, he'd never seen before. He hopped up onto the wooden sidewalk, which had been cleared of snow, thinking to himself that some new cowpoke had wandered into Marengo.

There were seven people lined up at the bar when Trey stepped into thc saloon. Tollie Stump, two whores from Josy's place looking for customers, the stranger, Big John the blacksmith, Calvin Clay the barber from next door, and at the end of the bar, Sally Jo.

All but the stranger greeted Trey when a place was made for him at the bar. Pete poured him a glass of whiskey and said with a grin, "A man could freeze his nuts off in this kind of weather, couldn't he?"

"He sure as hell could." Trey grinned back. "I'm not sure but what I didn't get one frozen on the way here."

When Sally Jo realized that Trey wasn't going to come to her, she started down the bar to join him. She had taken only a few steps when the burly-looking stranger grabbed her by the arm and jerked her back beside him.

"Stay here beside me, purty little whore," he leered. "Soon as I finish my drink, me and you are goin' upstairs and have ourselves a fine time. I ain't had a woman in over a month, so I be ready for a rough ridin'."

Trey started to push away from the bar to come to Sally Jo's aid; after all, he still liked her even if he didn't want to sleep with her anymore. He paused, though, remembering that the singer had a sharp tongue and he wasn't all that worried that she couldn't take care of herself.

And it looked that way as Sally Jo jerked free and said scathingly, "If you think I'm that woman, you'll wait a lifetime."

"Is that right, bitch?" the stranger grabbed her again and slammed her back against the bar, making her cry out in pain.

"Hey now," Pete called out, moving down the bar. "That will be enough of that, mister."

"You gonna stop me, baldy?" the man snarled, grabbing up a whiskey bottle and breaking its head off against the bar. "Come on, stop me." He glared at Pete, the jagged edges of the bottle gripped tightly in his hand, ready to strike out at the bartender.

This time Trey stepped away from the bar. "Hey, you mangy cur." His voice rang cold in the room. "I'll stop you!"

The heavy-set body spun around, the bottle held in front of him as he glared menacingly at Trey. Trey watched the narrowed slitted eyes of the stranger. They would tell him when the man was going to go into action.

In less than a second, the stranger came at him low and hard. Trey gripped the fingers of both hands together, side-stepped the lunging man, and brought his clubbed hands down on the back of his neck.

The man didn't make a sound as he slowly folded to the sawdust floor and lay there senseless. Trey shouldered his way through those who had gathered to watch the fight and walked over to Sally Jo, who was leaning against the bar, grimacing with pain.

"Are you hurt?" he asked with concern.

"A little," Sally Jo answered. "It feels like my back is broken."

"Do you mean it?"

"Not really. It just hurts like hell."

"Come on, I'll help you to your room." Trey took her arm and led her toward the stairs leading to the rooms above. "A hot bath will help you. Take away the soreness."

When Trey had settled Sally Jo into the room that had always seemed to smother him with the overpowering scent of perfume, ruffled pillows, and lacy curtains, he walked across the narrow hall and knocked on another door.

A redhead named Nell greeted him with a wide smile on her painted lips. "Come in, Trey." She tugged at his arm. "You haven't visited me in ages. Not since Sally Jo hit town."

Trey remained in the doorway, resisting the pull of Nell's hands. He ran a finger down her nose and, giving her a rakish smile, said, "We'll have to do something about that one day soon. For now I'd like for you to go downstairs to the kitchen and have the Mexican lad bring up some warm water for Sally Jo to soak in. A stranger got rough with her, and she hurt her back."

Since Sally Jo didn't fraternize with the prostitutes, she wasn't well-liked by them. Nell reluctantly nodded her head and went downstairs.

When Trey returned to Sally Jo's room, she had just stepped out of her last garment. Before he started the cattle drive, before he married Lacey, the singer's bare body would have had him striding across the floor, throwing her onto the bed and entering her, all in one movement.

But her amply curved body didn't stir him in the least. She could have been his friend Matt standing naked before him.

Sally Jo started toward him, her arms lifted, and he wondered what he could say to her that wouldn't hurt her feelings. Although he didn't desire her anymore, he wanted to break off their relationship without any hard feelings. She had to know that he was married now, but she would have also heard that he and Lacey weren't living together.

When Sally Jo slipped her soft arms around his neck and shoulders and pressed her body against his, Trey gently removed her arms and held her away from him.

"We musn't fool around until we see how badly you're hurt. You may have some broken ribs."

"I don't care if I do," Sally Jo pouted. "You haven't been with me since you came home from the cattle drive." She looked at him suspiciously. "Fact is, since you got married. Are you being faithful to the little wife?"

"My wife has nothing to do with it." Trey spoke sharply, not wanting to discuss Lacey with the woman he'd lain with so many times.

The singer sensed by his tone that she had spoken out of turn and turned her back so that Trey wouldn't see her displeasure. She pulled on a robe, and her voice was calm when she said casually, "You're probably right about my ribs. It does pain me a bit to breathe."

"I figured as much," Trey said and silently breathed his relief when the Mexican teenager knocked on the door, a pail of water in each hand.

"I've got to get back to the ranch now, Sally Jo," he said as the water was being emptied into the fancy hip tub. "You take it easy, and if your ribs continue to hurt, you'd better have Doc Carson take a look at them. They might need binding."

"Yes, I'll do that," his old lover said with a forced smile. She wanted to ask Trey when she would see him again but dreaded his answer—an answer that, deep in her heart, she already knew. Trey Saunders would no longer come to Whiskey Pete's seeking the comfort of her arms. He might not know it, but he was in love with his wife.

Sally Jo sighed as she sprinkled salts in her bath water. Should she look for a replacement for Trey, or should she move on when the snow cleared away?

Chapter Thirteen

Prince was stepping along at a good pace on the beaten-down snow path, and Trey let the reins drop across his proud, arching neck. He knew the stallion wouldn't stray off into the deep snow.

As always happened in an idle moment, his thoughts turned to Lacey.

What more could he do to win her over? he asked himself. It was true that he still hung around with his wild friends, but he hadn't been with another woman since he said his "I do's" in front of the preacher. If she hadn't responded so wholeheartedly to his lovemaking, he'd think that she plain out didn't like him. If that was true, it was a first for him.

"Maybe she just loves the way you make love,"

his inner voice pointed out.

"If that's the case," Trey mentally retorted, not liking that idea, "I'm dammed if I'll be her stud."

But as he rode on, he knew that he lied to himself. He'd be anything she wanted him to be if only he could be her husband in all ways— live with her, sleep with her, share his thoughts with her, listen to her when she spoke of hers.

A short time later, he saw Lacey's cabin at a distance, blue smoke coming from the chimney and going straight up in a thin column into the cold air. He wondered what she was doing, how she passed the time alone in the little place. If he was living with her, they could pass the time quite pleasantly, making love off and on all day.

Trey grunted at the foolish thought. When the ranch house came in sight, he was still mulling everything over in his mind. He rode to the barn and unsaddled Prince and removed the bridle, then went reluctantly to the house. He was in no mood to banter insults back and forth with his father.

He glanced into the parlor as he walked to the kitchen to make something to eat. Bull sat in front of the fireplace, his stockinged feet propped on the hearth. Trey hoped the old devil would stay there.

He was not to have his wish. He was laying a slab of ham in a frying pan when Bull entered the kitchen, a dark scowl on his face. He started complaining right off.

"I've been studying how, since your wife still refuses to move in with us, I don't know why I can't have me a woman move in. For one thing, I'm dammed tired of eatin' my own cookin', and the messes you throw together ain't fit to eat."

Trey twitched his shoulders impatiently. "Get it through your mule head that there will be no more women brought here for your pleasure. The cowhands will be returning home any day now, and we can eat with the men at the cook-shack."

"What about the house then?" Bull continued to argue. "It needs to be swept and dusted."

Trey turned the piece of meat over to cook on the other side before answering, "I'll hire Annie Stump to come in once a week to straighten things up. She'll knock you on your rump if you try anything with her."

"Bah! Who'd want to try anything with her? She looks like a man, wearin' men's trousers and flannel shirts."

"What's wrong with Ruby cleaning the place up after the pair of you finish wallowing around in bed?"

"Go to hell," Bull snarled. Wheeling around, he went back to his spot before the fire.

Trey grinned and cut into the under-cooked piece of meat, telling himself that ought to shut the old devil up for a while.

It was around ten in the morning, two days after the blizzard, when Annie, astride an old mule, came to Lacey's cabin to collect the milk. "The snow is too deep to get a wagon through," she explained in Lacey's warm kitchen as she struggled out of her heavy jacket, then removed the scarf she had had put over her hat and tied beneath her chin.

"Come stand by the stove and warm up while I pour us some coffee and put out some cookies," Lacey invited her.

"I ain't cold in the least," Annie said, and pulling a chair away from the table, she plopped down on it.

They talked of inconsequential things. Wasn't the blizzard bad and did Annie think it would snow again soon? Would Lacey give Annie the recipe for her sugar cookies? Then Annie said, almost too casually, "Tollie saw Trey in the saloon yesterday."

Lacey made no response, sipping her coffee and waiting for Annie to continue. She had a feeling she wasn't going to like what Annie said.

She discovered that she was right when Annie told her, "He got in a fight over that singer, Sally Jo. It seems a stranger was gettin' rough with her and Trey got into it with him. It wasn't much of a fight, though. Trey knocked him unconscious with one blow."

Annie gave a start when Lacey's cup clattered into the saucer. When she saw how white her young friend's face had grown, she said contritely, "I'm sorry, Lacey. I spoke without thinking." She squeezed Lacey's closed fist lying beside her cup. "It's true Trey and the singer used to be pretty close, but it ain't that way anymore. He would have stepped in no matter who the woman was if a man was mistreating her."

"It's all right, Annie." Lacey managed to smile wanly. "I know you didn't mean to hurt me. And I'm not really hurt. Ruby Dalton told me all about the romance between Trey and the singer. She said that Trey's marriage to me wouldn't stop their relationship."

"I hope you didn't believe that lyin' slut." Annie frowned. "Whatever that one tells you, just believe the opposite and you'll have the truth of it. Tollie said that Trey didn't spend hardly any time in Sally Jo's room once he helped her upstairs."

Annie wished she could take back her last words as soon as she uttered them. From the look on Lacey's face, she hadn't helped Trey's case at all. She jumped to her feet, muttering, "I'd better get out of here before my big mouth has you divorcing Trey. Just believe me that the singer means nothing to Trey anymore."

When Annie had left with her milk, Lacey sat down in the fireside chair. With a shove of her foot, she put it in motion, and while she rocked slowly she went over what Annie had said about Trey and Sally Jo.

Why had her friend's words been so upsetting to her? she asked herself. They had felt like the talons of an eagle clutching her heart, making it bleed. She didn't care what Trey did . . . did she?

She gave a ragged sigh and admitted that she did care. She cared deeply.

When had her feelings for Trey changed? Lacey stopped rocking and stared into the flames as though seeking an answer in them. Had it been after they made love, or before that?

She started the chair to rocking again. Was it possible that she had fallen in love with her husband? She had never loved anyone but her parents, and this newly developed feeling she had for Trey wasn't anything like what she had felt for them. Could the love for a man be so vastly different?

Lacey decided that whatever it was she now felt for Trey, she must be careful that he never knew about her confusion. She could at least keep her pride and hide her bitterness if he continued to see the singer.

The sudden distant sound of loud laughter brought Lacey out of her unsettling thoughts and questions. She rose and hurried to the window after she checked to see that the door was barred. The boiterous laughter had come from male throats. It could be a bunch of renegade Indians who had broken away from their tribe. Annie had mentioned once that the ranchers sometimes had trouble with them. They stole everything they could get their hands on, including a beef occasionally.

She shaded her eyes with her hands against

the glare of the sun and saw a long caravan of horses and wagons moving across the landscape. A wide smile curved her lips. The Saunders's cowboys were coming home from the cattle drive.

A man, whom she took for the trail boss, led the way, followed by eight men riding two abreast. A short distance behind them, the chuck wagon rolled along on the path made by the riders. The hoodlum wagon came next, and shortly behind it was the remuda, driven by a teenager.

Lacey watched until the whole outfit had disappeared behind a snow-covered knoll, then went back to her chair and stared glumly into the fire.

The cowhands would go into town tonight to celebrate their return. They would drink a while, then stumble their way to Josy's place to find comfort in the arms of one of her girls.

Trey would go with them, she though dispiritedly. He would drink with his men, then spend the rest of the evening with Sally Jo.

When the fire was burning steadily in the bunkhouse potbelly stove, Trey closed its heavy iron door. He had kept a fire going in the long building for three days running. Barring any unforeseen problems, the men should be riding in any day now.

He left the building and was nearing the house when he saw the long line of his outfit riding in, the horses' hooves kicking up great clumps of snow. The men saw him and gave a loud shout, snatching off their hats and waving them at him.

When all eight riders had reined in around him, he looked at the face of each man. They all looked pretty beat. He knew a stab of pain for the cowboy who had lost his life and now lay in a lonely grave.

He pushed away the sad thought and asked, "When did you men hit the heavy snow?"

"Late yesterday afternoon," Cole Stringer, the trail boss, answered. "I'm sure glad we missed the blizzard that put all this snow on the ground. It must have been a howler."

"It was a bad one," Trey said, then lowered his lids to hid the softness that came into his eyes. The storm's fierceness had given him the opportunity to finally make love to his wife.

Stringer stepped out of the saddle. "You men turn your mounts over to one of the men in the barn, then go to the bunkhouse and warm up. I'll settle up with Trey and join you later."

The men turned their mounts in the direction of the large barn, and Trey led the way to the house. When they stepped into the kitchen, Bull was waiting for them, sitting at the table. He barely nodded a greeting to Cole. As Trey splashed whiskey into three glasses, Bull asked, "How many cattle did you lose on the drive?"

Cole gave him a cold look. The old bastard didn't ask if they'd had any trouble with Indians or cattle thieves or lightning storms, or did they lose any men. He only cared about how many of his cattle had been lost.

"Smitty was trampled to death in a stampede," he said pointedly, hoping to shame the man for not asking about the welfare of his men.

But Bull's only response was an uncaring, "That's too bad. How many head did you lose?"

Cole looked at Trey's angry face, then answered coldly, "Around twenty-five head at river crossings."

"That's a damn lot of cattle," Bull said testily.

"And much less than we lost on the previous drives." Trey sat down across from his father. "You did a fine job, Cole," he said and lifted his glass. "Let's drink to it."

"Thanks, Trey." Cole smiled his appreciation. When he had downed his drink, he handed an envelope to Trey, in which was a check and a receipt for the cattle. He grinned at Trey and asked, "How are you likin' married life?"

"Hah!" Bull broke in before Trey could answer. "She refuses to live with him. Don't that frost your rump?" He laughed and slapped his leg. "Who'da thought randy Trey Saunders couldn't get his wife to sleep with him. The big man who can get any woman he wants."

Trey shot his father a furious look. The old bastard knew that he had slept with Lacey at least once. And though he wanted to reach across the table and punch Bull in the mouth, he retained his relaxed attitude and said with deceptive laziness, "Just because she won't live in this house with you doesn't mean I can't sleep with her in old Jasper's cabin."

He flicked a quick look at the trail boss. Did Cole believe him? He sighed an inward breath of relief. The knowing look on Cole's face showed that he believed Trey's story. No one would question why Lacey wouldn't live under the same roof with the old bastard.

"Bah!" Bull grunted and stood up. "If you was half a man, you'd drag her back here by the hair of her head." He took his jacket and hat from a peg next to the door. "I'm goin' to town," he said and slammed the door behind him.

Trey and Cole shared a laugh at Bull's abrupt leaving; then Cole filled Trey in on the details of the drive. He tossed the last of his whiskey down his throat and picked his hat off the floor.

"I'll be gettin' on down to the bunkhouse, take a bath, change into clean clothes, then go into town with the men and raise a little hell. You'll be comin' with us, won't you?" He asked the question as though it was a sure thing Trey would be accompanying his men.

He looked surprised when Trey answered, "I think I'll pass this time, Cole. I'm an old married man now, you know." His crooked grin took away the seriousness of his remark.

Cole laughed and said, "Somehow I can't see you in the role of an old married man."

When Cole had gone, Trey poured a couple

of fingers of whiskey into his glass and corked the bottle. As he sipped at the fiery liquid, the thought kept coming back to him that he wouldn't mind in the least living out the rest of his life as an old married man—if Lacey spent it with him.

Trey stood up suddenly and went into his mother's room. He opened her wardrobe and took from its bottom a small box. Inside it were Christmas tree decorations. They hadn't been used since he was a little boy. Christmas was ten days away, and tomorrow he was going to cut Lacey a tree. He hoped that she would let him help decorate it.

Lacey sat brooding before the fire until the striking clock alerted her that it was time she did her chores. With a sigh, she stood up, went into the kitchen, and pulled on old Jasper's ratty-looking jacket. Pulling a woolen cap down over her tawny curls, she picked up the milk pail.

Half an hour later, she was closing the barn door behind her and in the near dusk started making her way toward the cabin. Her attention was on the icy path, and she almost walked into the big stallion standing in front of the porch.

She looked up and blinked in surprise. Her father-in-law was looking down at her from his saddle. He smiled at her, but there was no warmth in his eyes. She supposed the thing to do was invite him into the house. After all, he was Trey's father.

But she remembered all too well that this man had once almost cost her her life.

With her hand in her pocket, her fingers curled around the trigger of her revolver, she looked up at Bull and asked, "What are you doing here?"

"Now that's a strange question." Bull pretended to be hurt. "Can't a man visit his daughter-in-law?"

"Not if that man wishes her dead, or out of his life."

"Now where did you get the idea I wish you was dead?"

"Look, Mr. Saunders, I'm not going to stand here bandying words with you. I'm getting cold, and I want to go inside. Why are you here?"

Bull laughed, a short and ugly sound. "I just thought that you'd like to know that Trey has gone to town with the men and will spend most of the night with Sally Jo."

A pain gripped Lacey in the chest with such force that she became dizzy with it. She had suspected that Trey would visit the singer tonight, and now it was a certainty. *Don't let him see your pain,* the little voice inside her whispered. No, she wouldn't give the old devil the satisfaction of knowing how fiercely his words had hurt her.

Lacey's knuckles grew white on the milk pail handle as she said with a calmness that surprised her, "If you think that piece of news bothers me, Mr. Saunders, you've made a cold ride for nothing."

Bull glared down at her a moment. Then, jabbing his heels into his mount, he rode away as fast as the horse could go through the snow.

Tears blinded Lacey's eyes as she stepped up onto the porch and entered the cabin.

Chapter Fourteen

Bull looked up from his plate of bacon and eggs when Trey entered the kitchen. He watched Trey place a box next to the door and asked, "What you got there?"

"Nothing that would interest you," Trey answered shortly as he laid strips of bacon in the same skillet Bull had used.

Bull frowned when the meat began to sizzle. "Be careful that you don't mess up the stove," he growled. "I spent an hour cleanin' it up yesterday."

"Is that so?" Trey said, delighted when the bacon started splattering grease all over the top of the range.

"Yes, dammit, it's so." Bull brought a fist down on the table. "Put a lid on the skillet."

"No use doing it now," Trey answered lazily, breaking three eggs into the frying pan. "I'm almost finished."

By the time he had dished up his morning meal, the top of the cookstove was covered with a film of grease. Pure hatred for his son shone out of Bull's eyes. Muttering a string of oaths, he pushed away from the table and stomped into the parlor.

Trey grinned. The one sure way of riling his father was to mess up his house—which his son did at every opportunity.

Trey looked gloomily out the window. He wished it could be different between him and his father, that there could be affection between them as there was between other fathers and sons.

That would never be, he knew. If it hadn't happened in thirty years, it wasn't about to happen at this late date.

Trey finished his breakfast, and leaving his dirty plate and cup on the table, he rose, shrugged into his jacket, picked up the box, and slammed the door behind him when he left.

It was early in the day, but he was going courting.

On his way to the barn, Trey remembered that he hadn't seen or spoken to Jiggers since the cook's return. He'd have to stop and visit with him for a while, for he knew the old fellow was probably feeling hurt that Trey hadn't stopped in to see him last night.

Jiggers was testy when Trey stepped into the cookshack; the old man barely acknowledged his greeting. "Look, Jiggers," he cajoled, "I'm sorry I didn't get around to seeing you last night." He paused a moment before telling his little white lie. "By the time I got over here, you had gone to town with the men. I hadn't expected you to go with them." He held his breath then, hoping that the old fellow really had gone with the men.

Trey let his breath out when Jiggers softened and said, "I felt like doin' a little celebratin' too. It took near a pint of whiskey to warm up my bones, I was that cold. The past three days have been hellish."

"I know. It's been a hard winter. I worry about the cattle still out on the range."

"They'll do what they always do; head for the foothills where the snow ain't so deep and browse off bush to keep themselves alive."

"I hope so," Trey said. Then, after a moment, he grinned at the old cook. "Did you and the men make hogs of yourselves, drinking and running next door to Josy's?"

Jiggers's lips lifted in a toothless smile. "I made a couple trips, but the others, they almost wore the path out runnin' back and forth between the whorehouse and the saloon."

Jiggers paused and chuckled. "Old Bull wanted to take the tavern whores upstairs, but none of them would take him on. Boy, was he mad when he went stomping out of the saloon.

It only riled him more when everybody laughed at him. I guess he'll go over to the Indian village and try to buy a young squaw to bring home."

"He'll not do that," Trey said grimly. "I've laid the law down. He's not to bring any more women into the house."

Jiggers gave a laugh. "He'll just have to use his hand from now on, won't he?"

Trey's lips lifted at the corners. "In between times when Ruby comes visiting."

"You let her come to the house? She's as much a whore as the ones at the saloon. The only difference bein', she don't charge the men."

"I only let her in because she claims she's making a neighborly visit."

"Back when you was around eighteen, you used to bed her, didn't you? I heard you up in the hayloft a couple times."

"I'll be dammed. I thought all along that it was a big secret."

"Old Bull thought it was a secret that he was humpin' her every chance he got. She couldn't have been more than sixteen the first time I saw them goin' at it."

"I found out about it too. That's when I dropped her."

"I wonder why Bull never married Ruby, instead of always pushin' her at you."

"I think it's because her Pa hates Bull so much, he'd disinherit Ruby if she married him. And money is Ruby's god, just as it is for Bull."

"You're probably right," Jiggers agreed, then

asked, "How are you getting along with that little gal you married? From a few things I heard in town, she's not what you thought she was."

"I was never more wrong in my life about anything," Trey said with a rueful grin. "I couldn't believe it when I found out she was a virgin."

"What are you gonna do about her? It's rumored in town that she won't live here at the ranch, that she don't like Bull at all."

"I'm still thinkin' on it. Right now she doesn't like me either. Ruby filled her full of lies about Sally Jo, and she thinks I'm still carrying on with her. If I can ever prove to her that I haven't touched another woman since I came home, I plan on taking my share of the ranch and starting up my own spread."

"Now that's a right good idea." Jiggers said, then grinned. "I'll come work for you."

"That's a deal." Trey grinned back. "Maybe I'll take all the cowpokes with me."

When they agreed that Bull would have a roaring fit if that came to pass, Jiggers changed the subject. "I've got to ride into town for supplies. I didn't come home with too much grub left over. I figure to take one of the pack mules. I had a hell of a time gettin' the wagon through some patches of snow on the way home."

"I've got to get going too. I'm going to cut down a Christmas tree for Lacey, then go on into town and do a little Christmas shopping."

Trey rode into the foothills where the pines grew and the snow wasn't so deep. It didn't take him long to spot a young fir about four feet tall and well formed—just the right size for the main room of the cabin, he thought, dismounting and taking a hatchet from where he had fastened it behind the saddle. As he started hacking away at the tree's trunk, he saw two bighorn sheep go bounding through the pines, headed for the upper regions of the mountain.

As the tree came down, he told himself that as soon as the snow melted a bit, he and Matt would go hunting for the big animals.

Lacey had just finished straining the milk and was carrying the crock to the storage room when through the window she saw a horse and rider approaching the house. She recognized the palomino-colored stallion at once and tried to repress the excitement that curled in her stomach.

She hated herself that Trey could still affect her this way when she knew he had spent last night with the singer. When he drew rein in front of the porch, she saw the tree the stallion was dragging behind him.

"What's he up to now?" she muttered, placing the milk in its usual place and hurrying from the cold room. Did he think he could soften her up with a Christmas tree, get her to do her wifely duty again?

Her full lips formed in a tight line. He was in for a big disappointment if he had that on his mind.

Lacey

It was a disapproving Lacey who answered Trey's knock. He gazed down at her, an uncertain look on his face as he stamped the snow off his boots before stepping inside. Her glinting eyes said he was not welcome. What had happened between now and the last time he'd seen her?

"I've brought you a Christmas tree," he said hestitantly. He took the box from under his arm and placed it on the table. "I also brought along my mother's ornaments to go on it."

When Lacey felt herself softening toward Trey, she snapped, "Are you sure Sally Jo won't object to you giving them to me? I wouldn't want her getting angry at you and barring you from her . . . room."

"What in the hell are you talking about, woman?" Trey's eyes glittered angrily. "Why should I give her a tree, or anything else for that matter?"

"Don't give me that innocent act, Trey Saunders. I daresay you can't count the times you've given her yourself. Including last night."

"You're crazy in the head," Trey exploded. "I never set foot off the ranch last night. What put that idea about Sally Jo in your hard head?"

Trey sounded so sincere that Lacey began to wonder if her father-in-law had told her the truth. She looked away from Trey's irate face and said in a small voice, "Your father told me that you were going to spend the night with Sally Jo."

"Damn his hide!" Trey's closed fist struck the table. "On his way to town yesterday, he stopped here long enough to cause trouble between us."

He looked down at Lacey and said soberly, "For some reason I don't know, my father hates me. He always has and he'll do anything in his power to hurt me. I wish you'd remember that from now on."

Lacey looked away from Trey. Matt had told her the same thing about Bull Saunders. "Bring in the tree," she said gruffly. "You're letting all the heat out."

Trey grinned at Lacey's imperious tone as he stepped outside and closed the door behind him. She knew she had falsely accused him but was too stubborn to say so.

It took Trey quite a while to untie the tree, sweep it free of snow, and make a trip to the barn for a hammer and nail and two pieces of flat board. He nailed the two pieces crosswise on the tree trunk, then opened the kitchen door.

"What a beautifully shaped tree," Lacey exclaimed. "Put it over there in the corner across from the fireplace."

Lacey wasn't satisfied until Trey had turned the tree three different times. She clasped her hands to her chest, exclaiming, "This is the first tree I've had in ten years. I can't wait to start trimming it."

"That will have to wait," Trey said, unbuttoning his jacket. "The tree has to thaw out first."

"I suppose you're right," Lacey said, disappointed. She turned around to go to the kitchen to inspect the ornaments Trey had brought and came up against his hard body. His hands darted out to grasp her arms to steady her. She looked up at him, startled, her lips parted. In the next second, his passionate mouth was moving over hers. Caught by surprise, her defenses down, Lacey's body responded to his kiss. She moved closer to him, her arms coming up around his shoulders.

Trey made a growling sound deep in his throat and pulled her tight into the vee of his spread legs. She could feel the hot, hard ridge of his arousal pressing and probing at her feminine mound.

He had trailed kisses down her throat and freed a breast when a knock came at the door. "Don't answer," Trey whispered huskily.

"I have to," Lacey whispered back as she covered her breast and began buttoning her shirt. "Whoever it is knows we're in here. He can see Prince standing out there."

"It's probably Matt," Trey growled, going to the kitchen. "I'll soon get rid of him."

When he flung open the door, expecting to see his friend standing on the porch, Trey stood and stared. The old handyman from Whiskey Pete's looked back at him.

"What are you doing here, Ike?" he asked. "Is something wrong with Pete?"

"Naw, Pete's all right. It's Sally Jo. She's in a

bad way. Seems like when that stranger slammed her into the bar, she got a couple of broken ribs. She seems to think one punctured her lung, and she don't think she's gonna make it."

Ike took a deep breath. "She's been askin' for you, and Pete said maybe I ought to go find you."

Trey sensed that Lacey had followed him to the door and had heard some of what Ike had said. He swore silently. What in the hell was he going to do? Although he didn't love Sally Jo, never had, he had slept with her for two years and he couldn't bring himself to deny her dying wish.

But what would his going to see the singer do to the fragile relationship he was trying to build with his wife? As it was, Lacey thought he regularly visited Sally Jo. If he went to her now, he might be jeopardizing any chance he had with Lacey.

"Are you comin', Trey?" Ike shuffled his feet.

With a bleak look in his eyes, Trey turned to Lacey, and held out a supplicating hand to her. "I'm sorry, Lacey," he said, "but I don't see how I can refuse to go to her."

Angry at herself for being taken in by Trey's lovemaking, Lacey struck back in the only way she knew how.

She pretended to shrug indifferent shoulders and said coolly with a mocking light in her green eyes, "Of course you must go."

"I'll be back just as soon as I can," Trey said earnestly.

Lacey made no response, but the icy look in her eyes told him not to waste his time.

He pulled on his jacket, slapped his hat on his head, and turned to give Lacey one last pleading look. He saw her back disappearing into the other room. His shoulders hunched, Trey walked outside, closing the door behind him.

He was afraid that his going to Sally Jo would be the last straw for his wife.

Chapter Fifteen

Lacey stood at the window, watching the light fade into twilight. There would be no moonlight tonight, she thought. The dark, lowering clouds would see to that. She hoped it wouldn't snow, for she planned on going into Marengo tomorrow to shop. She had seen some skeins of yarn in a basket at Doolittle's store and she wanted to purchase some of the dark blue wool to knit a scarf for Matt. She had noticed that the one he wore was looking a little ratty.

When it began to grow dim inside, Lacey lit the lamp on the kitchen table and then went into the main room to light the lamp on the small table next to her rocker. When she had held a flame to the candle on the mantel, she laid a log on the fire.

Straightening up and brushing the loose bark off her dress, she caught sight of the bare Christmas tree standing in the corner. She shook her head, thinking that it looked as sad as she felt.

She had no desire to open the box of ornaments. In fact she had shoved them out of sight. When Trey had left her to go to Sally Jo, he had taken the excitement of the coming holiday with him.

Lacey sat down in the rocker and stared vacantly into the fire. Three days had passed since the day Trey had ridden away to comfort the singer. Annie had told her yesterday that the woman wasn't going to die after all, that she had made a remarkable recovery once Trey was at her side.

"If you ask me," Annie sniffed, "I don't think the sly bitch was ever in that much pain. I think it was all a lie just to play on Trey's sympathy. She knew he would feel duty-bound to come to her if she was calling for him and he thought she was dying."

"Well, it worked," Lacey snapped, her face stony. "He lost no time hurrying to her."

"That doesn't mean he's in love with the woman," Annie pointed out. "Trey would go to any woman who called for him on her death bed. By now he'll have seen through her ruse and you can bet he raised hell with her. He'll be comin' back to you any day now."

"Hah!" Lacey snorted. "He'll be wasting his

time if he does, which I doubt." She looked at Annie, her green eyes stormy. "He shamed me, Annie, going to his lover. Everyone knows how he hurried to her side. Even a child would know where his affection lies."

"I think you're mistaken about that. I think you should give him another chance. I still think it's you he loves. After all, it's you he married."

Lacey gave a deep sigh. Her well-meaning friend didn't know the details of her marriage. She didn't know that on their wedding day Trey had gone straight to a whorehouse.

She set her chair to rocking. She had been making plans all week. Come spring, when the snow had melted, she would be leaving the first home she had known in ten years. She intended to get the medicine wagon in traveling condition and take to the road again. Trey could divorce her and spend all the time he wanted with Sally Jo. Not that he didn't do that now.

When Lacey went to bed, however, her cheeks were wet with tears as she fell asleep.

Trey had sat for the past hour staring out the window of the small room across the hall from Sally Jo's quarters. He only vaguely noticed the coming and going of Marengo's citizens on the street below.

He had occupied this room for a three days, and he had just realized that he'd been wasting his time. He had no doubt that Sally Jo had been uncomfortable at first, but when she hinted that he sleep in her bed instead of his own, he began to wonder just how serious her condition was. This afternoon, a private talk with the doctor confirmed his suspicion that she was in no danger of dying and never had been. Two ribs had been bruised, but neither was broken, so a punctured lung was impossible.

An angry frown marred Trey's forehead. Sally Jo had purposely scared Pete into sending Ike out looking for him.

He stood up, a look of determination on his face. Grabbing his jacket, he left his room and crossed the hall to Sally Jo's. When he opened the door without knocking, he saw the singer sitting in front of her dressing table brushing her hair. The long sweeps of the brush she was taking through her hair told him that there was nothing wrong with her ribs.

Startled by his unexpected entrance, Sally Jo dropped the brush to her lap; the face that had looked so serene a moment ago quickly took on a look of pain.

"Trey," she said weakly, "I was just about to call out for you. I foolishly got up to smooth some of the tangles out of my hair, and now I'm too weak to get back to bed." She held out a hand for Trey to assist her.

Trey ignored her silent request and instead sat down on the chair that had been brought into the room for his use. The only other chair there was too delicately constructed to safely hold his weight.

He lost no time in speaking his mind. "Sally Jo, you can stop this farce of being at death's door," he said bluntly. When she blushed guiltily and lowered her lids, he went on. "Your little trick has most likely cost me my wife, the only woman I've ever loved."

"I'm sorry, Trey." Sally Jo looked up at him, sincere apology in her eyes. "I didn't think your feelings for her were that deep. I thought that she was only a new body to you and that after a while you'd come back to me. It's happened before, you know."

"I know that." Trey nodded. "And I shouldn't be so angry with you. But Lacey is my wife and that makes her special to me. I intend to keep the marriage vows I made to her." His lips twisted ruefully. "I have little hope that she'll have anything to do with me from now on, but I won't be involved in your life anymore. You must believe that."

"I know." Sally Jo picked at the hair caught in her brush. "I've seen her on the street. She is very beautiful and young."

After a moment, Trey asked, "What will you do now?"

Sally Jo shrugged. "I don't know. I never should have come here."

"Why did you choose this small town? Your singing is much too good for Whiskey Pete's saloon."

"I was running from a man." The singer smiled briefly. "I chose Marengo because it was small. I knew he would never look for me in a saloon.

"Does this man follow you to harm you, or does he love you?"

"He loves me well enough, but he also loves to gamble. I warned him many times that if he continued to gamble away every dime he could get his hands on, I would leave him. When he took my week's wages from my bag and lost it all at the poker table, I packed up and caught the first train I could. I rode it to the end of the line, then took a coach that brought me to Marengo."

"So, I was right. You are from a big city."

"Yes, San Francisco."

There was so much sadness in the singer's eyes that Trey asked softly, "You still love him, don't you?"

"Yes, damn him, I do." She lifted tear-wet eyes to Trey. "I'm truly sorry if I've spoiled things between you and your wife. I know the feeling of losing someone you love."

Trey stood up and pulled on his jacket. "I'll be getting back to the ranch now. I've got to figure out what to say to Lacey. If I can ever help you in any way, Sally Jo, let me know—but no more tricks."

"Thank you, Trey." She followed him to the door. "I'll always remember the years we had." She watched his head and shoulders disappear down the stairs; then, with a sigh, she began to get dressed. It was time she got back to work. In the meantime she would figure out what she should do with the rest of her life. She couldn't be spending it here in this small town a million miles from nowhere.

The clock struck two and Lacey laid aside the half-finished scarf she was knitting for Matt. It was nearly time to go to the barn to do her chores. Darkness would come early today, for the clouds that had hung in the sky last night were still hovering overhead.

She poured a cup of hot coffee to brace herself to go out into the cold. Carrying the cup to the window, she gazed outside, watching two squirrels scamper about, looking for their supper before curling up in a hollowed-out spot in some tree.

Lacey's attention was caught by a black dot on the snow some distance away. As it grew nearer and larger, she made out a horse and rider. She frowned. She did not recognize the horse. Another grub-liner, she thought with a frown. She hoped he wouldn't stop at the cabin but would continue on to town. She was getting tired of refusing strangers her fire and a bite to eat.

When the rider was around twenty yards away and she could see him more clearly, Lacey saw that the man wasn't the usual type seen in the area. Certainly he wasn't a grub-liner. He was in his early forties, clean-shaven and dressed like a gentleman.

However, although he was quite good-looking, there was a roughness, an alertness about him that said he was used to looking out for danger.

The stranger halted the white horse in front of the porch steps and dismounted. As he stepped up onto the porch, he saw her at the window and flashed her a white smile.

"Miss," he called out in a genial voice, "can you tell me if this snowy trail leads to any town?"

"Yes, it does. Marengo lies about two miles straight on."

The man nodded, but lingered. "Is it possible I could get a cup of coffee from you, miss? I'm about frozen."

Lacey shook her head. "I'm sorry, but I never let strangers in."

A nod, and then, "I can't blame you." With one last smile, he turned to leave and his foot came down on a piece of ice. Suddenly he was on his back, grimacing with pain and clutching his leg.

Lacey could see by the way the leg was twisted at an awkward angle that it was broken. She flung open the door and knelt beside him. After she carefully felt the leg, she said gently, "I'm afraid it's broken. Do you think I can help get you inside?"

His face pale, the stranger nodded, then joked

over his pain, "Are you a doctor?"

"No"—she smiled back—"but we have a system for help out here on the range. I'll run a red rag up to the top of the cabin, and my friend from the neighboring ranch will see it and ride over. He'll ride to town and send a doctor out who will set the leg for you."

"Now," Lacey said, putting her arms beneath the stranger's, "let's see about getting you inside."

With the man pushing along with his good leg and Lacey pulling him, they managed to get into the kitchen and on into the main room. When she got him settled in front of the fire, she said, "I'll be right back as soon as I haul up the help sign."

As Lacey yanked on the pulley rope, she prayed that Matt was home and would soon see her distress flag. If he was in town and didn't get back until after dark, the man inside would spend a painful night.

She hurried back inside, her teeth chattering. The temperature was dropping fast. When the sun went down, it would soon be below freezing. The man moaned as she pulled off her shawl and went to the cupboard where she kept a bottle of whiskey for when Matt stopped by. She filled a water glass half full of the amber-colored liquid and, kneeling beside the pain-ridden man, she said, "Maybe this will dull your pain some until the doctor gets here. He'll probably give you some laudanum before he sets your leg."

The man gave her a grateful look, took a long swallow, then blinked as the whiskey burned its way down his throat. "Thank you, miss," he said, "it will at least warm me up." He offered Lacey his hand.

"The name is Jason Crane."

Lacey took his hand and shook it. "I'm Lacey Saunders."

Crane raised the glass to his lips again, swallowed, then looked around the cabin. "I don't see any evidence of a man around here. I take it you aren't married."

Lacey stood up and went to sit down in the rocker. "I'm married. I just don't live with my husband."

Crane smiled wryly. "We have something in common then. I'm married too, but I don't live with my wife."

Lacey wanted to ask him why that was, but decided it was too personal a question. Besides, he would then feel free to ask why she wasn't living with her husband. And that she didn't want to talk about.

Crane had finished the whiskey when Matt rushed into the kitchen, anxiously calling Lacey's name. "In here, Matt," she called back, then stood up as he hurried into the room.

"Are you all right?" Matt began. He stopped short at seeing a strange man sitting on the floor in front of the hearth.

"This is Jason Crane, Matt," Lacey explained. "He slipped and fell on my porch. His leg is broken."

Matt gave Jason's face a close scrutiny, seemed to approve of what he saw, and bent down to offer his hand. Straightening up, he said, "I'll get right into Marengo and send Doc Carson out. In the meantime, Lacey, you'd better get busy and do your chores before dark."

When Matt had left, Lacey looked down at Jason. "Are you warm enough for me to help you out of your coat?"

"Yes, I'm plenty warm." He unbuttoned his coat and Lacey slid it over his shoulders and arms. As she hung it on a peg on the wall, she asked, "Would you like some more whiskey before I go do my chores?"

"I'd appreciate some more, Lacey. My leg hurts like the very devil."

Lacey looked up at the sky as she began her chores. The clouds seemed larger and darker. "It's going to snow again," she muttered to the handsome white stallion clomping along behind her. When she opened the barn door and put him in a stall next to the mule, she said as she unsaddled him, "I'll give you a hefty helping of oats later."

Lacey had finished her outside chores and was bringing in the night's supply of wood when Matt returned with the doctor. Carson nodded a greeting to Lacey and then went straight to Jason, who was feeling the effects of the whiskey he had drunk.

Lacey introduced the two men, and the doctor grinned at Jason. "Another swig of whiskey and you'd be out." He felt along the broken leg and looked up at Lacey. "Where are your scissors?" he asked.

"Here in my sewing basket. If you're careful how you cut his pants leg, I'll be able to mend it for him later."

"Women." Doc shook his head. "Always looking ahead."

"I'm glad of that," Jason slurred. "These trousers set me back a good sum of money."

When the doctor began to snip at the inseam of the expensive material, Lacey left the room to strain the milk. She didn't want to watch the doctor set Jason's leg.

She was in the storage room placing the crock of milk on a shelf when Jason let loose a yelp. She sighed her relief. The broken bone had been set back in place. When she entered the main room later, splints had been put on the break and the doctor was wrapping strips of cloth around them.

"Now," Carson said to no one in particular, "where are we going to put him?"

"In my bed," Lacey said.

"I don't know about that." Matt frowned. "It hardly seems the thing to do."

"Are you suggesting that we carry him to the barn, Matt?" Doc asked dryly. "We sure as hell can't get him to town. He could very easily develop pneumonia."

"I guess you're right," Matt agreed reluctantly. "Anyway, he's in no shape to try anything on Lacey."

As they stood looking down at the unconscious man, Lacey said, "I don't think he's the kind of man who would try anything with me even if he were able. I'll go turn the covers down."

When Matt and the doctor had carried the unconscious man into the bedroom, taken off his outer clothes, and made him as comfortable as possible, they joined Lacey back in the main room.

"Was it a bad break?" Lacey looked at Carson.

The doctor shook his head. "It was a clean break. If he's careful of the leg and doesn't put any weight on it for a while, it should heal nicely. It's broken just above the knee."

"About your fee," Lacey began, but Doc shook his head.

"Crane already paid me. He's got quite a wad of money on him. He'll be able to pay you for nursing him too."

"I don't expect to be paid for taking care of him," Lacey protested.

"That's real Christian of you, Lacey." The doctor smiled at her as he pulled his jacket on. "But at least charge him for his board. He's a big man and will probably eat like a horse."

When Lacey walked him to the kitchen door,

she saw that it had started to snow. Before Carson rode away, he said, "I'll stop by in a couple of days to see how your patient is coming along."

Lacey went back into the main room and found that Matt had pulled his jacket back on. "I'm going back to the ranch to dig out an old army cot that's stored in my catch-all shed. I'll set it up in here. You should be comfortable enough in it until Doc stops by to check on Crane. He can help me move him out of your bed then."

Lacey's eyes showed her relief. She had been regretting giving up her bedroom and the loss of her privacy.

Matt left, saying that he would be right back, and Lacey went into her room to check on Jason Crane. She looked down on his handsome face and wondered wryly if he was sleeping normally, or passed out from the half bottle of whiskey he had drunk.

"Why do I feel that you're going to make a big change my life?" she thought out loud.

Chapter Sixteen

By the next morning, half the citizens of Marengo and the neighboring ranches knew that Lacey Saunders had a man living with her.

Doctor Carson put a stop to any gossip before it could get started. "If the man broke his leg on her porch, what was she to do? Let him lie there and freeze to death?"

No one could dispute the doctor's words. Not one of them would have acted differently had the same thing happened to them. Consequently, there was no whispering or looking askance at Lacey when she ran errands in town.

Three days later when Annie came to collect the milk, Matt and the doctor had moved Jason out of Lacey's bedroom and onto the folding cot.

He looked quite handsome when Lacey introduced him to Annie. He had just finished shaving and was still sitting up in the cot. He soon had Annie smiling and blushing like a young schoolgirl.

Lacey stood back, watching him flirting with her neighbor. *You are a devil, Jason Crane,* she thought.

When Annie finally left, staying an hour longer than she usually did, Jason called after her, "Don't forget that apple pie you promised me."

Annie was so aflutter at Jason's flattering attention that Lacey had to remind her to take the milk she had come for. "I'll be back tomorrow with the pie," she called to Jason before stepping outside.

Lacey watched her friend ride away, hoping that in her dazed condition she wouldn't ride past her house when she came to it. It was plain that it had been a long time since Annie Stump had had a man make a fuss over her.

"Annie is quite smitten with you," Lacey teased Jason when she went back into the main room to remove the wash basin and shaving material from the table beside the cot. "Shame on you, giving her all that sweet-talk."

"Annie is a nice person and I doubt that she's had a lot of *sweet-talk,* as you call it, in her life." Jason scooted back down on his cot. "All women need that once in a while. It lifts the spirit and makes their lives of drudgery a little more bearable."

Lacey looked at her guest with new eyes. Beneath his debonair demeanor, there lived a serious understanding of human nature. She thought that he would bring a lot of excitement to the marriage bed.

It was a week later before Trey learned of the man who was living with his wife.

Since his return from town and severing all ties with Sally Jo, he had hung around the ranch, checking branding irons, seeing that there was no rust on them, making sure they would leave a clean brand on the new calves. He examined bridles and bits and looked for weak spots on the many ropes hanging in the barn.

He did everything he could think of to keep his mind off Lacey. That included spending a lot of time in the bunkhouse playing cards with the hands. He was moody and bad-tempered, making the men privately express the wish that he would stay away.

"A feller never knows when he's gonna fly off the handle and cuss him out," one man said.

"It's because his wife won't have nothin' to do with him," another remarked.

"I wonder if he knows she's got that man with the broken leg livin' with her," yet another cowhand said.

"If he don't, it's damn sure I ain't gonna tell

him," the first man offered. "He's liable to pull that Colt of his and take a shot at me."

It was Bull who delighted in telling his son about the stranger in Lacey's cabin.

Bull had been gone all day, and Trey was wishing that he'd be gone all night as he relaxed before the fire. It had been very peaceful without the old devil around, needling him every chance he got.

Trey swore under his breath when he heard the kitchen door open. He tensed himself for the argument that was sure to come. Not only had he left his supper dishes on the table, he had deliberately splattered grease all over the stove, even onto the floor.

But when Bull plopped himself down in his favorite chair, one look at the smirk on his face told Trey that his father couldn't wait to hit him between the eyes with something that was sure to hurt.

Bull lost no time as he stretched his feet to the fire. "I heard in town that little wife of yours has got herself a man to live with."

Trey slid him a look from the corners of his eyes. "What in the hell are you talking about? There's not a man around here who would dare move in with Lacey."

Bull waved a hand in a dismissive gesture. "Maybe the natives would be afraid of you and your Colt, but this stranger don't know about you. He's snuggled in there tight as you please.

A handsome feller, I'm told. A fancy gentleman."

He gave Trey a sly look. "You might as well
go back to your singer. You ain't never gonna
get into your wife's bed."

"Shut your damn trap!" Trey shot to his feet.
He walked into the kitchen, jerked his jacket off
its peg, and stamped toward the door. Bull's
malicious laughter followed him as he stepped
outside and hurried to the barn. Matt would
know whether or not Lacey had a man living
with her.

As he rode past Lacey's little cabin on his way
to the Carlton ranch, the light from her kitchen
window seemed to mock him, to say how contented his wife was with the man Bull claimed
now shared her home. He reined the stallion in
and sat in the darkness, gazing at the lighted
window. Maybe he could catch a glimpse of her
moving around.

He finally saw her walk to the table, cup a
hand over the lamp chimney, and blow out the
light. He lifted the reins, signaling Prince to
move on. He didn't want to see the light go out
in the main room.

Matt had gone to town, José told Trey when
he knocked on the door. He climbed back in the
saddle and sat for some time, debating whether
or not to ride on into Marengo. His friends
would be in the saloon, and if what Bull said
was true, he didn't know if he could bear to see
the pitying looks they would give him.

He turned the stallion's head toward town. He had to know if Lacey was sharing her home with a man.

Surprisingly, when Trey entered the saloon, he was greeted as he always was. There were no pitying looks, only the usual, "Hey, Trey, come have a drink. Melt the ice out of your bones."

Trey saw Matt standing at the end of the bar and made his way there to push in beside him. When Pete had poured him a glass of whiskey, he looked at his friend and said in a low voice, "What's this I hear about a stranger moving in with Lacey?"

"Did you just learn about that?" Matt asked, surprised, seeing the rage simmering in Trey's eyes. "It happened close to a week ago. This Jason Crane stopped by Lacey's place and asked for a cup of coffee. Of course she refused to let him in. When he turned to leave, he slipped on a piece of ice and broke his leg. Doc Carson set it, and since the man couldn't sit a horse to get to my place, he's just naturally staying with Lacey."

Matt saw the relief that leapt into Trey's eyes and the concern that followed it. "I suppose everybody is talking about Lacey because he's there," Trey said.

"Not at all. They'd be talking plenty about her if she'd let the man lie on her porch and freeze to death. Don't worry about Lacey, Trey. A man with a broken leg poses no threat to her."

"I just don't want any gossip going on about her."

"There's not a scrap of talk, Trey." Matt gave a soft laugh. "Annie Stump would clobber anyone who said a bad word against Lacey."

"Tell me about this stranger. What's he like?"

Matt thought a moment before saying, "He's a very likable fellow. One of these men who draws his own sex as well as women to him. I'd say he's around forty, about as tall as you but more slender. He has a lot of gray in his hair. He's right handsome and very tight-lipped about where he comes from and where he's going. I've asked some leading questions, but he has a way of ignoring them."

"When do you think he'll be able to move on?"

"You've got me there, Trey. Doc said something about allowing him to walk around on crutches in a couple more weeks. 'Course, that don't mean he can mount a horse and ride out.

"I guess he'll be with Lacey for some time. Why don't you stop at the cabin and meet him?"

"Hah!" Trey snorted. "You must know that Lacey wouldn't even open the door for me."

Matt nodded. "She's mighty upset with you. She won't even talk about you."

"I can't say I blame her. I wish I could make her understand that I felt obligated to go to Sally Jo if she was dying and calling for me." He gave a derisive laugh. "More fool me, I found out in three days it was all a sham. Sally Jo wasn't dying—she wasn't even badly hurt. She had just used her bruised ribs as an excuse to get me to come to her."

"Yes, and she's very sorry about that now. I guess she hadn't realized how you felt about Lacey."

"Her feeling sorry doesn't do me much good, does it?"

"No, it doesn't," Matt agreed. Then he said, "Why don't you ride over to Lacey's cabin some afternoon at the time she goes to the barn to do her chores? Keep her there until she listens to you. If it doesn't work the first time, keep going back, wear her down, make her believe you. And in the meantime, stay away from the saloon and your rowdy friends. Word will get back to her how you're behaving yourself."

"You think?"

"I think."

When Sally Jo stepped out on the stage to sing, Trey slapped some money on the bar, said good-bye to Matt, and left. He wouldn't have anyone saying that he came to town to hear Sally Jo sing, he thought as he mounted Prince and rode down the street to the Doolittle store.

Trey had ordered Lacey's Christmas gift from Erwin, and the shopkeeper had assured him it would arrive in time for the holiday. He hoped it had arrived. Christmas was the day after tomorrow.

Erwin and Nellie greeted him with wide smiles when he entered the store. "I guess we know why you're here," Nellie said.

"Do you have it?"

"We sure do. It came in just before the last big snow," Erwin answered, "and it's just as pretty as the picture in the catalogue." He reached under the counter and brought up a long, thin flat box.

"Lacey's eyes are gonna sparkle when she lays them on these beauties," he grinned at Trey.

Trey snapped the lid open and gazed down at the string of pearls lying on black velvet. He ran a finger over the rich luster of the beads. How lovely they would look against Lacey's smooth throat, he thought.

"Do you think she will like them?" he looked anxiously at Nellie.

"Of course she will. What woman wouldn't. She may scold you, though, for spending so much money for them."

Trey doubted that. He'd be lucky if she even accepted them.

The crowing of the rooster awakened Lacey. She turned over on her back, stretched her arms over her head, then quickly pulled them back under the covers when the cold air hit her flesh. She lay a moment, gathering the fortitude to leave the warm feather bed and make a dash into the main room to roust up the fire she had banked before retiring last night.

Jason was still sleeping, snoring softly as she quietly poked among the live coals and added short pieces of wood to them. When the fire burned high, she stood up and turned her backside to the flames in order to warm the rest of herself. Her eyes fell on the bare tree sitting in the corner. A shaft of sunlight struck across its center and seemed to say to her, "Come on, put some pretties on me."

She dismissed the foolish notion and went into the kitchen to build a fire in the range. She had put on a pot of coffee, which was brewing when Jason called, "Good morning, Lacey. That sure smells good."

"It will be ready by the time I get dressed." Lacey smiled at him, entering the main room. "Did you sleep well last night?"

"Yes I did." Jason sat up. "In fact, I didn't wake up once. I think the bone is beginning to knit back together."

"That's good. Doc will be bringing you out a pair of crutches before long and you'll be able to get out of bed and move around."

"I certainly hope so. I'm not used to lying in bed. I can't wait to be able to climb on a horse and ride again."

"Where will you go when that happens?"

"I don't know," Jason answered on a sigh. "I'll visit your town of Marengo a few days, then move on, I guess."

"Do you ever think of settling in one place, putting down roots, so to speak? It must be a lonesome life, going from town to town like some lost soul. What are you searching for, Jason?"

"I've had a lot of time to think, lying here in bed, to look back at all the mistakes I've made. I'm forty years old and I've come to the decision it's time I made a change in my life—settle down in some town and become a respected citizen. I think I'd like the excitement of owning a small saloon." He grinned up at Lacey. "You know, knocking drunks' heads together when they get out of line."

"And you'd no doubt have dancing girls and a beautiful singer," Lacey teased.

A shadow passed over Jason's eyes. "Especially a beautiful singer," he said, as though to himself.

As Lacey went into her room to get dressed, she wished that Jason would meet the singer at Whiskey Pete's and take her far away from Marengo.

Chapter Seventeen

It was Christmas Eve and Trey had spent half an hour trying to decide what to write on the white paper-wrapped box lying on his dresser. Nellie had fastened a red ribbon bow on one corner, giving Lacey's gift a festive look.

He had come up with a half dozen things to write, but thought they sounded like something a teenager would write to his first girlfriend, although the words did express what he felt.

Trey glanced out the window. The range was darkening with approaching night. It was time he wrote something and got the package to Lacey's cabin. He intended to lay it in front of her door where she was sure to see it tomorrow morning when she went to the barn to do her chores.

Picking up a pencil, he wrote in big, bold letters: *Merry Christmas, Lacey. From your husband*. Taking up the package, he walked to the kitchen. He ignored Bull, who was sitting in the parlor. He pulled on his jacket, slapped his hat on his head, and in five minutes was riding toward Lacey's place.

When her kitchen light came in view, he pulled Prince in a few yards away from the building. He dismounted and looped the reins over a tree branch, then walked quietly to the cabin.

The curtains hadn't been pulled yet, and as Trey stepped up onto the porch he could see straight into the main room. He saw only the back of Lacey, who was sitting in front of the fire, but he had a full view of the man sitting on the raised hearth. His hands tightened on the package. The stranger had the kind of rakehell good looks that would attract women.

He leaned closer to the window, trying to hear what the man was saying to Lacey. He couldn't make out the words, but he did hear her merry laughter ring out at whatever had been said. She had never laughed like that for him, he thought sourly.

Trey stood in the darkness for a minute wishing with all his heart that he was the man sitting in there with his wife, the two of them laughing together. He heaved a ragged sigh and, laying the package in front of the door, quietly slipped away.

Astride Prince again, Trey turned the animal's head toward town. He needed a drink and the company of his friends to lighten the gloom that gripped him. If he went home feeling as he did, he might lose control and beat the hell out of his father. It was the old bastard's fault that Lacey wasn't living where she belonged. If she'd been welcomed into the family in the first place, everything would be different now.

If you hadn't gone off and left her to face him alone, things would be different, Trey's conscience nagged him as the stallion plodded along.

There were very few men at the bar when Trey entered the saloon, only the single fellows he drank with. He remembered then that it was Christmas Eve and the married men would be home with their families. As he ordered whiskey, he was wishing that he was one of those family men.

For some time now, the desire to carouse with his rowdy friends had lessened to a point that sometimes he didn't care whether he saw them or not. But tonight he needed their company—anybody's company other than that of the man who had sired him.

Tonight, however, the whiskey that burned down his throat and the racket of his bantering friends didn't do a thing for the pain that had driven him to the saloon. If anything, it only increased the heaviness in his chest.

He motioned for Pete to pour him another

drink, wondering why his old friend Matt hadn't shown up yet. He had no family to stay home with. And dammit, Trey badly needed to talk to the man he had taken his troubles to since childhood.

"Trey," Pete said as he recorked the bottle, "this is the last whiskey I'm going to serve you tonight. You've got a long ride home, and I don't want you fallin' off your horse and freezing to death in some snowbank."

Trey started to argue, to insist that he wasn't drunk. He snapped his mouth shut when Pete's face doubled in his vision. He knew then that he had had more than enough to drink.

He pushed away the drink he hadn't really wanted. His steps were only a little unsteady, though, as he walked to the door and stepped outside. He made his way to the lean-to where Prince waited for him. After two attempts, he managed to climb into the saddle, lift the reins, and ride out of town.

When Trey saw Lacey's lamplight shining through her window, he couldn't resist the impulse to peer inside the cabin again. Maybe this time he would see her lovely face. Tying the stallion to the same tree he'd used earlier, he slipped quietly onto the small porch.

He noticed immediately that his package was gone from in front of the door. Lacey had found it already. Had she liked his gift, he wondered, or had she thrown it into the fire?

Mingled laughter from the main room drew

him to the window. The curtains had been drawn, but not tightly. There was a two-inch gap he could peer through.

This time three people occupied the room. As they ate cake and drank something from a mug, Trey saw only Lacey's profile, the stranger's splinted leg lying outside the covers, and a full view of Matt. His friend was laughing just as loudly as Lacey and her guest.

With sagging shoulders, Trey turned and stepped off the porch. He was gripped with a loneliness he had never felt before. He'd have given everything he owned to be one of the group in Lacey's cozy little cabin. He was sunk in a gray gloom as he turned the stallion homeward.

Lacey had just lit the lamps and had joined Jason beside the fire when Trey peeped into the window on his way to town. "Matt is coming over later," she said, "and we'll have some of the eggnog Annie brought over this morning."

Jason raised an eyebrow at her. "I don't suppose she put any hard stuff in it?"

"I doubt it," Lacey laughed. "I doubt she's got any in the house."

"But you do." Jason grinned at her. "How about bringing out one of Matt's bottles and putting a little kick in Annie's Christmas drink?"

Her eyes sparkling, Lacey jumped to her feet. "Matt would appreciate that too."

Lacey had poured a good amount of whiskey

into the pitcher of eggnog when Matt rapped on the door. When he stepped inside, he removed two packages from under his arm and said with a smile as he handed one to her, "Merry Christmas, Lacey."

"Thank you, Matt," Lacey said, then looked at the long, thin package still in his hand. "Did you bring Jason a gift also?"

Matt shook his head. "Jason's too old to be getting Christmas gifts." He grinned at the man lying on the cot. "I guess it's another present for you. It was lying in front of the door. I almost stepped on it." He held it under the lamplight and said with some surprise, "It's from Trey."

"Trey?" Lacey squeaked, shocked.

Matt grinned and teased, "It's signed, 'from your husband.' You don't have another one tucked away that we don't know about, do you?" He shoved the package into her hand. "Unwrap it. Let's see what the rooster has brought you."

While Lacey unfolded the white square of paper with fingers that shook, Matt greeted Jason and took off his jacket. Both men waited to see what was in the long, thin box.

"Well I'll be dammed," Matt said when Lacey released the catch on the box and the lid popped open. "He's given her a string of pearls."

"And damn fine ones too," Jason said when Lacey handed him her gift. "He dug deep in his pocket to pay for these."

Both men knew fine jewelry, and Matt added, "He sure did."

Lacey only knew that they were beautiful and that Trey had remembered it was Christmas Eve and had brought her a present.

In the next breath, however, she wondered what Trey had given Sally Jo.

"Let me help you put them on," Matt said.

"No." Lacey closed the lid. "Let me see what you've brought me." She reached for Matt's package, which was lying on the table at her elbow.

She untied the twine wrapped around the brown paper. Folding it back, she exclaimed delightedly as she gazed down at a fleecy blue robe.

"It's beautiful!" She shook the garment out and held a sleeve to her cheek. "So soft and warm. I can put Jasper's in the rag bag where it belongs."

"I've been thinking that from the first time I saw you wearing it." Matt grinned. "That thing has got to be at least ten years old. I gave it to him that long ago."

"I'm sorry I haven't got anything for you, Lacey," Jason said, "but my best wishes will always be with the little nurse who took me in and cared for me."

Lacey smiled at him. "You will always have my best wishes too, Jason." She stood up and walked to her bedroom. "I have some gifts to pass out also."

A moment later she handed each man a package and watched them closely as they unfolded the wrapping paper. She would know by their expressions whether or not they liked what she had been working on in the evenings.

She could tell by the smiles that creased their faces that they were pleased. For Matt she had knitted a blue muffler, and a red one for Jason. "You little sneak." Jason smiled at her. "How did you manage to make mine without me being aware of it? I knew you were knitting one for Matt."

"I worked on yours in the afternoons when you were taking your snoring naps," Lacey teased.

"I'll have you know I don't snore, young lady." Jason wadded up the wrapping paper and playfully threw it at her.

"How do you know?" Lacey dodged the paper ball.

"Because none of my lady friends ever told me that I did." Jason winked at Matt.

"Probably they were snoring louder than you and didn't hear," Lacey came back.

"I think it's time we drank some of Annie's eggnog, you sharp-tongued little vixen." Jason gave up the battle of words.

"Annie's eggnog?" Matt's lips turned down at the corners. "Do we have to drink it? I've had it before and it's terrible."

"I think you'll find that she's improved on her recipe," Jason said as Lacey went into the kitchen. A short time later, she was back with cake and the drink that Matt dreaded. She and Jason watched him put a piece of cake into his mouth, then lift his mug to his lips with a grimace.

Matt swallowed, then looked amazed. "I can't believe Annie made this."

"She started it." Jason laughed. "Then Lacey doctored it up. She poured half a bottle of your whiskey into it."

All three laughed heartily. Then Matt turned his head toward the kitchen and said, "I thought I heard somebody on the porch."

They grew quiet, listening. When nothing broke the silence outside, Matt said, "It must have been my imagination." He took a long swallow of the Christmas drink.

Around ten o'clock, when the eggnog was all gone, Matt announced that it was time he got home. Lacey brought him his jacket and held it while he slipped his arms into the sleeves.

"We'll eat Christmas dinner around one o'clock tomorrow," she said, opening the door for him.

Matt aimed a kiss at her cheek, which ended on her ear, and called good night to Jason before stepping outside.

"That's a fine gift your husband gave you, Lacey," Jason said when she went back into the main room and began to gather up the dishes they had used.

"Yes, it is," she agreed. Worried that Jason

might lead the conversation around to Trey and ask questions she didn't want to answer, she said, "If you don't mind, Jason, I'm going to put these in the kitchen and go to bed." Her lips twisted wryly as she added, "I think I've had a little too much whiskey with my eggnog."

Jason hid a knowing smile. Lacey wasn't fooling him. She didn't want to talk about her husband.

Before she climbed into bed, Lacey lifted the pearls from their velvet bed, and stroking them, she wondered why Trey had bothered to remember her on Christmas Eve.

Likely out of a sense of guilt, she thought as she blew out the light and got into bed.

She lay staring into the darkness, telling herself that when spring came and she left Marengo, Trey would be happy about her leaving. She would no longer be an unwanted burden on him.

Chapter Eighteen

It was full daylight by the time Trey rolled out of bed. Although he had a splitting headache from the whiskey he had drunk the night before, he immediately remembered that it was Christmas and what he was going to do this day.

Before he'd fallen asleep, he had made up his mind that in the morning he was going to Lacey's barn to wait until she came there to milk the cow and feed the stock. If he had to tie her up to make her listen to him, then so be it. The stubborn little minx was going to let him explain why he had gone to Sally Jo.

After pulling on his clothes, he went to the kitchen, built a fire in the range, and filled the coffee pot with water and coffee grounds. While it brewed, he went back to his room, where he shaved and brushed his hair.

The coffee was ready when he returned to the kitchen. Pouring himself a cup of the fragrant brew, he sat down at the table and sipped at it until it was time to head out for old Jasper's place.

The rising sun had reddened the tops of the cottonwoods when Lacey came awake. Christmas morning, she thought without much enthusiasm. This day would pass in much the same fashion as all the others. She would do her morning chores, make breakfast, then she and Jason would sit before the fire, probably reading until it was time for her to start Christmas dinner.

Jason was an avid reader and had already gone through half of the many books Papa had made room for in the medicine wagon. She, of course had read them all, some of them several times, so they didn't hold much interest for her anymore. She enjoyed discussing them with Jason, though.

She had found him to be a very intelligent man; she had wanted to ask him if he had ever been a teacher, but the invisible wall he kept around himself had kept her from asking any questions. When his leg was mended and he left, she would probably know no more about him than she did now.

Lacey reached under her pillow and pulled out the string of pearls. As she ran them through her fingers, she thought that her husband was just as mysterious. Why had he given her this very expensive piece of jewelry when he was in love with another woman? It made no sense.

She stared up at the raftered ceiling. From the time she'd met Trey Saunders, nothing about him had made much sense—from the way he lusted after her, although he didn't love her, to the way he and his father hated each other.

Lacey sat up and swung her legs over the edge of the bed. As her feet felt for her fur-lined moccasins, she told herself that she couldn't wait for the time to come when she could get on the road again. She had known nothing but pain and misery ever since marrying handsome Trey Saunders.

Pulling on the robe Matt had given her and feeling its warmth and softness, she told herself that she was going to keep it on until it was time to start Christmas dinner.

"Merry Christmas, Lacey," Jason said from his cot as she punched up the fire and added wood to it. "It looks like it's going to be a fair day."

"Yes, it does. I haven't seen the sun this bright all winter."

"I wish spring would hurry up," Jason said, leaning up on one arm. "I'm itching to get on my horse and ride out."

"Where will you go? Do you have a destination in mind?"

Jason shook his head. "Not really. Maybe I'll just give my mount his head and let him decide where we'll go." He gave a small laugh and added, "It wouldn't be the first time."

"I'm going to head out too when the weather breaks," Lacey said, standing with her back to the fire.

Jason looked at Lacey, startled. "Where will you go? And more important, what will you do for a living? Are you a teacher?"

Lacey shook her head, amused at Jason's last question. "I'm no teacher. Before I married Trey, my father and I traveled around peddling his herbal vitamins. He died just before I got married, but I still have the medicine wagon and the old mule out in the barn. I won't get rich, but I'll make enough money to get by."

"That's a very dangerous undertaking, Lacey. You're much too pretty to be riding around alone. There's a lot of scoundrels riding the range these days, not to mention outlaws and renegade Indians. That little gun you carry around in your pocket wouldn't do you much good should you come onto a gang of outlaws."

"You're probably right, but I will not stay around here any longer than necessary."

"This crazy marriage you have with your husband—can't you get it straightened out?"

"There's nothing to get straightened out." Lacey turned around and stared into the flames.

"He's in love with another woman."

"Are you sure about that? He spent an awful lot of money on your Christmas gift. It doesn't look to me like he cares for another woman."

"Don't put any importance on the price of the pearls. He's a wealthy rancher and their cost was a trifling amount to him."

A silence fell between them, and Lacey was about to go into the kitchen to start a fire in the range when Jason spoke. "How would you feel about me going on the road with you, Lacey?"

"Would you?" Lacey ran over to the cot and sat down on its edge. "Having you with me would be such a relief."

"I think it's a good idea. Maybe along the way we'll both find what we're looking for."

"What are you looking for, Jason?" Lacey looked at him soberly.

"Who knows." Jason shrugged. "Maybe a wife."

"A wife is just what you need, Jason," Lacey said seriously.

"I agree with you, Lacey." He stared up at the ceiling. "And I hope I find one before too long. It's mighty lonesome making it alone."

Lacey was thinking about Jason's latter remark as she made her way to the barn a little later. She agreed with him. The weeks alone before he came along had been very lonely.

But Jason hadn't completely filled the void in her life, she thought, opening the barn door and stepping into the small, warm enclosure. He was fine company, and so were Annie and Matt; a person couldn't ask for better friends. However, you didn't tell them your innermost thoughts, your fears, your hopes and dreams. Those things were to be shared with a husband. Would she ever find a man who loved her? she wondered glumly, approaching the cow's stable.

She was lifting the latch on the stall door when she saw a shadowy movement beside a mound of hay. She gave a soft gasp, and her heart beat wildly when the shape of a man formed and came toward her.

"Who are you?" she cried out in breathless alarm.

"Don't be frightened, Lacey. It's only your husband." Trey came and stood in front of her.

"You scared me half to death!" Lacey's hands fluttered at her breasts.

"I'm sorry. I didn't mean to, but I have to talk to you and I couldn't think of any way other than to catch you here in the barn."

"That's a sneaky thing to do."

"You know damn well you wouldn't let me in the cabin to do any talking."

"And why should I after what happened the last time I let you in?"

"I tried to explain why I felt obligated to go to Sally Jo, but you closed your ears and mind to everything I said."

"And I'm glad I did." Lacey's eyes shot green fire at him. "She didn't die, did she? And yet you stayed with her for three days. Explain that, if she doesn't mean anything to you."

"I don't know if all men are as dumb as I am about a woman's duplicity," Trey began, "but it took me that long to realize I had been duped into coming to her."

He took Lacey's chin and lifted it until he could look into her eyes. "I swear by all that's holy, I've not been near her since, and nothing went on between us while I was with her. I have finally made her understand that it's all over between us."

He gave her shoulders a little shake. "I never loved her, Lacey."

"I wish I could believe that." Lacey searched his eyes and waited for him to say that it was she he loved.

Those words weren't uttered. "You can believe it, Lacey," Trey said instead, drawing her toward him. "You don't know how I hurt, how I need you. All I can think of is making love to you again."

Pulling her into his arms, he burst out raggedly, "Please, Lacey, make love with me."

"Wanting to make love to me is not enough," Lacey cried. "There have been many men who wanted to do that."

When she would have pulled away from him, Trey refused to let her go. He crushed her to his chest and bent his head, searching for her lips as she struggled to free herself from his embrace.

"For God's sake, Lacey," he said hoarsely, "hold still. You don't know what you're doing to me."

Lacey stopped fighting him immediately. A hard arousal was pressing against her. She looked up at his flushed face and shook her head vehemently.

"Yes," Trey whispered, and keeping an arm around her waist, he held her close while his free hand grasped her chin again.

In a split second his mouth was devouring hers.

"I hate you, Trey Saunders," Lacey managed to say before she relaxed in his arms and began to return his kiss.

But she hated her body more for wanting him, needing him, as he unbuttoned her jacket and slid it over her arms. When he picked her up in his arms, she sighed and placed her lips on the strong column of his throat.

When he had laid her down on a pile of fragrant hay, Lacey watched him pull off his boots, then his clothes. She held her breath as he came down to her and pulled apart her robe. When he slid his hands beneath the hem of her gown, she eagerly lifted her body to help him slide it over her hips, then up over her breasts.

He knelt beside her, feasting his eyes on the loveliness of her body before lying down alongside her and kissing her long and hard. The breath fluttered through her lips when his mouth left hers and fastened over one of her breasts. She moaned her pleasure as he nibbled and drew the passion-hard nipple. When she stroked his head, he took her hand and slid it down his body to where his desire for her jerked and throbbed.

Transferring his mouth to her other breast, he whispered huskily, "Hold me, honey, stroke me."

Lacey closed her fingers around his long, hard shaft, and squeezing it gently, she began to stroke her palm up and down its length.

It took but a minute for Trey to near the crest of his release. He removed Lacey's hand and positioned himself between her soft thighs. Hanging over her, he whispered, "Take me inside you, honey."

Lacey reached both hands down between their bodies and took his heavy manhood in them, then guided it to the opening of her woman's core.

Trey let out a low moan, and with one long stroke, entered her fully. He held still a moment, whispering as he throbbed inside her, "You feel so good, just like soft velvet. I could stay here forever."

Lacey bucked her hips at him, hinting that just being inside her wasn't enough. She wanted to feel the thrust of his hips against hers.

Trey gave a soft chuckle, and gathering her small rear in his large hands, he began to move rhythmically against her, almost fully withdrawing before plunging downward again. Lacey moaned her ecstasy, rising to meet each sliding descent.

With gritted teeth and determination to make their coming together last as long as possible, Trey stroked her until both were bathed in sweat and neither could push back the tide of passion that threatened to consume them.

On the point of withdrawing and spilling his seed in the hay, Trey changed his mind. With one hard drive and a low cry, he pumped his life-giving seed inside the well of Lacey's body. If he got her with child, she would have to live with him.

His breathing labored, Trey rolled over on his side, bringing Lacey with him, his manhood still jerking inside her. He ran a palm down her silky waist and hips, then brought his hand up to fondle her breasts.

"I'm not very large there," Lacey said with a small laugh.

"You fill my hands." Trey leaned down and flicked her nipple with his tongue. "Any more would just be wasted." He lifted a breast to his mouth and suckled it until Lacey's breathing quickened and he grew hard inside her. As her body responded, she whispered, "Again?"

"Yes, again," he whispered and rolled on top of her. "Again and again. I'll never get enough of you."

In the next fifteen minutes, Lacey knew two more releases before Trey allowed himself his own. As he lay limp on top of her, breathing raggedly in the well of her throat and shoulder, she said after a minute, "I'd better get my chores done and get back to the cabin. Jason will be worrying about me right about now."

Trey stiffened and rose on his elbows to gaze intently into Lacey's eyes. "What right does he have to worry about you?" he asked coolly. "Why should he care how long you stay in the barn and what you're doing here?"

Lacey stared back at him, her eyes glinting defiance. "Jason and I have become good friends. It's only natural that he would worry about what might have happened to me if I'm gone longer than usual." After a short pause, she added, "There *are* a couple of men who worry about my welfare."

"Are you saying that I don't care?"

"Are you saying that you do?"

"Of course I care. I worry about you all time."

"Oh, I'm sure you do," Lacey said scornfully. "Just like you did when you rushed off and left me alone to be with your lover."

"I did worry about you. You hardly left my mind."

"I can imagine what you were doing when I did leave your mind," Lacey sniffed.

"I was sleeping, damn you! And even then you were usually in my dreams."

Lacey looked at him and shook her head as if in bemusement. "You lie as smoothly as you make love." She gave him a hard push, grating, "Get off me, you bear, and don't come around here anymore. I'm sure Sally Jo is worried about you being so late getting back to her."

Before he could stop her, she scrambled to her feet, jerked her gown on, and retied the belt around her waist. Shrugging into her jacket, she jeered, "Merry Christmas, husband."

Trey watched her pick up the milk pail and let herself into the cow's stall. He didn't know which of his wishes was stronger. To shake her until she believed him about Sally Jo or to throw her in the hay and make love to her until she believed him.

He did neither. But as he climbed into his clothes and pulled on his boots, he hadn't lost his determination that some day, somehow, Lacey was going to realize that he loved her beyond all reasoning.

Also, he was going to check out this Jason fellow. It appeared to him that Lacey was just a little too interested in the man.

Trey left the barn without looking at Lacey and walked to where he had hidden Prince behind the barn. He swung into the saddle and sat there a moment deciding what to do. In his present mood, he didn't want to go home and spend the day with Bull. He lifted the reins and the stallion responded. Trey was going to drop in on his friend Matt.

Chapter Nineteen

Matt was eating breakfast when Lupe opened the door to Trey's knock. There was a warm welcome in the older man's eyes as he smiled at Trey and said, "Merry Christmas, Trey. You're just in time for breakfast. Have a seat and join me."

"I don't mind if I do." Trey took off his jacket and hung it on the back of the chair he pulled away from the table. "Riding over here in the cold air gave me an appetite."

He didn't add that his body also need refueling because he had just made love to Lacey until he was as weak as a new-born calf.

Lupe poured Trey a cup of coffee and Matt pushed a platter of bacon and eggs to within his reach. "Did you and Bull get into it this morning?" Matt asked as Trey helped himself from the platter, then spooned fried potatoes into his plate. "Is that why you're out so bright and early?"

Trey shook his head as he buttered a biscuit. "I didn't even see the old devil this morning. I just felt like getting away from the house. I wanted to avoid a row on Christmas day at least."

"Are you riding into town to spend the day with your wild friends?" Matt asked, concerned about his young friend.

"No," Trey said as he dug into his piled plate. "I thought I'd just hang around with you. If that's all right."

"Sure it is. The thing is, though, I'm going over to Lacey's around one o'clock. She's invited me to dinner."

A cup of coffee half raised to his lips, Trey gave Matt a startled look. A second later, a devilish glint appeared in his eyes.

"You know," he said, setting the cup back down, "I think I'll go with you. After all, a husband should spend Christmas with his wife, don't you agree?" he added at the doubtful look that crossed Matt's face.

"I agree it's the usual thing for a husband and wife to spend every holiday together. That is, if they spend all the other days in each other's company. But it's not like that with you and Lacey. It's possible that she not only won't let you in the cabin, she may not let me enter for bringing you along. And I've been looking forward to ham and sweet potatoes all week."

Trey picked up another biscuit and slathered it with butter. "She won't refuse to let you in, Matt. She thinks the world of you. Besides, if she kicks up a fuss, I'll tell her that I insisted on coming with you."

"If you get the chance to speak before she slams the door in your face. She's still plenty riled at you for going off and spending all that time with Sally Jo."

Trey knew that everything Matt said was true, and Lacey hadn't been all that happy with him when he left her. But he'd not miss the chance to spend more time with her. Matt saw the uncertainty in his eyes when he said, "I think Lacey is too polite to turn me away."

"Well, we'll know when we get there, won't we?" Matt grinned at him.

The aroma of sugar-cured ham and apple pie wafted throughout the cabin. Jason called from his cot, "My mouth is watering so much, I'm afraid I'm going to drown in my own saliva. I haven't smelled anything so good in too many years to remember."

"I haven't smelled a Christmas dinner cooking in the oven in over ten years," Lacey called back. "When my mother was still alive, our kitchen always smelled good."

Jason heard the sadness in Lacey's voice but didn't remark on it. Although they had devel-

oped a deep liking for each other, they still
hadn't reached that level of friendship where
they could ask personal questions of each other.

For instance, he would have liked to ask her
what had kept her so long in the barn that
morning, and why she had hay in her hair when
she returned to the cabin.

"Everything is ready." Lacey broke in on Jason's pondering as she lifted the ham from the
oven and placed it on top of the range. "Except
for the pie. It needs a few more minutes."

Jason sat up and glanced at the clock. "Matt
should be arriving any time," he said. "It's a
quarter to one. I hope he's not late. I'm starving."

"I think I hear him coming now." Lacey
walked to the window to look out. The glass
panes were steamed over from the potatoes
simmering on the stove, and before she could
wipe a spot clean, she heard footsteps on the
porch. She swung open the door and looked
stunned and incredulous at the sight of Trey
standing behind Matt.

"What are you doing here?" She scowled at
him.

"What do you think I'm doing here?" Trey answered tightly. "I'm here to have Christmas dinner with my wife."

"But your wife doesn't want you here."

"That's too bad for her. There's a lot of things
she doesn't want that are going to be changed,
starting with Christmas dinner."

"The devil it is, mister. You just get on your horse and ride back to town where you came from."

"I just came from Matt's place, where I've been ever since—the last few hours. I'm staying here," Trey said doggedly.

As Lacey glared mutinously back at Trey, Matt received the impression that they were continuing a fight that had started earlier in the day.

"Lacey," he said quietly, "what harm is there in letting Trey eat dinner with us? You have enough food, don't you?"

Lacey's eyes continued to spark anger at Trey another moment; then she said ungraciously, "Oh, all right, stay."

She turned back into the kitchen, ignoring Trey's mocking, "Thank you, ma'am. That's very generous of you, ma'am, to give a poor lonely man a place at your table on Christmas day."

Matt jabbed him in the side with his elbow and said in an undertone, "Shut up, you jackass, before you make her change her mind."

"Go on into the other room and say hello to Jason," Lacey said when they had taken off their coats and hats. "I'll have dinner on the table in just a few minutes."

Trey got his first close look at the man sharing his wife's home, and his eyes took on a dangerous glint. He didn't like what he saw. The man was handsome—too handsome. He had none of the rough edges Trey Saunders had. His world-wise eyes said that he had experienced much in his life, good and bad.

Jason met Trey's hard look and thought, *So this is the great Trey Saunders, the man Lacey refuses to live with*. What a fool he is not to be fighting for her.

He gave Matt a genial smile and said, "You're just in time to sit down and enjoy the meal Lacey has been preparing for the past three hours."

Trey's lips drew into a tight line as he thought, *Who in the hell does he think he is, the man of the house?* Then Matt was saying, "Jason Crane, meet Trey Saunders."

The last thing Trey wanted to do was shake the handsome stranger's hand. He knew, however, that if he refused, Lacey *would* order him out of the house.

It was the barest of handshakes. Amusement glittered in Jason's eyes. Lacey's husband didn't like having him here one bit. It would be an entertaining few hours.

Trey took a seat on the raised hearth, where he had a clear view into the kitchen and he could see Lacey moving back and forth between the stove and table. The red dress she wore fit her to perfection, shaping her breasts and tiny waist. As she smoothed a tablecloth over the table, then laid out the plates and flatware they would use, he felt a stirring in his loins. He was remembering how her breasts had felt in his hands that morning and how they had tasted in his mouth.

"I think I'll go give Lacey a hand with getting the food on the table," Matt said in the tense silence.

"I wouldn't do that," Jason spoke up. "Lacey told me she doesn't like a man underfoot in the kitchen."

It was all Trey could do not to take a swing at Jason Crane. He had no right to know all those intimate things about Lacey. Only he should know what his wife liked and didn't like.

Matt was thankful when Lacey entered the room and said it was time to come eat. Trey was about to burst; the air was full of his anger. Matt hoped that before the day was over, the hot-headed fool would not attack the injured man. Not that Jason wouldn't deserve it. He was purposely needling Trey.

"I would like Jason to join us at the table for the meal," Lacey said. She looked at Matt. "Could you and Trey get him on a chair and carry him to the table?"

"What a kind thought, Lacey," Jason smiled at her. "And it will save you from running back and forth serving me." He slid a sly look at Trey.

"Bring a damn chair in here and we'll get his ass in it," Trey ground out at Lacey.

When he and Matt had lifted Jason and got him into the chair Lacey had brought in from the kitchen, Trey was tempted to drop his side and let the bastard fall, hoping he would break the other leg.

But Jason was carried to the table without mishap. As Trey and Matt took their places, Trey looked up at Lacey's stern face, and a wickedness came into his eyes. "It's a fine-looking meal you've made for us, Mrs. Saunders."

Lacey shot him a fiery look but made no response. She would not look at him fully. She could not bear to see the mocking look she knew would be in his eyes, nor the sensual curve of his mouth. They would remind her of a time she preferred to forget. As it was, she would have to call on all her pride to get her through the day.

When everyone was seated, Trey across from Lacey and Jason and Matt facing each other, Lacey frowned. She didn't want to sit across from her husband. Every time she lifted her gaze, she couldn't help looking at him. Out of frustration and orneriness she said, "Jason, will you slice the ham?"

"It would be my pleasure, Lacey," Jason said when the big platter was placed before him.

Rage gnawed at Trey. He wanted to snatch the knife from Jason and plunge it into his heart. He should be the one doing the slicing. Lacey had asked Crane to do it only to aggravate him. A nudge of Matt's foot under the table brought him back to a semblance of sanity.

As the meal was eaten, only Jason seemed at ease. Trey was in a black mood and didn't try to hide it. Matt was nervous and on the edge of his seat in fear that Trey might lose control, and Lacey wanted to knock Jason's and Trey's heads together for acting like two spoiled little boys.

"When do you think your leg will be healed enough for you to move on?" Trey spoke to Jason directly for the first time.

Jason unconcernedly helped himself to a biscuit, and as he broke it open, he answered, "I haven't given it much thought. Truth is, I'm not in a hurry for it to mend." He slid a glance at Lacey. "I kinda like the scenery around here."

In the tense silence that followed, Lacey wished that she could stretch her foot far enough to give Jason a hard kick on his good leg. He was deliberately baiting Trey, and it was only his broken leg that had kept Trey from inviting him outside.

She shot Matt a reproachful look for bringing Trey with him. Matt could only give her a helpless shrug in return.

"Where do you hail from, Crane?" Trey broke the code of never asking a stranger where he came from.

Jason raised a surprised eyebrow, but after a moment he answered, "I come from many places. Name a town, and I've probably been there."

"In your many travels, have you left a wife and children behind?" Trey continued to jab at him.

A cold glint was growing in Jason's eyes. "I

have no children scattered about in my wake, but there is a wife somewhere."

"She kicked you out, did she?" Trey jeered.

Jason gave him a hard look, then said somberly, "No. She left me." He looked at Lacey and added, "A woman can only take so much mental cruelty from a husband, so much of his carelessness of her feelings." He looked back at Trey. "I'm sure you know what I'm talking about."

Trey jerked forward in his seat. Lacey, in her nervous irritation, jumped to her feet, knocking over her empty coffee cup. "I hope you all saved room for some apple pie," she said, a slight tremor in her voice.

The two men knew that their goading of each other had ruined Lacey's Christmas dinner. Trey stood up. It was his fault. He'd had no business coming here uninvited. Matt had warned him not to come.

"I'm afraid I ate too much ham, Lacey. I'll have to pass on the pie." He walked over to the rack of pegs on the wall and took down his hat and jacket. "I'll be getting on home now." He smiled at Lacey, who stood staring at him. "Thanks for the dinner. It was the best I've eaten in a long time."

He was gone then, closing the door quietly behind him.

Matt saw the tears glimmering in Lacey's eyes and said with a forced smile, "I haven't done diddly in the making of this fine dinner, so I'll serve the dessert."

While Matt was slicing the pie on the workbench, Jason took Lacey's hand and urged her to sit back down. "I'm sorry, honey, for my part in ruining your meal, but he came marching in here so sure of himself and as belligerent as hell. I couldn't resist knocking that smug look off his face."

"I know." Lacey swiped at her tears. "A lot of it was just bravado, though. We'd had a big argument in the barn this morning, and he knew he wasn't welcome when he walked in here."

"I know it's none of my business, but what goes on between you two? It's as plain as my broken leg that the two of you love each other."

"You're crazy!" Lacey exclaimed. "There's no love between us."

"Lacey, you're lying and you know it. You love that big buffalo. As for your husband, anyone with eyes can see that he's crazy as hell about you."

"Oh really? A lot you know about it. If he's so crazy about me, why is it he spends most of his time with that singer in Whiskey Pete's saloon?"

"Now, Lacey." Matt placed the pie on the table. "How many times do I have to tell you that he hasn't had anything to do with Sally Jo since he married you?"

As Lacey and Matt argued back and forth, neither noticed how quiet Jason had grown.

The pie was eaten mostly in silence. Lacey

was considering what Jason had said about Trey being crazy about her, and she was trying to make up her mind whether there was any truth in his words.

Jason's mind was spinning with what Matt had said about a singer named Sally Jo. Could she be *his* Sally Jo? The woman he had been searching for? Surely it was stretching coincidence that two singers would have the same name. He wished he could ask Matt to describe the woman without raising his and Lacey's curiosity. It was going to be hell waiting until he was able to sit a horse and ride into town to find out for himself.

Matt was thinking he couldn't wait to get the hell out of there, away from the two who moodily picked at their pie.

Trey sat motionless in the saddle, his eyes moving unseeing over the featureless white range. He had come to the fork in the snow-beaten path. The way to the right would take him home, and the path straight ahead would lead him into Marengo.

He didn't want to go back to the ranch and listen to Bull grumble about not being allowed to have a woman in the house, nor did he especially care for the company of his friends right now. What he would really like to do was strike off and just keep riding, forget about the little vixen who was driving him crazy.

Trey knew that he would not leave the territory. He would carry on as usual, never giving up the battle to meld Lacey's life with his own. She was a fever that burned in his blood.

The stallion moved out at the pressure on his reins, plodding along the narrow path that would take his rider into Marengo.

Chapter Twenty

When Trey walked into the saloon, he saw at a glance that the only patrons in the place were his single friends—those who had no real home or near relatives they could spend Christmas with.

There was a bunkhouse where they worked, but that building could sometimes be a cheerless place, especially on a holiday. A man had too much time to think back, to remember a time when his mother was preparing a Christmas dinner and friends would stop by throughout the day. He would try to remember how it had come about that he had left home and ended up with a life that was going nowhere. He would worry about what was to become of him when he grew older and was too stove up to ride and rope or to help drive a herd of cattle to some distant market.

Trey was comparing himself to those men as greetings were called out and a place was made for him at the bar. His life differed only in that he would always have a home, but like the men laughing and talking now, someday age would catch up with him and he'd be alone, a bitter old man who hadn't had the good sense to hang on to the woman he loved.

"The drink is on Sally Jo," Pete said, placing a glass of whiskey in front of Trey.

Trey frowned and thought that he had made it as clear as he could to the singer that he was interested in only one woman—his wife.

He looked down the bar to see where the singer was standing, but Sally Jo spoke from behind him. "Trey, I want to talk to you," she said. "Can we go sit at one of the tables?"

"Look, Sally Jo," Trey began, but she shook her head and walked toward a table off in a corner. Trey hesitated a moment, then followed her. He geared himself up for tears and pleading. He'd gone through this with other women who would not accept the fact that he was tired of them, that another woman had caught his interest.

"You can take that wary look off your face, Trey," the singer said when he sat down. "I know it's over between us, but I hope we can remain friends. It pleases me that at least I was dropped because of a wife and not some young whore who showed up one day."

"That would never have happened, Sally Jo. I was perfectly contented with you before I got married."

"It's your wife I want to talk to you about. I've been doing a lot of thinking about her, how she knows about us and thinks we're still seeing each other.

"I'm so ashamed of the trick I pulled on you, pretending that I was dying. I didn't stop to think how it would affect your young wife. It must have made you look guilty as hell when you came to me and stayed on so long."

"You're right, it did," Trey said, "and I'm afraid that little ruse of yours put a finish to her ever thinking that it's all over between us."

"I was afraid of that," Sally Jo sighed, "so I'm going to ride out to her place and stay there until I make her believe that nothing has gone on between us since the day you married her."

Trey gave a short laugh. "As soon as she realizes who you are, she'll slam the door in your face. That is, if you're lucky. She might attack you. She looks gentle as a kitten but when she's riled, she's like a mountain cat, spitting and scratching."

"I'm pretty good at dodging," Sally Jo laughingly said, "so I'm going to chance her claws."

His face quite serious, Trey said, "If you're able to convince her, I'll never be able to thank you enough."

"You really love her, don't you, Trey?"

"Yes." Trey nodded. "I only realized it recently. I thought it was just lust I felt for her. I get all roused up everytime I look at her—or think about her for that matter." Trey ducked his head and grinned. "Then slowly it dawned on me that she was the most important thing in my life."

He stared glumly at his glass of whiskey. "I can't imagine a life without her." He looked up at Sally Jo. "How could you tell, when I didn't even know?"

"I know all the signs." Sally Jo gazed down at her own glass. "I've been in love myself . . . still am."

"Not with me, Sally Jo." Trey looked alarmed.

"No, not with you, you conceited cowboy." Sally Jo pinched his arm. "I'm still in love with my husband." She cupped her chin in her palm and stared out the grimy window at the equally grimy street. "I miss him so much, Trey."

Trey didn't know how to comfort his old lover, so he said, "Let's get drunk and forget about wives and husbands." He hurriedly added, "But no trips upstairs."

The singer nodded. "No trips upstairs."

It was around nine o'clock in the morning, the day after Christmas. Lacey had just returned from the barn and placed the pail of milk on the table when she heard the frightened bray of the old mule and the angry scream of a mountain cat.

"Don't go out there, Lacey!" Jason called anxiously as she made for the door on a run.

"I have to, Jason. It sounds like the beast managed to get inside the barn," Lacey cried as she grabbed the rifle leaning beside the door. "If I don't shoot him or scare him away, he'll kill every one of the animals."

The slamming of the door behind her cut off any further arguments from Jason.

Lacey saw at a glance that the cat had jumped from a tree through the small loft window. A deafening racket was going on inside. Her sorrell and Jason's stallion had joined their high whinnies to the frightened braying of the mule and the cow's bawling. And over it all was the hysterical cackling of the chickens. The angry squalls of the cat were growing louder and more vicious by the second.

Praying that she would be successful in scaring the cat away, Lacey unbarred the door and swung it open. Raising the rifle to her shoulder, she aimed at the sky and squeezed the trigger.

The echo of the shot hadn't died away when the long, lean body streaked past her, headed for the foothills. She called soothing words to the animals as she hurried to the mule. The old fellow was trembling, and his eyes were rolling in terror and pain.

When Lacey stepped inside his stall, she cried out in pity for the old fellow. Blood was trickling from deep claw marks on his rump and haunches. She jerked up an empty oat pail and, running outside, scooped it full of snow. Hurrying back inside, she patted handfuls of snow on the wounds, continuing until the blood had almost stopped flowing. When she was able to examine the claw marks, she saw that her faithful friend needed serious attention.

It took her just a few minutes to heave a saddle on Red and tear across the range toward the Carlton ranch. Fifteen minutes later, she was knocking on Matt's door.

"I'm sorry, Lacey, but you just missed him," Lupe said when she opened the door. "He left for town not more than fifteen minutes ago."

Lacey nodded her thanks and turned the sorrell's head in the direction of Marengo.

Matt picked up his mail at the small store that was also the post office. After he had purchased a bag of tobacco, he walked down the street to the saloon.

The first thing he saw on entering the building was Trey and Sally Jo asleep at a corner table. He looked at Pete. "How long have they been there?"

Pete grinned wryly. "All night and yesterday afternoon. They passed out around midnight. I just let them sleep it off. Trey was in no shape to ride."

Matt glanced significantly at the steps leading upstairs. "Did they stay here all the time?"

"Yeah." Pete nodded. "They didn't budge from the table. Just kept drinkin'."

Matt walked over to the pair and bent a frowning gaze on them. "You're sorry-looking pieces," he muttered, taking in Trey's whisker-stubbled face resting on the table, his lips slack as he snored gently. He turned his gaze to the singer, looking at her mussed hair and smeared face paint.

Matt was about to shake Trey's shoulder, wake him up, and cuss him out, when the door opened and Lacey hurried inside. "Matt," she said, coming forward, "I need you to come—" She stopped short, her face blanching at the sight of Trey and Sally Jo asleep at the table, their heads touching.

"Now, Lacey," Matt said gently, seeing the shattered look in her eyes, "It's not what you think. I'm sure Trey can explain everything."

"He won't be explaining anything to me," Lacey said, her voice as cold as ice. "I don't care diddly who he consorts with. I only care about my old mule. He's been attacked by a mountain cat and his wounds need attention. Will you come take care of him, Matt?"

"Of course, honey," Matt answered. "But don't you think . . ." His voice trailed off, for at that moment, simultaneously, Trey and Sally Jo raised their heads and looked up at the two people standing beside the table. Their bloodshot eyes widened. Trey swore softly, and Sally Jo blushed in embarrassment.

Before either could speak, Lacey was halfway to the door, her chin up and her back ramrod straight. Trey tried to call after her, but his mouth and throat were so dry, he only made a croaking sound. By the time he had worked up enough moisture to call her name again, she was gone, the door slamming behind her. When he would have risen and gone after her, Matt pushed him back down in the chair.

"You look like hell, man. You don't want to try to talk to her now. Go home and get yourself cleaned up."

"It's not what she thought, Matt." Trey groaned, running his fingers through his hair. "Sally Jo and I were both real down, and we decided to get drunk. And that's all we did."

"That's true, Matt," Sally Jo said, gazing earnestly at him.

"Look." Matt held up a silencing hand. "I believe both of you, but it doesn't matter what I think. The important thing is what Lacey thinks." He looked at Trey. "I'm sure you know what she's thinking. I'm afraid you've done it this time, son."

"Damn, don't I know it." Trey's hands fisted on the table. He stood up, pulled on his jacket, and slapped his hat on his head. "I'm going home to wash up and change my clothes. I must smell like I've been sleeping with a bear."

"Huh." Matt snorted as Trey walked past him. "You smell worse than that." He said good-bye to Sally Jo and followed Trey.

*　　*　　*

Lacey

As soon as Lacey walked into the cabin, Jason could tell by the stony look on her face that something had happened to her since she'd left for town. He had seen her return to the barn, with Matt close behind her. Had her old mule died?

"How's the mule?" he asked as she took off her coat and shawl.

Holding her cold hands out to the leaping flames in the fireplace, she answered, "He's going to be all right once he calms down. Matt cleaned his wounds and put some salve on them."

"What about the cow and our horses? Did the cat get at them?"

"No, but they're still very nervous."

When Lacey sat down in the chair next to him and stared into the fire, Jason said gently, "Something else has upset you, hasn't it, Lacey?"

Lacey drew a long breath and stopped rocking. In as few words as possible, she told him how she had to track Matt down, and how she had found Trey and Sally Jo together.

"So you see, Jason, you were wrong about Trey caring for me. He went straight from here to spend the night with the singer."

Pain and anger flared in Jason's eyes, and it was a full minute before he said gently, "I'm sorry, honey. I'd have sworn that the bastard was crazy in love with you."

After a short laugh, Lacey said, "You've got

part of it right. He is a bastard. It was lust you saw in his actions, not love."

"I'm still not completely convinced," Jason said. "I'm seldom wrong about people. I do know that he's as jealous as hell of me. When he left here, he was as mad as a wild horse cornered in a canyon."

"Well, all I know is that I can't wait for spring to come, so I can get away from here."

Jason made no response. He wasn't sure he'd be going with Lacey after all. He might be traveling with another lady.

Chapter Twenty-one

Lacey moved about the kitchen putting lunch on the table. January had come to an end, and they were now in the first week of February. She glanced into the main room, where Jason was staring into the fire.

Dr. Carson had called this morning, and after examining Jason's leg, announced that it would be safe for his patient to get out of bed and move around a bit with the crutches he had brought along.

"But don't put any weight on the bad leg yet," he cautioned after he helped Jason to stand and showed him how to use the crutches. "You don't want to end up with a limp. By early spring you can throw them away."

Jason had quickly gotten the hang of the

crutches. He walked around the cabin until he was exhausted and now sat before the fire resting.

Lacey and Jason had just finished eating warmed-over stew with freshly baked bread when a light knock sounded at the kitchen door. As Lacey stood up and walked to the door, she heard the clump of Jason's crutches behind her. When she opened the door, Jason drew in a sharp breath and Lacey gasped in outrage.

Sally Jo stood on the porch, a tentative smile on her face. Ready to order her away, Lacey paused. The singer's face had blanched, making her cold red cheeks stand out in contrast.

"Ethan," she gasped softly, grasping the door frame to keep her suddenly weak legs from folding beneath her.

His face alight with joy, Jason stepped up beside Lacey. "I have been hoping that the Sally Jo I've been hearing so much about was my Sally Jo," he said softly.

Stunned and full of questions, Lacey was jostled aside as Sally Jo rushed through the door to throw her arms around her Ethan. "I've missed you so," she cried, raining small kisses on his face.

"I've been looking for you for over two years," Ethan said, hugging Sally Jo fiercely.

"I didn't think I would ever see you again," Sally Jo said, smiling at him through happy tears.

"I'd just about given up ever finding you."

One answer to the questions running through Lacey's mind was answered. When Jason—Ethan had said that he might find a wife as they traveled the countryside, what he had really meant was that he might find *his* wife.

She couldn't understand why he was so enthusiastic about finding Sally Jo. He knew that she had been Trey's lover for a long time. Didn't that bother him? Lacey hadn't changed her mind about Trey. For even if the singer loved only her husband, that didn't mean that Trey loved his own wife.

She hoped fiercely that Trey would feel the same pain he had caused her to feel.

Completely ignored by the couple gazing adoringly at each other, Lacey sighed and pulled on her jacket. She'd go to the barn until the other woman left.

As she stepped through the door, closing it behind her, Sally Jo was saying, "When I left San Francisco, I was so mad at you, I deliberately looked for a small town to settle in. I knew you would only search for me in large cities."

Her teeth chattering, Lacey sat in the barn for more than an hour before Sally Jo finally left the cabin and rode toward town.

Ethan's happiness still shone in his eyes when she returned to the cabin. "I never dreamed my search for Sally Jo would end here," he said when Lacey sat down beside him. "I can't believe that all this time, she's been only a few miles away."

"Why have you been using a false name? Are you running from the law?"

"Not at all, Lacey. I started using that name when Sally Jo left me and I went looking for her. I was afraid she might hear that Ethan Reed was searching for her and she would take off again."

"Why did she leave you in the first place?"

"I'm a gambler, Lacey. For years, Sally Jo put up with my gambling away every dime I could get my hands on. Finally she'd had enough, and one night while I sat at a poker table, gambling away her money, she packed her bag and caught a train. I've been looking for her ever since."

"I suppose the two of you have made plans to leave Marengo as soon as possible."

"Yes. We're returning to San Francisco as soon as the weather permits. I never stopped gambling as Sal hoped I would, but I stopped the reckless betting and began to quit the games when I was ahead. I've saved enough money to set us up in our own place. Sally Jo will take care of the entertainment part of it and I will oversee the gambling end."

Lacey didn't say anything until she had poured herself a cup of coffee and sat back down at the table. She took a swallow of the strong brew, then said, "Doesn't it bother you that your wife and Trey have been lovers ever since she came to Marengo?"

"I'd be a liar and a damn fool if I said it

didn't," Ethan said after a thoughtful pause. "But how can I hold that against her when I've been no angel myself since we parted? There have been numerous women since Sally Jo walked out on me. Everybody has his, or her, way of dealing with hurt or disappointment. I feel very lucky that I'm still the one she loves.

"Of course I'd like to shoot Trey Saunders between the legs," he added, an angry glint in his eyes.

"I'd like to shoot him there too," Lacey said unhesitatingly, "and do the same thing to your wife."

Ethan chuckled, then after a while he said, "It's going to be hard not to see Sally Jo while my leg is still mending. I don't suppose . . ."

"You suppose right," Lacey cut him off in mid-sentence. "I won't have that woman in my home. I let her stay this morning for your sake, so you could have your reunion with her, but that's the end of it."

"I'm disappointed, but of course I don't blame you."

Letters passed back and forth between Ethan and Sally Jo during the following month, with Matt acting as the courier. March arrived then, and the doctor told Ethan he could discard the crutches. The bone had mended nicely and he barely limped.

The next morning, Lacey watched him packing his clothes in his saddlebag. He would join

Sally Jo at the saloon. They would remain there until the snow melted enough for them to move on.

She would miss Ethan terribly, Lacey thought as she broke eggs into a skillet of bacon grease. He had been such good company during the cold winter months; she had enjoyed his easy ways and the tales he regaled her with as they sat before the fire in the evenings.

"Put it out of your mind," Lacey told herself as she slid the eggs onto a platter. "There's nothing you can do about it." She poured two cups of coffee and called Ethan to the table to eat their last meal together.

Ethan was his usual joking self as they ate, but later, as he stood beside his stallion ready to mount, all levity left him. He gazed down at Lacey and with tenderness in his eyes, he said, "I love you, Lacey Saunders, like the sister I never had.

"I wish I could stay and watch over you, but I will think of you often and worry about how you are."

He drew a sobbing Lacey into his arms, held her close for a moment, then put her away from him. "I still think I'm right about Saunders," he said. He swung into the saddle and Lacey watched him ride away through tear-filled eyes.

When Ethan had disappeared from sight, Lacey looked up at the low, murky sky and sighed. It was going to snow yet again, and from the looks of the dark clouds, it would be a heavy one.

She turned and entered the cabin, heavy-hearted and dreading the long evening she would once again spend alone.

Her mouth opened in a wide yawn as she cleared the table. The knowledge that Ethan would be leaving today had kept her from a deep, restful sleep last night.

As Lacey finished drying the few dishes and hung up the dish towel, she glanced out the window at the sky. Black clouds hung there, looking threatening. There was no doubt about it—more snow was on the way.

Her eyes fell on Ethan's cot when she walked into the main room. She wanted to get it out of sight as soon as possible and started stripping it of sheets and pillowcase. When she had folded the blankets and stored them away, she dragged the mattress out on the porch, then folded the cot and took it into the storage room.

By the time Lacey had made up her bed, she decided to give the two rooms a good cleaning. They hadn't had a real scouring since Ethan's arrival.

She tied a scarf around her hair and grabbed the broom. Dust flew as she swept out her room and then the main room. By the time she finished dusting the few pieces of furniture, it was time for lunch.

After she had a sandwich of ham and biscuit, she went into the main room and took her usual seat in front of the fire. She yawned again as she took a thin book of poetry from the table beside the chair. She turned the pages until she came to the last one she and Ethan had read out loud last night.

Her lids grew heavy as she read a poem by an unknown author. She began to nod, and presently the book dropped into her lap. In seconds she was sound asleep.

The bawl of a cow with a full udder awakened Lacey with a jerk two hours later. She opened her eyes to a dusk-filled room.

"My goodness," she exclaimed, "what time is it?" She looked up at the clock and couldn't believe it was almost four o'clock. She went into the kitchen, looked out the window, and sighed. While she had slept, the snow had arrived.

A few minutes later, dressed in her outer wear, with the milk pail in her hand, she stepped outside and discovered that the snow had come in on a strong wind.

Altogether, what with milking the cow and feeding the stock and chickens, more than an hour passed. When Lacey pushed the barn door open, she found it pitch dark outside. The only thing she could see was a blanket of snow in front of her.

"Drat," she muttered under her breath as she closed the door, "I'll have to light the lantern."

She was thankful that Matt had impressed upon her the importance of always keeping a lantern in the barn for just such a happening.

It hung next to the door, with a tightly capped jar of matches sitting on a bracing beam below it.

With the lantern lit, Lacey stood a moment thinking. She would need a free hand to hold on to the lead rope that would guide her to the cabin. Although it would freeze, she would have to leave the milk behind.

She forced the door open again and stepped outside. The wind almost took her breath away as she felt for, and found, the guiding rope. With it in hand, she took a step, then cried out in alarm. The rope hung limp in her hand. The other end wasn't fastened to the cabin. The wind must have torn it loose.

For a moment panic overtook Lacey. "Dear Lord," she whispered, peering through the white wall of snow, "can I find my way back to the cabin?"

She hadn't taken the time to light the lamp in the cabin before she left so she wouldn't even have that small glimmer to guide her. She stood a moment trying to fix in her mind exactly where the barn was located in relation to the cabin. It would not be a straight course because the path wound around a stand of pine halfway to her small home.

She could walk a straight line for several yards before she came to the trees, she thought, then bear to the left around them, then walk straight again.

Confident that she could make it home, Lacey

323

started walking, struggling against the wind, her feet crunching new snow.

But a short time later, however, Lacey's panic returned. She had been walking for at least five minutes and she hadn't bumped into the trees yet. Somehow she had strayed off the course. She had no idea where she was or even if she was going in the right direction. She reluctantly accepted the fact that she was lost and might not make it back to the cabin.

"I can't just stand here," she muttered after a while, and she continued in the direction she thought she should go. The wind-driven snow stung her face, her feet grew numb, and her fingers ached as she plodded on.

She grew desperately tired and only wanted to lie down and sleep. Suddenly she was no longer cold. The big white bed looked so comfortable, she thought, as she lay down and curled her body into a snowdrift.

"I'm afraid it's getting set to snow again," Matt said to Trey as he glanced out the saloon's window. He drank the last of his whiskey and set the glass back down on the bar. "I'm gonna head for home, try to beat the storm."

Trey looked down to the end of the bar, where his father was trying to talk one of the whores into taking him to the bawdy house. He decided he didn't want to hang around either.

"I'm gonna leave, too, as soon as Sally Jo finishes her song. It would be rude of me to walk out while she's still singing."

Matt nodded. "I guess it would, considering that the two of you were pretty close once. How do you feel about her husband coming back into her life?"

"I'm real happy for her. She never stopped loving her husband, even though she had left him. I guess I'm just glad that they will be leaving town when the weather permits. Without Sally Jo as a constant source of irritation to Lacey, I have a chance to make our marriage a real one."

Matt slapped Trey on the back. "Keep working on it, son. She's worth fighting for." He buttoned up his jacket, pulled his hat low on his forehead, and left the saloon.

Sally Jo was coming to the end of her song and preparing to leave when the door opened and Ethan Reed stepped inside. The singer saw him at once, and with a happy squeal, she jumped off the stage and into her husband's arms.

A few minutes later, after many hugs and kisses, Trey watched the pair climb the stairs to Sally Jo's room, a smile on his face. He was imagining the reunion that would take place between them.

It occurred to him then that Lacey was once again alone in the little cabin. Although he hadn't liked the idea of Ethan Reed sharing her home, he had felt easier in his mind that someone was there with her.

He desperately longed to see Lacey and wondered if she would let him in. It had been a month since he had seen her. He decided that he would at least try.

Trey finished his drink and was about to leave when he saw Bull stamping out of the saloon. His face was black with fury, and amusement glittered in Trey's eyes. The old man had been unable to convince the whore to spend any time with him.

He decided he would stay a little longer and give Bull time to ride far enough away so that he wouldn't have to ride along with him. Right about now, the old devil would be blaming his son for the itch between his legs and would start an argument between them.

As Trey lingered over his drink, Cole Stringer, his trail boss, came into the saloon. "I passed Bull a couple miles back as I rode in," Cole said, pushing in beside Trey. "He looked proddin' mean. Didn't even speak as he sat his mount in the middle of the path waitin' for me to go into the deep snow, out of his way."

Trey smiled briefly. "He's mad because none of the whores will take him on."

"He's got a bad reputation with the ladies," Cole agreed. "They say he's too rough with them."

"Rough is the only way the old bastard does anything."

One of the ladies they had been discussing sidled up to Cole and, stroking his leg, asked huskily, "Cole, honey, do you feel like havin' a little fun?"

"I'm always ready for some fun, Myrtie." Cole gave her a wide smile as he ran a hand up her short skirt.

Trey watched them go through the saloon door and disappear into the winter storm. He remembered the times he had escorted a soiled dove to the house behind the saloon and hoped he'd never have to do that again. All he wanted was Lacey, his wife. He wanted to make love to her until they were both too old to do anything but sit on their porch and play with their grand-children.

I'd be around a hundred years old by then, he thought with a wry smile, pushing away from the bar. He said good night to Pete and walked out into a blinding blizzard.

As usual, Trey gave Prince his head, trusting the animal to take him home. He'd have to be on the alert for the path that branched off to Lacey's cabin.

When he felt they had traveled about a mile, Trey started peering closer to the ground. He was anxious not to miss the turn-off.

He had just spotted it when the wind and snow lessened. His spirits lifted. He could now see about a yard in front of him.

When the stallion suddenly stopped, Trey peered through the snow and saw Lacey's porch. Why wasn't there a light in her kitchen? he wondered as he dismounted. He knocked on the door, and when there was no answer, he walked into the dark cabin. He went through the three rooms, calling, "Lacey, are you here?"

The cabin was eerily silent, the only sound the crackling of the fire in the fireplace.

Trey wasn't too alarmed as he lit the lamp on the kitchen table, then the lantern that sat in a corner of the main room. She had probably gotten a late start with her chores.

He stepped out onto the porch, closed the door behind him, and felt for the rope that was always attached to the iron ring nailed to the door frame. When he couldn't find it, he raised the lantern to look for it.

Trey sucked in his breath. The rope had been untied and now lay crumpled on the porch, half covered with snow. A savage oath ripped out of his mouth. He knew instinctively that it was Bull's dirty work. He had stopped here on his way home, and discovering that Lacey was in the barn, he had deliberately removed the means of her making it back to the cabin.

Anxiety gripped him. Was Lacey still in the barn, or had she tried to make it back to the cabin? Was she now lost, wandering around in that white wilderness?

A wolf's yowl split the silence, making Trey shiver. If Lacey was out there, the beast would find her. He climbed back in the saddle. First he would check out the barn. She might be waiting in there for the storm to abate.

A swift inspection of the outbuilding revealed what he had dreaded. Lacey had left the barn. God knew where she was.

Back in the saddle again, Trey sat a moment, wondering how best to track Lacey down. There were no visible footprints to follow; the snow had seen to that. He decided he'd ride the stallion in an ever-widening circle, hoping to come upon her. He felt certain that she was walking in circles.

He had ridden about five minutes, calling Lacey's name over and over, when suddenly Prince pricked up his ears. Trey reined the stallion in and slowly scanned the area as far as he could see.

He almost missed the dark shape lying in the snowbank. He hurriedly stepped out of the saddle, sinking in snow past his knees. He struggled his way to Lacey and bent over her with held breath, afraid he'd find her dead.

For a moment he thought she was. Her face was as white as the snow. He shook her shoulder and called her name in a trembling voice. When she moaned faintly, he knew a gladness that made his heart pound.

Scooping her up in his arms, he plowed his way back to the stallion. Prince was patient as Trey made two attempts to mount before finally settling into the saddle with his precious burden.

Trey found that Lacey hadn't traveled far, because in just a short time Prince was stopping in front of the barn. As he slid out of the saddle,

Trey shook his head in bemusement. The snow had stopped as suddenly as it had begun. It had been a spring snow squall.

The barn door stood open, and the stallion hurried inside to get out of the cold. "I'll stable and feed you later, fellow," he called after the animal, "but right now I've got to take care of Lacey, and pray God she hasn't been in that snowbank too long."

Trey managed to get the cabin door open and to carry Lacey into the main room. He laid her down on the rug in front of the fire and quickly added more wood. He then knelt down beside her, and in his hurry to get her out of her frozen jacket, tore off two buttons.

As he took off her boots and pulled off the men's trousers he so hated, he talked gently to her, most of it nonsense. His thought was to keep up a running string of words, hoping that she would hear him and hang on to the fragile thread of life.

When he had her bare of all clothing, he sighed in relief. Even though she was shivering violently, her flesh still had a pink flush.

He stood up, hurried into the bedroom, and turned back the covers on the thick feather mattress. Returning to Lacey, he picked her up and carried her to the bed. When he had her settled on her back, he pulled the covers up to her chin. Kneeling beside the bed, he shoved his hands beneath the covers and began to massage her toes. After a while he moved up to her arches and then to her ankles.

Trey continued to rub Lacey's cold flesh, moving up her legs and thighs until his fingers felt as if they were going to fall off his hands.

Finally Lacey began to moan with the pain of returning circulation.

With a heartfelt sigh, Trey stood up, took off his boots and clothes, and slid in beside her. Taking her in his arms, he held her close, realizing with surprise that the lovely bare body wasn't stirring him. All he had on his mind now was getting the warmth flowing through her veins again.

Of course, he thought with a crooked grin, tomorrow morning could be a different story.

Chapter Twenty-two

Lacey came slowly awake. One bare arm lay outside the covers, and she pulled her chilled flesh back into the warm cocoon of the feather mattress. She gave a startled jerk when her arm came in contact with her bare waist and hip.

Her eyes widened. What was she doing in bed without any clothes on? And how had she got here? The last thing she remembered was wandering around in a raging snowstorm.

As she asked herself these questions, there was a movement beside her. She turned her head and gasped softly. Her husband's head was lying on the pillow next to hers.

She tried hard to remember how she had ended up in bed, naked. Clearly Trey must have found her and brought her to the cabin. She vaguely remembered the pain caused by a pair of massaging hands on her limbs, but nothing else.

Lacey wondered nervously if anything else had happened in her unaware state. Had she and Trey made love? Surely not. She would remember that. It wasn't possible, regardless of what state she might be in, to forget being made love to by Trey Saunders.

Why had he come visiting after a month's absence? she asked herself, frowning thoughtfully. The answer came quickly. Now that the singer was back with her husband and had no time for him, he had decided he would try again to get into his wife's bed.

Well, she declared angrily to herself, *it isn't going to work*. She eased out of bed and stole noiselessly out of the bedroom. She hurried to the fireplace, where the fire was almost out. Shivering in the cold air, she pulled on the clothes that Trey had stripped off her.

As quietly as possible, Lacey stirred up the remaining live coals and laid small pieces of wood on top of them. When they flamed, she added some split logs, then went into the kitchen where again, making as little noise as she could, she built a fire in the range.

The clock struck seven and she reached for her jacket. It was time to milk the cow.

Trey had come awake about five minutes before Lacey had. He lay quietly, breathing in the rose scent of her body. She lay only inches away from him, and in his mind's eye he could see her lovely body curled in sleep. He felt a stirring in his loins. Never had he wanted anything as badly as he wanted to pull her into his arms and make love to her until they were both witless.

Trey sensed when Lacey awakened, and from the corners of his eyes he watched her draw her arm back under the covers. His lips stirred in amusement when her soft gasp told him she had discovered her naked state. He could almost hear the questions running through her mind. She would realize soon that she had company in bed.

He made himself breathe quietly, to feign sleep as he heard the faint rustle of her head turning to look at him. He swore softly to himself when, moments later, he felt her push back the covers. She was leaving the bed. Gone was his chance to seduce her into making love with him.

With an aching hardness, Trey listened to Lacey stir up the fire in the fireplace, then the faint noise of her firing up the range in the kitchen. She was being very quiet, afraid of waking him up, he thought sourly.

In a short time he heard the kitchen door open and close, and he knew Lacey had left the cabin. He rolled out of bed, and as he pulled on his clothes he tried to convince himself that he might be able to coax her back into bed. If he could only get her in his arms, kiss her, he could do it.

He walked into the kitchen, washed his stubbled face, then brewed a pot of coffee. Pouring himself a cup, he sat down at the table to wait for Lacey's return. As he sipped at the hot drink, he rehearsed in his mind how he would go about his seduction of Lacey.

When Lacey opened the barn door, Prince whinnied a welcome to her. "Poor fellow!" she exclaimed as the animal came toward her. "You're still saddled." She rubbed the spot between the soft brown eyes, murmuring, "I bet you're hungry too." She removed his bridle and gave him a big helping of oats. As the stallion chomped away at his meal, she tried to remember riding home on him. Nothing came to mind, so she picked up the milk pail.

Lacey didn't linger over her chores. Her feet and hands were sore from being nearly frozen, and it was difficult to draw the milk from the cow. The animals got their usual amount of food, but she didn't take the time to pet and talk to each as was her custom.

On her way out of the barn, Lacey saw the pail of milk she had left behind yesterday afternoon. As she had predicted, it was frozen solid. But it would thaw out, and Annie's pigs would never know the difference, she thought as she grasped the pail's handle. She trudged back to the cabin, a gallon of milk pulling at each shoulder.

As Lacey stepped up onto the porch, she caught sight of the rope lying loose on the floor. She set the pails down and picked it up. Fear shadowed her eyes as she studied the crimped end where it had been tied to the iron ring. The wind had not torn it loose; it had been deliberately untied. Someone wanted her dead, and she didn't have to guess who. Her father-in-law was the only person who wanted her out of the way.

You old devil, she thought, opening the door. If Bull would just be patient for a while, she'd be out of his life forever.

Lacey wasn't too surprised to see Trey sitting at the table waiting for her.

He gave her a wide, white smile. "I hope you don't mind that I brewed a pot of coffee," he said.

"Of course not. It smells good."

"How are you feeling this morning?" Trey asked with real concern as she set the pails on the work bench. "I was going to do your chores, but you beat me to it."

"My hands and feet are a little sore," Lacey answered, her expression cool and withdrawn.

"You came close to freezing to death last night."

"Yes, I know, and I thank you for saving my life."

"Dammit, Lacey, I'm not looking for thanks.

I'm only trying to point out how dangerous it is for you to be living here alone."

"Look," Lacey said sharply as she poured herself a cup of coffee. "If you'd stay away from me and convince that father of yours that you have no interest in me, I wouldn't be in any danger living alone. The only reason I got caught in the storm last night was because someone untied the guide rope. I imagine that you know as well as I do who did that."

"I have my suspicions and you can bet I'll take care of it. But what if I don't want to tell the old bastard I'm not going to stay away from you?

"Lacey," he said earnestly, "I want our marriage to work. If you'd only let me move in with you, he'd know better than to try anything else."

"You're a fool if you believe that," Lacey said, her voice full of sarcasm. "You've threatened him before, and it hasn't made a speck of difference. That man won't stop until he sees me dead."

She took a sip of coffee and looked at Trey, who stared broodingly out the window. *He's so handsome,* she thought, gazing at his dark hair still mussed from sleep, the morning shadow of stubble on his lean jaw. Her gaze drifted to his firm, yet soft lips, lips that could stir her to mindless rapture when he kissed her.

Lacey gave herself a mental shake, and with a trace of a weary smile on her lips, she said emptily, "I know why you happened to come here last night, Trey. With Sally Jo back with her husband, you've decided that you will try to get over the loss of your lover by replacing her with your wife."

Trey jerked his head around, his eyes boring into hers. "Is that what you really think, Lacey?" he demanded angrily.

Lacey nodded. "That's what I know."

Rage contorting his features, Trey jumped to his feet and jerked his jacket off the back of his chair. "I'm tired of playing this game," he ground out savagely, and before she could argue further, he slammed out of the cabin.

"At least she doesn't hate *you*," Trey said to Prince on entering the barn and walking up to the stallion, who was still chomping at his breakfast. "I'm sorry I forgot to take care of you last night, fellow, but all I could think of was tending to that little witch I'm married to.

"For all the scant thanks I got for it," he added, settling the bridle back over Prince's head. He led the stallion out of the barn, swearing to himself that he would never again come near the beautiful vixen he had married.

Yet, as he rode toward the ranch, the thought never entered his mind to divorce Lacey.

Trey's mood was black when he stomped into the ranch house. Bull, cleaning the stove of any grease his breakfast of bacon and eggs might have left on it, opened his mouth to demand that Trey wipe his feet, then snapped it shut. The big man looked mad enough to kill.

"All right, you old bastard," Trey started right

in as he jerked off his jacket and slapped his hat on the table, "tell me why you tried to kill Lacey again."

"What in the hell are you talkin' about?" Bull gave him a startled look. "I ain't been near that woman all winter."

"Maybe you haven't been around her, but you sure as hell were around her cabin yesterday. When you left the saloon, you stopped by there long enough to untie the guide rope to the barn. Lacey near froze to death trying to find her way home. If I hadn't come along and found her sleeping in a snowbank, you'd have gotten your wish."

"I didn't go near that damn cabin!" Bull slammed his fist down on the table. "I came straight home and I had a hell of a time doin' it. I doubt if I could have found my way there had I wanted to."

Trey knew there was a lot of truth in what his father said. He'd had a hard time seeing the turn-off path to the cabin himself.

As Lacey made up the bed, trying to ignore Trey's scent, she kept remembering his hard and implacable face as he stormed out of the kitchen. Had she accused him unjustly all this time? she asked herself. He always sounded so sincere when he denied having anything to do with the singer since their marriage. Had her jealousy blinded her to the truth? Matt and Ethan always insisted that Trey loved her.

Lacey

Were they right and she wrong?

Lacey was about to sit down and give in to the tears she had repressed ever since Trey left when she saw Annie riding up to the cabin. She wiped at her wet eyes and went to open the door. Annie's cheerful company was just what she needed today.

Chapter Twenty-three

Lacey stood at the kitchen window, watching the rain running down the glass panes. It had been raining all week. Spring had arrived, wet and muddy. Old-timers complained to each other that they couldn't remember it ever raining so much in April.

She moved from the window after a while, and walking across the floor to the stove, she opened the oven door and took out a sheet of cookies. There wasn't much a woman could do in such wet and gloomy weather but bake something. She had given Matt so many pies, cakes, and cookies that he had jokingly said he was thinking of opening a bakery.

Lacey placed the cookies on the work bench to cool, then walked back to stare out the window. The rain still fell steadily, and from the looks of the lowering skies it wasn't going to stop soon. She sighed. She might as well make up her mind that she would have a wet ride to Marengo.

She had put off the trip all week, but now the kerosene pail was empty and she had used the last of her salt on the eggs she made for breakfast. She had no desire to sit in the darkness tonight, nor to eat unseasoned food for supper. Also, she needed to purchase some heavy axle grease for the wheels of the medicine wagon.

Lacey had spent some of the rainy days in the barn readying the vehicle for the road. She had scrubbed it out, thrown away her father's thin pallet, then stuffed her own with sweet-smelling hay. It was made up with clean linens waiting for her to use it again. Lastly, she had dusted off the bottles of herb vitamins and carefully repacked them in the wooden boxes. They were to be the means of her survival.

After she had repainted the faded words her father had put on the sides of the wagon more than ten years ago, she had begun, bit by bit, to stock her home on wheels with the staples she would need as she rolled along between towns—farther and farther away from Wyoming Territory and her husband.

A wariness came into her eyes. When Trey settled his monthly bill at the grocer's, he would probably wonder why she was suddenly needing so many supplies. He had been so angry with her the day he stamped out of the cabin, she was surprised she was still allowed to use the Saunders's credit line.

Lacey had seen Trey from a distance several times since their angry confrontation, and once they had come face to face on the street in Marengo. Her heart had begun to pound like a crazy thing. Although his face looked strained and thin, it looked so dear to her that it was all she could do not to throw herself in his arms and pull his face down to rain kisses all over it.

But she wouldn't have had the chance even if she had gathered up the nerve to do it. Trey had given her a cool look, nodded his head slightly, and walked on without a pause. Tears had blurred her vision, and she stumbled slightly on an uneven board in the sidewalk.

Ethan and Sally Jo had left Marengo as soon as the snow melted enough for the coach to run again. Ethan had come to the cabin to say goodbye and to say again that he felt sure Trey loved her.

Lacey had given a bitter laugh and said, "He loves me so much he hasn't been by for weeks."

Ethan gave Lacey a stern look. "Do you always make him feel welcome when he does come visiting?"

"Why should I? He only comes for one thing."

"That doesn't mean that he doesn't love you. It's only natural for a man to want to go to bed with the woman he loves."

Lacey had wanted to ask, "Is that why he went

to bed with Sally Jo for two years?" But she knew the words would hurt Ethan. He didn't need to be reminded that his wife had slept with another man.

So she had shrugged her shoulders indifferently and changed the subject.

Before Ethan left, he gave Lacey a serious look and said, "I hope you're not still planning on traveling around alone, peddling your father's vitamins."

To save him from worrying about her, Lacey lied, saying that she had given up that idea. Her eyes twinkling, she said, "I've been thinking that maybe I'll go to Big Josy and ask her for a job. Do you think a beanpole like me would make the madam very much money?"

Ethan grinned. "You wouldn't get the chance to find out. Trey would jerk you out of the bawdy house so fast you'd think you'd been caught in a whirlwind. Anyway, you're hardly a beanpole these days. You've put on weight, and your face is quite blooming."

"It's from the sweets I've been eating all winter," Lacey said and pushed the platter of cookies closer to him. "Have some more."

"I've had enough," Ethan said. "Anyway, I've got to get going. I promised Sally Jo to help her get packed."

A minute later, Lacey stood on the porch watching her friend ride away until he was out of sight. She knew she was going to miss him dreadfully.

Lacey

As Lacey pulled on her slicker, preparing to brave the weather, she wondered how Ethan and his wife were faring in San Francisco. Knowing Ethan, she was sure they had their own place by now and that everything was going well for them.

"Looks like it'll fair up soon," Jiggers said, walking up to where Trey sat on a scarred bench straightening out ropes before forming them into loops to be hung on saddle horns. Spring roundup was approaching, and preparations were being made for it.

Trey laid aside a coiled rope and looked up at the old cook as he began to fashion a hobble. "It looks that way," he agreed. "In a way, though, the rain has been a help, driving the cattle in."

"I don't know if the men would agree with you. They've been ridin' in lookin' like drowned gophers."

"That's true, but in the meantime the rain is keeping the buffalo gnats down. If the weather was dry, swarms of them could madden the cattle, make them stampede for hours."

"I'd forgot about that." Jiggers sat down beside Trey and picked up a saddle that needed mending. "Has the grub wagon been overhauled yet?"

Trey nodded. "Couple of the men finished with it yesterday. It only needs to be stocked with supplies."

"I'll take the buckboard into town tomorrow and pick up what I need."

The two men worked in silence for a while. Then, after clearing his throat, Jiggers looked at Trey and asked, "What are you gonna do about that little wife of yours, Trey? You gotta know you can't go on like this forever. It's draggin' you down, man."

Trey laid down a finished hobble and picked up a piece of rope to start another one. "I don't know what to do, Jiggers. I've been hoping that time would take care of everything, but I'm beginning to have my doubts. It's been so long and nothing has changed yet."

"You damn fool, Trey, ain't nothin' gets taken care of if a feller don't work at it. If I was crazy mad about a woman the way you are about your wife, I'd be over at her cabin ever day, tellin' her how I feel and insistin' that she be my wife in every way."

"Damn it to hell, Jiggers," Trey snapped, "do you think I haven't tried? A man can only take so much scorn and accusation. She's got it in her head that I continued to bed Sally Jo after we were married."

"Well, the way I look at it, that's a good sign. Your wife is jealous and that means she cares for you. If she didn't, she wouldn't care how many women you sleep with. You're just gonna have to keep after her, wear her down."

"I don't know if that's possible, Jiggers. I haven't treated my wife the way I should have right from the beginning. Thinking that she was a whore the first time I saw her, I married her just to spite the old man. Then I rode off to let her find her own way to the ranch, to face Bull alone. And if that wasn't enough, she saw me stop at a whorehouse when I left her, only minutes after we were married.

"I've acted like a real bastard toward her ever since. I don't know if any woman would have it in her to forgive a man who has treated her so poorly."

"But hell, Trey, she's got to know by now that you care for her."

"She doesn't. She thinks I only want to get into her bed. She's heard a lot of stories about how I used to be, and she thinks all I do is chase whores."

Jiggers shook his head. "Decent women can be a real pain, cain't they?"

The wry twist of Trey's lips said that he agreed.

Jiggers laid the mended saddle aside and walked over to the open barn door. "It's finally stopped rainin'," he said over his shoulder, "and the sun is tryin' to come out. Maybe my bones will stop achin' a little."

Trey made no response as he tossed another hobble on the pile at his feet. He was thinking that he would take the old cook's advice. He was going to ride over to the cabin and try once again to make peace with his wife. If he didn't succeed today, he'd keep trying until she got it through her stubborn head that he loved her, that he had never loved any woman before her.

Marengo was in sight when the fall of rain lessened, then ceased altogether. By the time Lacey rode down the muddy street, the clouds had dissipated and the sun was once again shining.

Lacey lifted her head to let its warmth bathe her face. Everything would dry out now, and everyone's spirits would rise.

Certainly she felt better, she thought, reining Red in at the general store. Even her stomach had settled down. She'd had a touch of stomach flu for the past month. Annie had brought her a small bag of camomile and the tea she had brewed from it had been soothing to her stomach.

Lacey swung out of the saddle, stepping into mud that reached several inches past the ankles of her boots. She removed her slicker, rolled it up, and tied it onto the cantle. She checked the front of her shirttail then, making sure it hung straight below her waist. She had gained so much weight lately, she couldn't close the last button on her trousers.

After she had removed her sopping wet hat and hung it on the saddle horn, Lacey stepped up onto the wooden sidewalk and entered the store.

Nellie Doolittle looked up from dusting the counter and called her a friendly greeting. Her husband Erwin left off talking to a customer to greet her also.

"Say hello to your daughter-in-law, Bull," he said, a twinkle of mischief in his eyes. Everybody in the Marengo area knew about the dislike the rancher held for his son's wife.

Bull looked over his shoulder at Lacey and then turned back to Erwin without a word to her.

Giving Lacey a broad wink, Nellie said, "Ain't it good to see the sun shinin' again, Lacey?"

"It certainly is. I was beginning to think it would never stop raining."

"What can I get for you?" Nellie laid aside her duster.

Lacey hesitated, shooting a glance at Bull. She wanted to linger in the store until her father-in-law left. She was afraid that if she went first, he would follow her and maybe try to kill her again.

Nellie caught on to Lacey's unease and said, "Maybe you'd like to look at the new yard goods we got in last week before you give me your order."

"Yes, I would," Lacey answered gratefully, and looked through the material until she heard Bull stamp out of the store. She went to the counter then and asked for the salt and kerosene.

"You shouldn't let that ornery old man bother you, Lacey," Nellie said as she wrote Lacey's purchases down on the Saunders's account. "To my knowledge the man doesn't have a friend to his name. Except maybe that Ruby Dalton. They're two of a kind. Rumor has it they're also bed partners sometimes."

Lacey thought the same thing but didn't say so. Nor did she say that she was afraid of her father-in-law, that twice he had tried to kill her and she was afraid he might try again.

She breathed a sigh of relief when later she stepped outside and saw Bull riding out of town.

Lacey's new ease soon left her, however, for as she, too, left Marengo, she saw Trey's big stallion galloping toward her. Tensed up again, she gripped the reins, wondering what to say to Trey if he spoke to her this time. The last time he had barely nodded his head at her.

When they grew even, Lacey's pulses quickened. The smile on Trey's handsome face said that his pleasure at seeing her was sincere.

"I just came from your place," Trey said as they both drew rein. "I figured you'd either gone to visit Annie or you'd ridden into town."

His eyes ranged hungrily over her face. "How have you been?" he asked pleasantly. "You're looking good."

"Thank you," Lacey answered, thinking that he was thinner than the last time she'd seen him. "I had a touch of stomach flu for a while, but I think I'm recovering from it."

"Lacey, we've got to talk," Trey said earnestly. "I mean talk like normal adults, not get angry and shout at each other the way we usually do. We can't go on like we've been doing. It's not natural and it's wearing me down."

Lacey felt an emptiness in the bottom of her stomach. Trey was going to ask her for a divorce.

"Yes," she managed to say calmly, "I guess it's time we talk."

"Every year around this time, Matt and I go up into the mountains and hunt for longhorn sheep. We'll be gone for about a week. I hope that while I'm gone, you'll give a lot of thought to our situation, and that you'll agree to what I have to say to you when I return."

Numb, Lacey could only nod agreement as she lifted the reins and rode on. It was a good thing she had the old medicine wagon ready, she thought with slumped shoulders, for she was going to be asked to leave the area.

Chapter Twenty-four

Lacey sat on the porch fanning her face with her hat. The past few days had been unusually hot for the time of year. What had been mud and puddles in the yard and around the barn a short time ago was now dry and dusty hard clay.

She looked down toward the closed-in pasture where the cow, the old mule, and the sorrel cropped at the tall, green grass. I'm going to miss Red, she thought. They had grown quite fond of each other. From the first, the big horse had liked her gentle handling of the reins, her soft voice. She felt sure that old Jasper hadn't mistreated the animal, but like most men, he hadn't pampered his mount.

"I think Red and I will go for one last long ride," Lacey said, standing up and slapping the hat on her head. It was a week today since Trey and Matt had ridden away for the hunt of long-horns. They would be returning sometime to-day, and when they did, she and Trey would have their talk. She'd be on her way then. Where to, she didn't know. She hadn't thought that far ahead. Her only intent was to get as far away as she could as fast as she could. She wanted to put as many miles as possible between her and Trey.

She lugged the saddle from the barn to the pasture and whistled for Red. The horse raised his head, looked at her, then came galloping up to the fence, his tail and mane shining bright red in the hot sunlight.

"You know we're going for a ride, don't you, fellow," Lacey said softly as she let herself through the gate and tugged the saddle across Red's broad back. When she had tightened the cinches, she led the mount outside the pasture, closed the gate behind her, and swung into the saddle.

Red wanted to go at a full gallop, but Lacey held him back to a slow, relaxing lope. "It's too hot to run today, boy." She reached down and patted his sleek neck. "Maybe we'll go for a run after the sun goes down and it cools off a bit."

Red had covered two or three miles when they came to a basin full of water. Lacey pulled him in and let him drink until he lifted his head, his thirst quenched. She turned him homeward then. The sun had swung westward quite a distance, and soon it would be time to bring the stock in for the night. Several times this week, as she lay in bed, she had heard the screams of the big cats up in the mountains. It would never do to leave the animals outside after dark.

Lacey was only about half a mile from the cabin when she stood up in the stirrups and peered ahead. Black smoke was rolling from the direction of the cabin. With her heart in her throat, she kicked her heels into Red's sides and sent him flying across the range.

"Oh, God," she whispered when she topped a rise and saw the cabin and barn engulfed in flames. She saw right off that the cabin was beyond being saved. The roof was ready to cave in at any second. She looked at the barn, and though she could see the flames licking the inside of it, she thought it might be possible to pull the medicine wagon to safty. The wagon and the vitamins it held were her future.

She vaulted out of the saddle, sprinting through the wide barn door. Through the heavy smoke she could make out the wagon; the flames were dangerously close to it. She grabbed the shafts, and throwing all her strength into the motion, she leaned forward, pulling with all her might. The wagon began to move, but slowly. The smoke had become more dense, smarting her eyes and burning her throat.

"Oh God, I can't do it," she cried and let go of the two long poles. Coughing and choking, she started making her way to the door. When she was only a few feet away from the opening she stumbled on a pitchfork handle. She fell to the floor, hitting her head hard on the milk stool as she went down.

Everything went black as she lay there, oblivious to the fire creeping ever closer toward her.

"Go lie down, Cy," Matt said to his hound. The dog was hungry and whined around his legs, nosing at his hands. "There are no more scraps for you. Go catch yourself a rabbit."

Matt and Trey were breaking camp. They'd been up in the mountains for seven days, stalking the bighorn sheep. They hadn't bothered to kill one until yesterday afternoon around dusk. Their annual trek up the Rockies was an excuse to get away from cows and the never-ending work involved with them. They would return to their ranches, refreshed enough to throw themselves into the drudgery of daily ranch life.

As Matt tossed their camping gear into a burlap bag, Trey tied their rolled-up bedrolls onto the little jackass that had patiently climbed behind them, carrying their supplies. The bighorn was already strapped across the animal's sturdy back.

Matt knew it had been a hardship for Trey to stay for the usual seven-day hunt. He had confided the first night out that he was going to make one last try at making his marriage work. His frequent preoccupation told Matt that he was anxious to set his plans in motion.

"I guess that just about does it," Matt said as he kicked dirt over the campfire, making sure no live coals would be left behind. "Let's get started down the mountain." He grinned. "Show off our trophy."

As the horses and little jackass picked their way around boulders and stunted pine, Matt felt a stirring of pity for Trey. His companion's face wore conflicting emotions. There was a mixture of eagerness and uncertainty on the handsome features.

"Don't torment yourself, Trey," he said when they reached the valley floor. "Play your cards right and Lacey will come around."

"There's never been anything this important in my life before," Trey said, "and I'm scared to death I'm not going to be dealt a winning hand this time."

"Then you've got to pull an ace out of your sleeve. Bend that proud, stubborn head of yours and beg a little."

Trey was about to say, "Damned if I will beg," then kept his mouth shut. If it came down to it, he would beg.

They lifted their mounts into an easy canter, facing the red ball of the sun that would set before long. They had almost reached the place where Matt would turn off to his ranch when Trey, shading his eyes with his hand, asked uneasily, "Does that look like smoke coming from Lacey's cabin?"

Matt peered intently, then burst out, "It sure as hell is! From the looks of it, a building is burning."

His face suddenly pale, Trey thumped the mustang with his heels and started down the valley at a run. Matt was hard behind him.

They came to a skidding halt in front of the barn. They saw Lacey's sorrell standing with hanging head and heaving sides, but no sign of Lacey. Trey leaped from the saddle, wildly calling her name.

"Be careful, son," Matt yelled anxiously as Trey rushed inside the barn. The roof threatened to cave in at any second.

The smoke was so dense, the flames so near and so hot, that Trey could only feel his way, praying he was going in the right direction.

He heard a low moan and almost stepped on Lacey's inert form at the same time.

"Thank God," he whispered, scooping her up in his arms. He staggered through the barn door just as the building collapsed.

As Trey laid Lacey on the ground a safe distance away from the burning buildings, Jiggers came thundering up. "I saw the smoke and near to killed my horse gettin' here," he panted, jumping to the ground and running over to Matt and Trey, who were kneeling beside Lacey's limp form.

"We've got to get her to the ranch, Matt," Trey said hoarsely.

"I don't think we should move her, Trey,"

Matt said soberly. He had noticed that the front of Lacey's trousers were soaked with blood. He directed Trey's attention there. "I'm afraid she might be hurt inside."

"Oh, dear Lord." Trey's eyes grew wet. "What are we going to do?"

Matt took charge. Trey was beyond anything but kneeling beside his wife and stroking her head. Matt stood up and looked at Jiggers. "Take my horse and ride as fast as you can to town and bring back Doc Carson."

As Jiggers swung stiffly onto his horse's back, Matt knelt down beside Trey. "Trey," he said, "I'm going to unroll your bedroll for Lacey. We'll make her as comfortable as possible until Doc gets here." He squeezed Trey's shoulder as he stood up. "That's about all we can do, son."

Trey nodded and Matt could see his lips moving. This proud, wild man was begging God to spare his wife. Matt stood a minute; then, taking off his bandana, he uncorked his canteen and poured water on it. As he squatted back down and gently wiped Lacey's face, he saw the lump near her forehead.

He nudged Trey. "I think this is why she's unconscious. She must have fallen and hit her head on something."

"But why is she bleeding?"

"I don't know, son."

Trey grew impatient. It seemed like hours had passed since Jiggers rode off. He was about to ask for the third time where the hell they were, when Jiggers and the doctor arrived.

Flinging himself out of the saddle, Doctor Carson hurried to kneel beside Lacey. While Trey and Matt watched anxiously, he examined the lump on her forehead, then turned back the blanket covering her.

"What have we here?" he said, his tone concerned as he saw the blood-soaked trousers.

"We think she's bleeding inside," Matt said, worried.

"We'll see," Carson said, then added, "Trey, help me get these damn britches off her." Matt and Jiggers walked away to stand under a tree, so the doctor could examine Lacey in privacy.

His fingers trembling, Trey gently peeled the trousers down over Lacey's legs as the doctor removed her boots. He reached to untie the drawstrings of her blood-soaked bloomers, but Carson saw his face blanch at the sight and stopped him. "I'll take over now, Trey. Go stand with your friends until I finish examining her."

"I'm her husband," Trey protested. "I want to stay with her."

"Well, you're not going to. I'm going to be too busy with your wife to worry about you."

"Come on, Trey," Matt called, "do as Doc says. You're only going to be in the way."

Trey reluctantly went over to the tree, but he paced about, never taking his eyes off the doctor, who worked over his wife. When some time had passed and Trey was about to go and demand how badly Lacey was hurt, Carson stood up and came to join them.

"Trey," he said gruffly, "I've got the bleeding stopped, and your wife is going to be all right." He paused and looked away from Trey. "I'm sorry, son, but she lost the baby."

Trey stared at the doctor, stupified. "Lost the baby?" he whispered huskily. "I didn't know she was in a family way."

"Neither did she. She's just as surprised as you are. She's been thinking that her morning sickness was stomach flu. She's awake now and you can take her home whenever you're ready."

Still stunned at the doctor's revelation, Trey walked over to where Lacey lay. He knelt down beside her and gently drew his fingers across the tears spilling down her cheeks. "Are you in pain?" He took her limp hands in his.

"Some," Lacey answered, then asked, "Where is Matt? I guess I'll be staying with him until I recover."

"Like hell you will," Trey spoke sharply. "You're coming home with me, where you've always belonged."

"But I'm afraid of your father." Lacey tried to sit up.

Trey gently pushed her back onto the blanket. "I give you my solemn promise that he won't harm you in any way. I'll put the fear of death into him."

Lacey knew it was futile to argue further. Anyway, she felt too weak to buck Trey this time. She would wait until she was stronger.

When Trey climbed into the saddle, she didn't resist when Matt lifted her and handed her up to her husband.

"I'm sorry about your baby, honey," Matt said softly, looking up at her. "And don't worry about Bull. Trey will take good care of you."

Lacey gave him a weak smile, wondering just how long Trey would be patient with an ailing wife, one he wanted to be rid of. "Will you come visit me?" she asked wistfully.

"Every day." Matt smiled at her, then stepped back as Trey gathered up the reins.

Lacey lay in the crook of Trey's left arm and shoulder while he steered the mustang with his right. "Are you comfortable?" he asked solicitously.

Lacey nodded her head against his chest. She couldn't speak. Her voice was choked with tears. She cried because of the baby she'd never know. She cried over the loss of her wagon, her only means of making a living. She cried over the loss of the little cabin which had been her only real home in more than ten years.

But mostly she cried because Trey was now forced to put off asking her for a divorce. *I'll recover as fast as I can,* she promised herself. She would not be a burden to him any longer than she could help. In the meantime she'd think of something to do when she left him.

Emotionally and physically drained, Lacey's lids drooped and she slept.

Trey had known that Lacey cried, even

though she tried to conceal her tears from him. But holding her close against his chest, he felt every little quiver in her soft body.

He felt like crying too. He wondered about the baby that hadn't made it into the world. Had it been a little boy who might have grown up to ride beside him during roundups, go hunting with him for the bighorn sheep? Or maybe it had been a girl child, all pink and soft, looking like her mother.

He prayed silently that he and Lacey could make more babies, boys *and* girls. He would be the best father he knew how. Never would he treat a child of his the way his father had always treated him.

He felt Lacey grow limp in his arms and knew that she slept. His arms tightened around her protectively. If Bull so much as gave her a dirty look, he'd knock him on his fat ass. He knew he'd have to keep a close eye on Bull, for he was almost certain the evil man had set fire to old Jasper's buildings. He had recognized a hoofprint among the others trampled in the dirt around the barn. The right front shoe on his father's horse had a vee-shaped nick in it.

As Trey kept the mustang at an easy, steady walk, he wondered what Bull had hoped to accomplish by setting fire to Lacey's buildings. He didn't want her living at the ranch. Had he hoped that she was inside one of them and would burn to death, or had he thought that if he burned her out of her home she would leave the area?

Whatever his devious plans had been, nothing had come of them, Trey thought, his face set in grim lines. Lacey was still alive, and he intended that she remain so. If he could convince Lacey to stay with him, he was going to have their own home built when the roundup was over.

They reached the ranch house at last, and when Trey reined in, Lacey stirred and raised her head. He felt her stiffen and said softly, "Don't be afraid, Lacey. Nothing bad is going to happen to you, I swear it."

He tightened his arms more securely around her, and as he slid out of the saddle, Bull stepped out on the porch. A flash of surprise shot into his small, slitted eyes, then quickly disappeared.

"What's wrong with the girl?" he asked in his usual gruff voice.

"The *girl* has a name," Trey said coldly. "You can refer to her as Lacey, or my wife. And don't act innocent with me, you miserable old reprobate. Just be thankful that you didn't succeed in your dirty scheme."

"I don't know what you're talkin' about." Bull followed along beside Trey as he carried Lacey onto the porch. "I don't have any scheme toward her," he said, stopping in the doorway.

Trey shot Bull a look of loathing. The man was lying. For beneath his blustering, denying words, a thread of fear was evident in his voice. His face and stance threatening, Trey ground out, "I'm going to tell you this just once, so pay close attention. If you ever so much as lay a finger on Lacey, it will be the last thing you ever do." He stepped into the kitchen, kicking the door shut in Bull's face.

When Trey eased Lacey down onto the edge of a bed, she looked around and realized she was in his mother's room. She kept the blanket wrapped around her while he rummaged through the big dresser drawers. When he came toward her with a thin dimity gown, she held out her hand for it.

"Do you need any help getting into it?"

Lacey shook her head vehemently. "Thank you, but I can do it." When Trey continued to stand beside the bed, uncertain what to do, she said smartly, "Either turn your back or leave the room."

"Dammit, Lacey," Trey swore, turning his back to her, "I've already seen every part of you. Do you think I'm so crude I'd want to make love to you at a time like this?"

Lacey's head was throbbing and her fingers were weak and fumbling as she tried to unbutton her shirt. A sweat broke out on her forehead and she was near helpless tears as she said weakly, "Of course I don't think that. Didn't you ever hear about a woman's modesty?"

Trey was a minute answering her. He'd never been with a woman who showed any shyness in baring her body to him. For the first time he realized another difference between a decent woman and one who had lost all sense of respectability.

"I'm sorry, Lacey," he said finally, "I forgot that we're practically strangers. I just thought that you'd need help changing into the gown."

Lacey gave a rueful laugh. "It seems you thought right. I can't even get my buttons undone. I'll need your help after all."

A humorous smile curved Trey's lips as he turned around and sat down on the edge of the bed. Pushing her hands away from the shirt, and beginning to undo the buttons, he said, "Lacey, I don't know what to do with you. Sometimes you're so stubborn, I could shake you."

"I can put your mind at ease about one thing," Lacey said lightly as Trey slid her arms out of the shirt sleeves. "You'd better not lay a hand on me."

"Oh? Do you think a little ole scrap like you could stop me?" Trey bantered, pulling her camisole up over her head.

"I guess I'd have to shoot you," Lacey answered in the same tone as the gown was pulled over her head and she automatically shoved her arms into the short sleeves.

"I guess I'm gonna have to hide that little gun of yours," Trey said with mock severity as he tugged the dainty garment down past her waist.

"Don't you dare," Lacey retorted as she lay

down, lifting her rear so that Trey could pull the gown down to her ankles.

"There." Trey straightened up. "You're all changed. It didn't hurt you a bit, did it?"

Lacey looked startled; then she smiled. Trey had made undressing her such a simple act, she'd forgotten to be shy about him seeing her nakedness.

"You're a slick one, Trey Saunders." She smiled up at him.

"Not at all. I just handled you like I would a frightened yearling bogged down in mud."

"And how do you do that?"

"I just keep talking to it gentle-like so as to keep its mind off the rope I'd tossed around its neck in order to pull it out of the muck."

"Well"—Lacey grinned crookedly—"I don't know if I like being compared to a cow."

"Lady," Trey said, trailing a finger down her cheek, "there's no comparing your lovely body to that of a cow."

Lacey blushed furiously, remembering that he had just seen her body in all its nakedness.

Trey chuckled and bent to lightly kiss her forehead. "Don't worry, wife. I didn't look once at your beautiful curves."

She looked into his teasing brown eyes and couldn't help smiling at him. "Of course you didn't, you liar," she snorted.

Grinning, Trey walked over to the dresser and took a key from a small drawer. Returning to the bed he handed it to Lacey. "I'm gonna ride over to Annie's now and have her come over and change your dressing. I'll lock the door behind me, so don't feel afraid to take a nap if you want to. No one will get in here to bother you."

"Thank you for all your kindness, Trey," Lacey said in a small voice.

"You don't have to thank me, Lacey." Trey frowned. "I'm your husband. I only did the natural thing a man would do for his woman."

His woman, Lacey thought as the door clicked shut behind Trey. It had such a permanent sound. Her lips were curved in a smile as she drifted off to sleep.

Chapter Twenty-five

Three weeks had passed since Lacey lost her home and baby. She had been slow getting her strength back, even though Annie came to the ranch at least three times a week with dishes to whet her appetite. And Trey provided a daily supply of beef broth for her to drink.

He wasn't much of a cook, Lacey thought with a half smile. Everything seemed to lack seasoning. But she had eaten and drunk everything he brought her. After all, he was trying, and she had a feeling he had never before had to tend a woman for such a lengthy time.

The doctor had allowed her to get out of bed on the second week. "Take things easy the first couple of days," he had warned. "As you feel your strength returning, you can start doing light housework and take over the cooking."

He looked at Trey standing at the foot of the bed. "Your husband is no chef. That steak he served me the other evening was as tough as the soles on my boots."

"His cooking isn't that bad." Lacey found herself defending Trey. "He makes a fine breakfast of bacon and eggs."

"Of course you'd side with him." Doctor Carson closed his little black bag. "Women are noted for sticking up for their husbands, regardless of what they're guilty of."

"That's right." Trey jumped in before Lacey could deny the doctor's charges. He wanted to think that Lacey would side with him in all things.

Lacey remembered that conversation as she made up her bed. She and Trey had gradually drifted into a more easy relationship after that. They talked to each a lot these days, especially in the evenings when they sat out on the porch trying to catch a cool breeze. He talked about his mother with a gentle yearning in his voice. It was plain that he still missed her, yet Lacey sometimes got the feeling that he was relieved at her passing. She was more sure of that when Trey told of Bull's cruelty to the mother he had adored.

She in turn spoke of her mother, how it was sometimes hard to remember exactly what she looked like, but that a smell of roses or tinkling laughter always brought her to mind.

She also talked about her father, describing him as a gentle, honorable man who would never have fit into the harsh life of ranching, who was most happy reading the books that had burned in the fire.

Lacey smoothed the quilt over her bed and left the room. She had already made up Trey's bed and straightened his room. She never went near Bull's room. She couldn't have brought herself to touch anything that had been near the body of that man. It was hard enough to sit at the same table with him when they ate their meals. Sometimes she would catch him looking at Trey, sullen hatred in his eyes.

She was beginning to think that her husband was in more danger from his father than she was.

As Lacey sat down at the table in the big, immaculate kitchen, she heard the cowboys preparing to ride out to the roundup camp. With her chin resting on the heel of her palm, she watched them through the window as they rode past with the jingle of spurs and bridle bits.

Every time she watched them ride out, she worried about Trey. It was a dangerous job, rounding up half-wild cattle. A man could be kicked by a horse, charged by a steer, trampled in a stampede, or killed by lightning in an electrical storm.

The men had to search every draw and hollow to collect the cattle and drive them in, in order to brand the new calves. It seemed that Trey was always in the saddle, riding early and late. The longhorns were as wild as deer, hiding in the thickets by day and browsing by night.

Trey had told her that the best method of rounding up was to find a herd when the moon was full and bright and stampede the cows out of hiding with gunshots. The cowboys would let them run until they slowed down to a walk. But sometimes they came to a spot where manzanita and bucklebrush formed an almost impenetrable thicket. That was when Matt's hound was sent in to rout them out.

The grub wagon rolled past the window, and Lacey wondered if she would be here another spring to watch all the hustle and bustle of roundup time. Trey was very caring about her welfare and sought out her company whenever he got home, tired and dusty from fourteen hours in the saddle. But he never even hinted that he would like to share her bed.

Lacey's lips curved ruefully. Sometimes he fell asleep in the middle of a conversation. She didn't fault him for that, though. She knew how hard he worked.

Unlike that lazy Bull, she thought, who did nothing but ride around issuing orders, making the men swear silent, dire threats at him.

She and Mr. Saunders got along together simply by ignoring each other. She still kept her door locked at night when she went to bed and when she took a nap in the afternoon.

She cooked good, hearty meals and kept the

house spotless, giving Bull no cause to complain about anything. It was no hardship keeping the house neat and clean. It was a beautiful home, and she often marveled that Bull had chosen such lovely furniture to go with it. He looked so out of place in the parlor, as he insisted on calling the room. The delicate flowered upholstery of the sofa and two matching chairs would not easily hold his great weight, and the graceful tables with milkglass lamps sitting on them were at odds with his rotund figure and rough clothing. There was a large rocker he always used when sitting in front of the fire.

Lacey thought of Ruby Dalton and how she hated it when the woman came visiting. Trey was so rude to her, Lacey was surprised the woman continued to come to the house. She remembered the time Ruby showed up on the pretext of extending her condolences to "poor Lacey" on the loss of her home.

Trey had barked a short laugh, then said that "poor Lacey" wasn't receiving visitors.

Annie, who was visiting at the time, gave a loud burst of laughter at Trey's surly lie. That Ruby had heard her was evident by the silence that settled in the parlor, only to be broken by the sound of rapid footsteps and the slamming of a door. Ruby had left in a snit.

"Shame on you two," Trey had said with mock severity when he came into the bedroom and found her and Annie giggling. "Can you imagine how embarrassed I was to have Miss

Dalton catch me in a lie?"

"Oh, I'm sure." Annie grinned up at him. "I can see by your face that you're just mortified."

Ruby had returned three days later but hadn't made any pretense of visiting Lacey. A big row erupted between Trey and his father when Bull and Ruby started toward Bull's bedroom.

"I warned you about that, old man." Trey's voice was hard. "I'll not have Lacey exposed to your carrying on in the house. You can just take yourselves off to the barn and wallow around in the hay."

Bull had let out an angry roar, declaring that Trey should tend to his wife and keep his nose out of his father's business, that he and Ruby only wanted a little privacy to talk over a business deal.

"Yeah, I can just imagine what kind of business you two want to discuss," Trey said contemptuously. He turned to Ruby then. "Unless you want to take a walk to the barn, you might as well go on home."

Loud and angry words had been hurled at Trey, but he had stood firm against the barrage, and in a short time Bull and Ruby had stamped out of the house, heading for the barn. From then on, Ruby's trips to the ranch had been few.

When the grub wagon rolled out of sight, Lacey stood up and started clearing the breakfast dishes off the table. When they were washed and dried and put away, she wandered around the house, trying to find something to do. There was nothing she could turn her hand to. She decided to ride out to the camp where the branding was going on. Trey had suggested a couple of times that she might find it interesting to watch that part of ranching.

That had sounded encouraging to her. Would he have invited her to learn more of ranching if he didn't plan on having her around next spring?

Jiggers saddled the sorrell for her and helped her to mount. "Don't stay out in this heat too long," he advised her.

The roundup camp was hot and dusty when Lacey arrived, and she reined Red in several yards from the fire where the irons were being kept heated. She winced at the wails of frightened calves as branding irons hissed against hair and skin. She wanted to clap her hands across her ears to shut out the sound of a bawling, anxious mother whose calf had been separated from her, the roar of steers, and the whinny of horses.

Trey saw her arrive, and after he had neatly tossed a loop of his lariat over a calf's hind leg so that it could be thrown and branded also, he came riding toward her, the cattle scattering before his mustang's hooves.

"Man," he said, wiping a sleeve across his sweating face, "this hellish heat is blistering my very soul. Maybe you shouldn't have ridden out. You look kinda peaked."

Lacey took her canteen from where she had looped it around the saddle. Uncapping it, she handed it to Trey. "I filled it just half an hour ago. It's got to be cooler than yours."

Trey lifted the flat, round vessel to his lips and took a long swallow. He handed it back to her and wiped his mouth with the loose-knotted, faded bandana that sagged at his throat. "There's nothing like a drink of cool water when your throat is parched." He smiled at her.

Lacey agreed as she recorked the canteen and tied it back on the saddle. Trey's name was called then, but before he rode away he said, "Why don't you ride over to that grove of cottonwoods and rest for a while? It will be cooler under the trees."

Lacey nodded and turned the sorrell's head toward the shady spot.

When Trey rode back to join the men around the branding fire, they shot him sidelong glances and winked at each other. "Wonder what his little bride promised him tonight," one man said in an undertone as another hunkered down beside him.

"From the goofy look on his face, I've got a pretty good idea."

Lacey rode Red into the center of the grove and dismounted beneath the largest tree, which would give the most protection from the sun. Taking the bridle and saddle off Red, she looped the reins over a branch and spread his blanket on the ground. She wasn't as strong as she had thought; it would feel good to lie down and rest for a short time.

As Trey had promised, it was cooler in the grove, and once Lacey had stretched out on the blanket and relaxed, the din and racket of yelling cowboys and loudly complaining cattle gradually faded away. Moments later she gave an unconscious, contented sigh and dozed off.

Dusk was falling and Jiggers had supper almost ready before Trey shouted out to the men that they would call it quits for the day. The cowboys dusted off their clothing and then scrubbed themselves in basins lined up on a bench beside the water barrel.

Trey took his turn, ran a comb through his hair, then filled a basin with water and walked over to the grove of trees. The men watched him, big grins on their faces. Old Trey had it bad. He was used to women waiting on him.

Lacey lay curled on her side, her head resting on her bent arm. Trey hunkered down beside her and spent a minute just gazing down at her. A yearning grew inside him. Would she ever let him make love to her again? He couldn't go on much longer, seeing her every day, trying to treat her like a sister.

It hadn't been too hard at first; they were both grieving over the loss of their baby, and Lacey's body was mending. But she was recovered now, and every minute he spent around her was an aching hell. If she didn't let him share her bed soon, he'd have to set her free. He couldn't stand much more without going crazy.

Trey broke off a blade of grass and drew it across Lacey's lips. She frowned and brushed at it, but kept on sleeping. He grinned and flicked the grass across her nose. Again she brushed it aside as though swatting at a fly.

When he drew it across her lips once more, she sighed impatiently and opened her eyes. She looked up at Trey with slumberous eyes, her soft lips curving in a smile. "So you're the pesky fly." Her voice was husky from sleep.

By sheer willpower, Trey kept himself from gathering her up in his arms and crushing her lips beneath his. He nodded with a grin. "I'm the pest."

Lacey sat up, finally realizing that it was near dark. "I've slept the afternoon away," she exclaimed. "Why didn't you wake me up? Now I'll have to ride home in the dark."

"You know I'd never let you ride home alone." There was reproach in Trey's voice. "I've been thinking, why don't you spend the night with us?"

"You mean, sleep outside?" Lacey's eyes widened.

Trey nodded. "There's nothing like sleeping under the stars, all cozy and warm in a bedroll. You'd like it, Lacey. What do you say?"

The thought of sleeping out in the open strangely appealed to Lacey. It would be a new experience for her, and she was sick to death of being shut up in the house for days on end.

"I think I'll try it," she said, making up her mind. "I'll finally get to eat some of Jiggers's cooking."

"Well"—Trey grinned—"he doesn't cook like you do, but he's fair. Watch out for his coffee, though. It can cut your throat."

"I'll be careful," Lacey promised with a chuckle.

"You look rested from your sleep. Are you hungry?"

"I'm famished. What has Jiggers cooked up for us?"

"I know he's got steak on the cookfire, and I think he's made some rice pudding." Trey took Lacey's hand and pulled her up beside him.

He kept hold of her hand as they walked to the campfire. Lacey smiled at the cowboys waiting in line to have a steak plopped on their tin plates. Most of them shyly returned her smile. When she and Trey took their places at the end of the line, Trey whispered, "We'll take our steaks a distance from the men. Your presence will keep them from eating like a bunch of hogs."

Lacey choked back a laugh. She didn't know about the remark that the men ate like hogs, but she could tell that her presence made the cowboys uneasy. After all, she was the boss's wife and they had to be on their good behavior.

Jiggers's meal was by no means fancy, but the steaks were tender, the potatoes baked just right, and the rice pudding as tasty as any she had ever made. Lacey found herself eating with an appetite she hadn't enjoyed in a long time. She reminded herself to slow down or Trey would think *she* was eating like a hog.

With their stomachs replete, they rested their backs against a tree trunk. Trey rolled a cigarette and smoked it as they drank their coffee. At least Trey drank his. After one swallow, Lacey set hers aside with a grimace of distaste.

Trey laughed. "Tomorrow morning I'll add a lot of hot water to yours."

They joined the men at the campfire then, placing their empty plates on the tailgate with the others. Lacey complimented Jiggers on his steak, making him blush with pleasure.

Settled around the blazing campfire then, with the distant yowling of coyotes coming faintly on the air, Lacey moved close to Trey, seeking the warmth of his large body. The spring evenings were still cool.

Cole, the trail boss, came and sat down with his guitar. When he began to softly strum the strings, the cowboys sang along.

Lacey had a peaceful, contented look on her face that Trey had rarely seen there before. When she leaned closer to Trey, his heart pounded. Would the men never go to bed? he wondered irritably. Until they bedded down, he and Lacey couldn't seek their bedroll. He wasn't about to lead her away while they remained at the fire. There would be sly looks and snickers as the men told each other ole Trey couldn't wait to bed his wife.

Would he get to make love to Lacey tonight? Trey wondered, looking at the glowing end of his smoke. Surely he would. They would be lying close together under one blanket; how could it not happen? He knew that if she gave him a chance, he could rouse her to a fever pitch.

After what seemed hours to Trey, Cole finally laid his guitar down and the men began to stretch and yawn. At last they were ready to roll up in their blankets.

When only Jiggers still remained up, washing dishes and laying out what he would need for tomorrow's breakfast, Trey took Lacey's arm and helped her to stand. "Time we turn in too, I guess." His voice was husky and uncertain as he wondered if Lacey would object to sharing his blankets. She could very well refuse to do so.

He picked up his bedroll, and he and Lacey made their way to the grove of trees where Lacey had taken her long nap. As he raked up a thick pile of leaves and then spread one of the blankets over it, Lacey watched him uneasily. The makeshift bed looked pretty narrow. When she'd agreed to spend the night in camp, she hadn't thought of the sleeping arrangements. Naturally, she hadn't brought along her own bedroll.

"Do we sleep in our clothes?" she asked hopefully.

When away from the ranch, the only clothing the cowboys removed was their boots. But tonight Trey wanted as little as possible between him and his wife.

"No," he lied. "Take off your boots and strip down to your underclothing."

Lacey turned her back and did as she was told, neatly folding her trousers and shirt close to the bed; they both finished undressing at the same time. Lacey glanced at Trey and noted that he wore his short summer underwear. The only thing covering his broad chest was a sprinkling of curly hair.

Surely he would be cold.

But when they were settled in and the top blanket was pulled up over their shoulders, Trey's body radiated heat like an open fire. Lacey felt that no harm would ever come to her as long that magnificent body was near. Not even with Papa had she felt so protected, so safe. Suddenly, she was silently praying that Trey wouldn't send her away.

Lacey lay quietly on her back, watching Jiggers's silhouette as he moved about camp. The fire died down, then winked out, and the old cook unrolled his blankets under the wagon. The only sound then breaking the silence was the low hum of night insects.

Was Trey asleep? Lacey listened to his even breathing. If he was, she didn't know whether to feel relieved or insulted. Until recently, he had been relentless in pursuing her, cajoling or demanding that she do her wifely duty. But since she'd moved into the ranch house, it appeared he had lost all romantic interest in her.

Trey was not asleep, Lacey discovered when he turned over on his side facing her and whispered, "Are you asleep, Lacey?"

"No," she whispered back, her pulses beginning to race.

"Are you afraid, sleeping outside?" He tentatively moved his arm to lie lightly across her waist.

"No," Lacey managed to answer in a normal voice. "I just have to get used to it." She laughed lightly. "I miss my pillow."

"Why don't you lay your head on my shoulder?" Trey's arm tightened slightly, pulling her closer. As Lacey raised her head and shoulders and moved to do as he suggested, he slipped his other arm behind her, drawing her onto her side.

Lacey could feel Trey's heart pounding against hers and felt the heat of his body increase as his hand stroked up and down her back. She grew still when his hand wandered over to her waist, then inched up her ribcage. When his palm fitted itself over her breast, she made a motion to remove it, then stopped as his fingers gently kneaded it, making the nipple swell and grow hard.

A soft sigh of relief feathered through Trey's lips when he felt her body relax and fit itself into his. He gathered her close and lowered his head to capture the red lips lifted to his. After he had pulled her soft underlip between his teeth and suckled it for several seconds, he began to trail his mouth down the white column of her throat. A soft, low moan escaped her as his lips settled over her breast.

Trey started out being gentle in his lovemaking, kissing and stroking her body, becoming reacquainted with it. But his long-suppressed desire for her soon burst loose. He became like a man possessed, raining kisses over her body as though he couldn't get enough of her. And sometime during his wild seeking, Lacey began to respond with an abandonment that made his blood sing.

When she sobbed his name and tossed her head about, he parted her thighs and climbed between them. "Oh, Lord, you feel so good," he whispered huskily when she took his pulsating length and guided it inside her.

Sliding his hands beneath her bottom, he held her steady to take his powerful thrusts. She eagerly rose to meet every slide of his swollen member. His mouth captured her passionate cry when together they reached a heart-stopping release.

The sky was turning gray in the east when the lovers had exhausted themselves.

But even as they slept, Trey held Lacey close, not really finished with her. He would only rest a while, he told himself.

Chapter Twenty-six

Trey and Lacey awakened to the sound of the cowhands bantering to each other as they washed up for breakfast.

Lacey still lay clasped tightly in Trey's arms, and as he leaned over and bent his head to kiss her long and hard, she felt his need for her rise and press against her thighs.

When he thrust his hard erection against her, she whispered nervously, "We can't do anything now, Trey. It's broad daylight and the men will see us."

He pulled the blanket up over their heads. "Now they can't see us," he whispered huskily, and lifted her leg so it lay across his hip.

"But they'll know what we're doing," Lacey

whispered in protest as Trey took his member and slid it inside her.

"They can only see my back, which will not be moving. They won't be able to see you as you do all the work," Trey whispered back. "Come on, honey, move on me."

As Lacey began to buck against Trey, sliding her tight sheath up and down his long, thick manhood, she found an extra pleasure in realizing that she was in charge for a change. She had the power to decide when Trey would receive his release.

Twice she brought him to the peak of soaring away to the clouds, only to pause a moment before thrusting at him again.

Finally, he'd had enough and growled, "If you don't stop that teasing, I'm going to flip you over on your back and ride the hell out of you, and I don't give a damn who sees me."

"I'm sorry." Lacey chuckled softly. "I'm only paying you back for doing the same thing to me last night."

"Well, we're even now." Trey slid his hands down to cup her rear and pull her tighter into him. "Now, you little witch, let's finish this."

The cowhands were almost done with breakfast when Lacey and Trey joined them. Lacey wished them gone when she saw the amused looks the men tried to hide. Damn Trey, she thought, a dark red washing over her face. He had lied to her. The men had known darn well what they were doing. When she looked at Trey accusingly, he only grinned and winked at her.

When the hands saddled up and rode out in different directions to search out the wild cattle, Lacey and Trey lingered at the chuckwagon, sipping a second cup of coffee. Lacey hoped that now Trey would say the words she so longed to hear. She knew he loved her body— there was no question of that after last night and this morning.

But that wasn't enough. She wanted him to love her as a person as well.

The word so important to Lacey wasn't spoken. Instead Trey said, with a twinkle in his eyes, as he prepared to join his men, "I'll be riding up to the house for lunch. Maybe you can think up something good for dessert . . . in the bedroom."

For a split second, Lacey wanted to declare angrily that there would be no dessert for him in bed. That desire soon left her. She knew that to refuse him, she would hurt herself as well. If he should suggest they crawl under the wagon and make love right now, she knew that she would follow him.

So she said with a matching twinkle in her green gaze, "I'll ponder on it."

With a quick, hard kiss, Trey walked to the little mustang waiting for him and swung into the saddle. With a wave of his hand, he galloped away to the branding fire the men had started.

"It's about time you two started gettin' along together," Jiggers said as Lacey prepared to return to the ranch house. "Life is gonna be much easier around here now. Trey's been a very devil to be around ever since he come home from the cattle drive last fall."

Lacey gave the old man a startled look, and as she rode off she mused on his words. He had more or less said that it was her fault that Trey had been so hard to be around. Had she misjudged her husband all this time? Had he been true to her, as he claimed?

When she rode up to the barn and turned Red over to one of the stable hands, she was thinking with excitement about the dessert she would serve her husband for lunch . . . in bed.

A pattern was set from that day to the last day of the branding. Not only did Trey ride in for his lunch and "dessert," he rode home at night to share his wife's bed. They made love late into the night, and usually by the time Trey arrived at camp, the cowhands were already branding calves.

When Jiggers remarked one morning, "You're gettin' thin, son. You'd better stop some of that night work."

Trey only grinned and said, "I'd give up my right arm before I'd do that."

One day Lacey decided to brave the scorching heat and ride into Marengo to buy some thread. Trey had a pile of shirts that had needed mending for a long time. It appeared that when he tore a hole in one, he went out and bought another.

When she walked into the store, Nellie Doolittle greeted her with a wide smile. "I've got a letter here for you." She reached under the counter and brought up an envelope. "The return address says it's from San Francisco."

As Lacey carefully tore open the white square, she knew it was from Ethan.

Her eyes scanned the masculine scrawl on the paper.

"Dear Lacey, I hope this letter finds you well and that you and Trey have stopped squabbling and are together at last. I also hope that the two of you are as happy as Sally Jo and I are.

"Prepare yourself for the next sentence. Sally Jo and I are expecting. You can imagine our surprise. We had never wanted children, thinking that they would never fit into the way we lived.

"But now that it has happened, we can't wait for the little scutter to get here. I have already told Sally Jo that if we have a little girl, we are going to name her Lacey. Sal agrees.

"We have our saloon as we had planned, with living quarters above. It is small but quite classy. There are no soiled doves in it.

"Please write to me and let me know how

things are with you. You have my address if ever you need me. Fondly, Ethan."

A soft smile curving her lips, Lacey folded the letter back into the envelope and lifted her gaze to Nellie, who waited expectantly. "It's from Ethan Reed," she explained, then went on to say that he and his wife had their saloon and were expecting their first child.

Nellie only said, "Now ain't that nice." She sensed that Lacey didn't want to discuss it further. After all, Trey and that woman had carried on for two years.

As Lacey rode homeward, her thoughts were on Ethan and his letter. He seemed content and she was happy for him. He loved his wife and was wise enough to put the past behind him and build a new life.

"Why can't you do the same?" her inner voice asked. "Maybe your husband doesn't speak the words you want to hear, but could you ask for better treatment than he gives you? You could be much worse off."

Lacey knew that was right. If Trey hadn't come along when he did, only God knew where she would be today. *Count your blessings, girl,* she thought, riding up to the ranch and dismounting.

The morning of the last day of the branding, Trey and his father got into such a heated argument that Lacey escaped to the bedroom. She was afraid that this time they would come to blows.

It was their same old argument. Her father-in-law wanted to bring a young Indian girl into the house as a housekeeper.

"Don't give me that bull, old man," Trey had sneered when the subject was brought up. "Lacey keeps this house as neat as a pin and she cooks us some damn fine meals. You just want to move a woman in here so you can vent your lust and meanness." He had ended with, "I'll not have Lacey insulted the way you insulted my mother all her married life."

The argument had gone on and on, Trey accusing, Bull denying. At last Trey's father had slammed out of the house, muttering dire threats.

Trey didn't seem to pay any attention to his father's angry words, but Lacey, who had come and stood in the doorway, had seen the look of pure hatred Bull shot at his son before stamping out of the house.

Trey dropped a kiss on top of her head, and she followed him to the door. As he prepared to mount the little stock horse waiting for him, she said earnestly, "Please be careful today, Trey. I know he's your father, but I don't trust Bull not to harm you if he gets the chance."

"Don't worry about me, honey." Trey swung into the saddle. "I learned a long time ago to keep watch when that old bastard is around."

Lacey watched him ride away, a heavy uneasiness gripping her chest. It was with some relief that she saw Annie riding toward the house. Mrs. Stump's cheerful chatter and neighborhood gossip would take her mind off Trey and stop her worrying about him for a while.

"Good morning, Annie." She smiled at her plump neighbor as the woman heaved herself off her mule. "I hope you came only for a visit. My cow has gone completely dry."

"I knew it was time for that," Annie puffed as she climbed the porch steps. "Have Trey bring her over to my bull. It's that time of the year."

"Trey said he was going to do that," Lacey said, leading the way into the kitchen, "but he's been busy from first light to dark with the branding. Thank goodness today will see the last of it for a while."

"The men had the irons in the fire when I rode by," Annie said, taking a seat at the table. "I was surprised to see Ruby Dalton there. She and Bull were off by themselves, their heads together, talking about something." She laughed and added, "They were probably makin' plans where to meet later on."

When Lacey had poured her a cup of coffee, Annie asked, "Is it true that Trey has barred Ruby from the house?"

Lacey nodded. "It's true. She can come no closer than the barn."

"I bet that riled old Bull." Annie grinned. "You

know about the gossip that goes on about him and Ruby, don't you?"

"Yes, Trey told me. He says that it's not gossip, that it's the plain truth. From what he says, it's been going on for years."

"Bull Saunders is an evil man, Lacey. He's capable of anything. It wouldn't bother him one whit to kill Trey if the notion hit him. You see, nothing has gone his way since Trey's mother died. The old devil hadn't expected that she would leave her half of the spread to her son. It was a big shock to him and an added insult when that son put a stop to his bringing women into the house when he married you."

Annie took a swallow of her coffee. Looking earnestly at Lacey, she said, "You can't caution Trey enough to watch his back trail."

"I know." Lacey nodded solemnly. "But I can't understand why the man hates his son so. You'd think he'd be proud of him. Trey works like a dog on the ranch."

Annie shook her head. "That has baffled everybody. It just don't make a lick of sense."

She changed the subject then and began to discuss her family. "We started putting in our garden patch yesterday. My Glory, who is only ten, has taken over the household chores, and Franklin, who's fourteen, is doing his father's work. That Tollie"—Annie shook her head—"is the laziest man that ever drew breath."

Lacey hid a smile. Everyone knew how lazy good-natured Tollie Stump was. His father had left him a fine ranch when he died, but out of mismanagement and laziness, the son had soon lost everything except for a small tract of land. Annie had taken over then and turned the few acres into a thriving farm. Tollie spent most of his time hunting and fishing.

But the love the Stumps shared for each other was deep and strong. Even when Annie spoke of Tollie's laziness, it was said with affection. Lacey hoped that someday she and Trey would know that kind of love.

As Annie chattered on, a queer, cold chill came over Lacey. She felt driven to ride out to the branding camp, to keep an eye on Trey.

She could barely hide her relief when Annie finally said that it was time she got home. "I told Tollie to start plowing the potato patch, but if I'm not there to keep an eye on him, he'll take off up the mountain and stay there all day."

After Annie rode away, Lacey flew about the house, making up her and Trey's bed, straightening the parlor, and washing the dishes. Then she hurried into the bedroom and changed from her dress into the men's garb she now wore only for riding.

At the barn she waited impatiently for the sorrell to be saddled. She was gripped with the conviction that she must get to Trey, that something bad was going to happen to him. When Red was led out, she swung onto his back, and with a nudge of her heels the big animal moved out, breaking into a hard gallop at Lacey's command.

As she rode into the branding camp, everything looked the same as the other time she had visited it. The dust was still ankle-deep, choking the men and coating their sweating faces. The horses were affected as well, their eyes red-rimmed from the dust, and when they were momentarily pulled to a halt, they shook their heads and blew thin streams of dust from their nostrils.

Lacey gave a smile of relief when she saw Trey riding toward her out of a shimmering haze of heat.

His eyes said that he was happy to see her. "I didn't know you were riding out today," he said, his eyes twinkling mischievously. "I don't think I can spare the time right now to take a trip to the cottonwood grove."

"Really?" Lacey pretended to be disappointed, making Trey laugh.

"You just can't stay away from your man, huh?" he teased.

"I'm worried about you, Trey," Lacey said soberly. "I had this terrible feeling that something was going to happen to you."

"So you've come out here in the heat to protect me," Trey teased.

"I'm serious, Trey. I feel it in my bones that you shouldn't be here today. Why don't you take the day off?"

"Now, honey, you know I can't do that. We

need every hand in order to finish up the job today. Why don't you ride back home? I'll be just fine."

The bawling and bellowing of longhorns took Trey's attention from Lacey. The cowboys were trying to keep them bunched and moving away from the wilds where they had been all winter. He touched spurs to the little quarterhorse he rode today and raced the half mile to help the men.

Undecided what to do, Lacey wavered between what instinct told her and Trey's assurance that he would be all right. She saw that the men had managed to turn the steers toward camp, and she was about to turn Red's head homeward when she paused in the action of lifting the reins.

She had seen a movement in the cottonwood grove. As she squinted her eyes, peering, the sun glinted off a shiny object. She saw a puff of smoke, followed closely by the sharp report of a rifle.

She let out a little dispiaring cry as the wild cattle immediately spooked and, as one, swerved around, heading back toward the men driving them.

"Oh, dear Lord," she gasped, a sick feeling of terror gripping her. Trey was right in their path.

Horrified, Lacey could only sit and watch, biting her lip until it bled. The frenzied cattle were almost upon Trey and the outriders when they drew their guns and started shooting in the air, yelling at the top of their lungs and popping their ropes.

Almost at the last minute, it seemed, the long-horns swerved and stampeded toward the grove—straight toward where the shot had been fired.

Standing up in the saddle and staring intently ahead, Lacey saw two figures scrambling to-ward a couple of horses tied to a tree. From this distance, they looked like a man and a woman. Ruby and Bull! They had deliberately turned the stampeding cattle against Trey.

As she watched, her heart pounding, the pair reached the horses and grabbed at the reins. Frightened from all the noise, the horses reared up, tore loose, and raced away. Bull and Ruby were left just yards away from the thundering herd. She caught a glimpse of Bull's big body being tossed in the air and heard Ruby's shrill scream. Lacey kicked Red with her heels and sent him racing to catch up with Trey and the men following the herd.

When the last of the cattle had disappeared over a rise, Lacey and the men rode up to the crumpled figures lying in the dust.

They came upon Ruby first. They swung out of their saddles and hurried to kneel beside her. Although Ruby's body was broken and blood trickled from the corner of her mouth, her gaze fastened on Lacey, hatred for her shining hot in her eyes.

With her dying breath, she whispered, "I almost got you once, you little bitch. I was the one who cut your guide rope." Her mad stare became fixed then, and Trey moved his hand over her lids, closing them. Ruby Dalton had passed out of this life.

He looked at Lacey, shaking his head. "It never entered my mind that she cut the rope."

He helped Lacey to stand and they walked over to where Bull lay, more dead than alive. Like Ruby, his body was badly broken, his legs twisted unnaturally beneath him. As Trey squatted down beside him, pure hatred stared up at him.

"You're dying, Father," Trey said with difficulty, trying to find some pity in his heart for this man who had never in his life given him a kind word. "Before you go, I'd like to know why all these years you've hated your only son, your only child."

Bull continued to glare his hatred at Trey, then finally managed to gasp out, "You damn fool . . . you're not my son."

"I'm not?" Trey sat back on his heels, stunned. "If not you, who then?"

Bull closed his eyes, and Trey grabbed his shoulders and shook him. "Don't you dare die until you tell me who my father is!" he shouted.

Bull opened eyes that were glazed with pain. "The man who has always hung in the background of your life . . . and your mother's. Your grandfather paid me to marry her, because . . .

the man who had put a brat in her belly was nowhere around."

Bull closed his eyes again. It looked as though he had drawn his last breath until Trey's fingers bit into his shoulder and he demanded sharply, "Who was that man, you old bastard? Who is my father?"

Bull opened his eyes, and with his last, shuddering breath gasped out, "You come from . . . the seed Matt Carlton put in your . . . whorin' mother's belly."

While everyone stared down at the dead man in disbelief and shock, Trey stood up, his face cold and stony. When he strode toward his mount, Lacey ran after him. "Where are you going, Trey?"

"Where do you think I'm going?" Trey ground out, swinging into the saddle. "I'm going to shoot the man who is the cause of the hell my mother and I lived in all those years."

"Trey!" Lacey grabbed hold of his knee. "Matt loves you. I'm sure there was a good reason he didn't marry your mother."

"Don't follow me, Lacey," was Trey's only response as he put spurs to his mount.

Matt was sitting on his porch, ready to pull off his boots, when Trey pulled his horse to a rearing halt in his yard. "What's wrong, son?" he called anxiously, springing to his feet as Trey strode toward him, his face working with all the emotions churning inside him.

Trey hopped up onto the porch and gave Matt a rough push that sent him back into the chair. "Even though you have the right, don't ever call me son again," he grated out.

Matt's face went chalk white. "So," he said slowly, looking down at the floor, "he finally told you."

"Yes, he told me. Now you have five minutes to tell me why you ran out on my mother before I put a bullet in your heart."

"I don't know if I can tell it all in five minutes," Matt said gravely, "but I'll try."

He wasted a few seconds of his allotted time thinking back over the years. He looked up at Trey then and, with suffering in his eyes, began to speak.

"I was several years older than Martha and never paid much attention to my pretty little neighbor until I noticed all the young men who were suddenly calling on her. I rode over to her father's plantation one day and discovered what was bringing the young bucks to her veranda.

"Your mother was the loveliest woman I'd ever seen. Not only was she beautiful, but she was also sweet and innocent. I fell madly in love with her that day, and I couldn't believe my good luck when she returned my love. With our parents good wishes, we began making wedding plans.

"There was an Indian uprising around that time, and it became pretty bad; a lot of men were killed. A month before our wedding date, all able-bodied men were ordered to go help stop the killing, burning, and looting.

"On the evening I rode over to tell Martha good-bye, we walked along the river, our spirits low. We turned to each other for comfort, and before we knew it our kisses and caresses got out of hand. You were conceived that night.

"I had no idea that Martha was in a family way the day I rode away to fight the Indians. When I arrived back home six months later, I was desolated to learn that my love had married Bull Saunders three months before.

"Why him of all men? I asked myself. He was quite a bit older than Martha, and it was well known that he was a brutal man who treated all women shamefully.

"A short time later I saw Martha and Bull on the street. She was big with child and I knew then why she had wed Saunders. Not knowing when or if I would return from fighting, she had married him out of desperation. I took a step toward her and that bastard grabbed a fistful of her hair and sneered, 'Hurry along, whore—I got a itch that needs scratchin'.

"I started to lunge at the bastard, to fasten my fingers around his thick neck and squeeze the life out of him. But I stopped at the pleading look in your mother's eyes."

Matt drew a deep breath before continuing. "You were two months old the first time I saw you. Martha sent me a note by a young darkie,

403

asking me to meet her at our favorite place down by the river.

"She was so thin and haggard-looking that I hardly recognized her. But love for me still shone out of her beautiful eyes as she unwrapped you and held you out to me. 'Meet your son Trey,' she said softly.

"As I held you, my heart filled with love and despair, she told me how ashamed her parents had been about the coming baby, how they had paid Bull to marry her.

" 'I had to let you see your son, Matt,' she said in her lovely, quiet voice, 'for next week, Bull is moving us west.'

"When we parted a short time later, I knew that I would follow her and my son. I could at least watch my son grow up, and maybe scare Bull into treating your mother right."

Matt sighed. "Of course I was wrong. Sometimes I wondered if my following her only worsened her life. She forbade me to intervene in her marriage. She was afraid Bull would only treat you more harshly.

"So, Trey, I don't much care if you do shoot me. I'm worn out with the hell I've lived most of my life."

His eyes wet, Trey sat down in the chair next to Matt. Only sorrow for the man he loved remained inside him. He grinned at the grey-haired man and said, "Before nightfall arrives, everyone in the area will know that you're my father. How does that set with you?"

Lacey

Matt gave him a startled look and smiled back. "That sets right well with me, son. I'd be proud to shout it to the whole world."

They spotted a cloud of dust rolling toward the house, and Trey shook his head. "Here comes your daughter-in-law. I told her not to follow me, but she doesn't pay a speck of attention to what I have to say."

Matt smiled to himself at the pride in Trey's voice. "Have you gotten around to telling her that you love her yet?"

"Well, no. Not in so many words, but I'm sure she knows it."

"How would she know if you don't tell her?"

"My body tells her almost every night," Trey answered, his tone saying he was convinced of the truth of his words.

"Maybe she thinks your body is only looking for release, and that love doesn't enter into it. I advise you to tell her how you feel. All women, especially wives, want to be told that they are loved."

"You think so?" Trey looked surprised.

"I know so, you idiot. You tell her that as soon as possible."

When Lacey pulled the sorrell in and dismounted, she saw at a glance that all was well with father and son. Matt rose and folded her into his arms. "I'm happy to see you, daughter. Will you and my son have some coffee and Mexican pastry with me?"

* * *

The whole ranch house seemed to take on a new character after Bull and Ruby were laid to rest in the small cemetery, well away from where Trey's mother was buried. Ruby's parents had showed up for her burial, but there was no one for Bull.

For two days, Lacey had Trey moving furniture about, arranging the pieces into a more homey look. Trey was careful not to track mud into the house, but if he sometimes forgot, Lacey didn't scold him. A house was meant to be lived in, not just looked at, she believed.

Besides, she meant to fill the big house with the sound of children's happy voices and pattering feet. She was almost sure she was expecting again. Two mornings in a row she had lost her breakfast.

Only one thing marred Lacey's happiness. If only Trey would say he loved her, she wouldn't ask for anything more. He treated her like a queen, exhausted her every night with his lovemaking, and never went to town except on business, yet those desired words never came.

A week later, when Trey said that he loved her, the words came so naturally that they were both surprised.

It was twilight and they were sitting on the porch after supper. Matt had taken the meal with them and had just ridden away. When he and his horse had disappeared from sight, Lacey said dreamily, "What a grand love he had for your mother."

"Yes," Trey agreed, "but no grander than the love I have for you."

Tears sprang to Lacey's eyes. Finally he had said the word she had waited for so long. She stood up and, taking him by the hand, tugged him out of the chair.

"Let's go to bed," she said huskily.